To Ke... we... ...ept your prom...
Marie Axx

Broken Bonds

Marie Anne Cope

Published by Scarygirl Ltd

First published in Great Britain in 2015 by Scarygirl Ltd.
Reg. No. 8336470

A CIP catalogue record for this book is available from the British Library.

Paperback ISBN: 978-0-9575359-6-1

To those who believe a promise is a promise, whatever the cost.

ACKNOWLEDGMENTS

Although I left BONDS open for a sequel, I never believed it would be so soon. Somewhere, in the deep dark recesses of my mind, Antony and Becca would have another outing; I just had no plan as to when that would be.

It is all down to you, dear reader, that BROKEN BONDS has come into being so soon. It is also to you and your unwavering support that I extend my deepest gratitude. For, without your requests, BROKEN BONDS may still be recessed somewhere dark and scary.

My eternal gratitude, once again, goes to three very important people, who helped me bring BROKEN BONDS to you, dear reader. To Stephan, Jenny-Lee and Neil – I toast you!

And finally, to my family, my friends and my partner. Thank you for supporting me, for believing in me, but more importantly, for encouraging me to be me.

MAGICAL REFERENCES

Summoning

By my Goddess and by my God
I call upon the power of the four elements
Of earth, of air, of fire, of water
I call upon you to aid me and to protect me

Spell O' Unbinding

By my Goddess and by my God
I ask for your power to strengthen my spell
By my Goddess and by my God
I ask for your power to heed my promise
Help me to free this being from this evil curse
Through my actions, through our power
We release him from his tomb

Spell O' Manumission

You who are bound within this tomb
Will rise again and commit to me
To aid my quest to set thee free
As I do will, so mote it be

Completion and Thanks

By my Goddess and by my God
My humble thanks for supporting me
I bid you take the intention behind my actions
And see it executed for all time
As I do will, so mote it be

PROLOGUE

'Thank you, Mr Withers. I'll take it from here.'

'Are you sure, Miss? He's dangerous. I heard what he did…'

'I'm sure. Now, for your own safety, it would be best for you and your men to get out of sight.'

'But you might need our help, you know, if…'

'I won't. Now, please, I need to get on with this. There isn't much time until dawn.'

'Have it your way, but don't say I didn't…'

Becca stood and stared at the stone sarcophagus, the light from the moon lending it a ghostlike appearance. She shuddered as she looked at it; remembering as her hand moved to touch the bite marks on her neck – just scars now.

Taking a deep breath, she stepped forward and reached out to touch the cold rough granite. Nothing. The ground was consecrated. The spells still held.

She turned her face towards the star strewn sky and closed her eyes. Feet planted firmly and palms turned upwards, she summoned the protection she hoped would be enough.

'By my Goddess and by my God, I call upon the power of the four elements. Of earth,' she said and turned her palms downwards, feeling the earth shudder and the energy spike upwards and into her body.

'Of air' Becca whipped her hands around in a circular motion and she braced herself just in time as the wind picked up, dragging the clouds across the sky to collide; the resulting thunder resonating through her.

'Of fire' she said and pointed her power fingers heavenwards to meet the bolt of lightning that shot towards the earth.

The taste of sulphur triggered her gag reflex, but she willed her body into stillness. There was no going back now.

'And of water.' She clapped her hands three times and the heavens opened, releasing their burden onto the parched earth.

Becca felt the power as it pulsated in the centre of her palms. She needed to do this while the energy remained strong.

Placing her palms against the seal, she said the Spell O' Manumission. She held her breath, but she needn't have worried. The elements were with her. Lightning shot down, connecting with her core, before exiting through her palms and radiating around the seal. Becca stumbled backwards, her palms charred and burned from the exit wounds, and watched as the light pulsated three times and then went out.

Taking her Maglite out of her pocket, she directed its beam to the seal. The spell worked. The seal was broken.

'Mr Withers? I'm ready for you now,' she shouted through the veil of rain, but there was no response.

'For goodness sake,' Becca muttered as she pulled out her phone and dialed his number.

'I'm ready for you. Didn't you hear me? Just hurry.' She disconnected and squinted through the rain. Within a few minutes she saw the men she hired, lumbering across the now muddy ground.

'It's the noise of this rain. Came out of nowhere. Bloody forecasters can't get anything right…'

'Yes, yes. Can you slide the lid downwards, if you can? Just about half way.'

'Why are you..?'

'I'm not paying you to ask questions, Mr Withers,' Becca said and felt a stab of guilt for being so harsh. 'I'm sorry, I…'

'It's fine. Let's get it done and then we can all go home and get out of this God awful rain,' he said and smiled at her, before directing his men to the task.

The lid pushed back, the men hidden once again in the cover of the trees, Becca stared down at the vine wrapped form of Antony Cardover.

It's not too late to go back, a voice sounded in her head.

'I can't. I made a promise,' she muttered to herself. Closing her eyes, she placed her hands above the vine covered body and began to chant the Spell O' Unbinding. As she chanted, she drew her hands away from his body towards the earth in a rhythmic motion. Slowly, the vines began to loosen and unwrap themselves and, as she finished the spell, Becca watched as they disappeared back into the earth.

As the last vine vanished from sight, she closed her eyes and turned her face heavenwards.

'By my Goddess and by my God, my humble thanks for supporting me. I bid you take the intention behind my actions and see it executed for all time. As I do will, so mote it be.'

The rain ceased, the thunder fell silent and the clouds parted ways, allowing the moon to light the scene once again.

As she waited, her heartbeat thudding, her breath shallow as she looked at him, really looked at him. There was no denying it, he was exquisite. His rugged features and ebony hair were one thing, but it was his eyes; set deep under hooded brows that drew you in, that enveloped you, that caressed you, that possessed you. Those eyes, as dark as his hair, were mesmerising. Becca couldn't ever remember seeing eyes like his before.

She stood and stared, unaware of the goose-bumps that had erupted across her skin; oblivious to the breath that caught in her throat; completely blind to the warnings her body was trying to alert her to.

'Hello, Rebecca.' The sound of his voice snapped her out of her trance and she went to step backwards, away from him, but her movements were too sluggish, her responses too slow; the movements of someone who had been drugged.

She screamed as his hand clamped around her throat and dragged her to him, into the sarcophagus.

'It's been too long, my dear, and this time I'll get what I want.'

Holding her above him, almost at arm's length, he slit open her throat, across her carotid artery. It didn't take long for the blood to start pumping out, the increasing pace of her heartbeat aiding the flow.

Becca struggled against his grip, but her strength was waning, her oxygen supply cut off, her body growing numb.

Bending his elbow, Antony lowered her towards him, until her lips were inches from his. She could smell the fetid stench of his breath, as she struggled to focus her blurring gaze on him.

'Time to reclaim what is mine,' he whispered and jerked her over his head. Her mind whirled. *What the hell was he..?*

Becca screamed again as she felt his teeth puncture her heart. The pull was excruciating, like she was being dragged beneath the surface of the sea; the pressure on her chest squeezing the life out of her.

Her survival instincts kicked in and she flailed her arms as she tried to catch hold of the sides of the casket. She kicked her legs out towards him. She opened her mouth and screamed at the top of her lungs. Surely Mr Withers would hear her; he couldn't be that far away. But all of that was only in her mind, for Antony was draining the life out of her far too quickly for her to respond.

She felt tears form in the corners of her eyes and slowly plummet to the ground. She heard her breath rattle in her chest, becoming more shallow and wheezy with each effort. She heard echoes of the night around her; the sounds hollow and far away.

Suddenly, Becca felt a rushing feeling in the pit of her stomach, the same feeling she got when she rode a roller-coaster. The night span around her and what little air she had in her lungs was knocked out, as she landed flat on her back. Her head connected with an object and everything went black.

'Welcome back, Rebecca.' Becca heard his muffled voice as she blinked her eyes to try to clear her vision.

Shapes swam above her, making her dizzy, before they settled into stillness and she became lost in the dark ebony pools she had been staring down into not so long ago.

'You need to be awake for this,' he said.

'For…what?' she murmured, her eyes closing again. She felt so tired.

'For this,' he said and clutched her jaw with one hand, causing her to yelp. He squeezed, none too gently, forcing Becca to open her mouth. Her gaze followed his other arm as he raised it above her head, crossing in front of the moon, blocking what little view she had.

She tried to twist from his grasp, as warm liquid dropped onto her face, but she didn't have the strength.

Antony forced his arm down to her mouth and she tried to yank her head from his grasp, but she couldn't. The warm liquid – blood; his blood – was running into her mouth.

She closed off her throat, but her body was more concerned with breathing, with surviving, than with what was in her mouth. Her throat yielded and she swallowed.

Becca prayed for her body to reject the blood, but it didn't. It craved it and she found herself sucking on his arm, drawing his blood inside her, pulling his essence into her being. As she drank, she felt stronger and she gripped onto him, pulling on him, hungering for him. Somewhere, far away, she heard laughter, but she didn't care. She had what she wanted, had what she needed.

'And that's enough,' he said and ripped his arm away from her, leaving her reaching for him, begging for him.

'It won't take long now,' she heard him say, his voice far away. 'Your body will die; is dying. But my blood…well, let's just say you're soon going to know what I've felt like for over four hundred years.'

Becca tried to speak, but she couldn't. She tried to respond, to lash out, but she was immobile. All she could do was watch as, without any effort at all, Antony slid the lid of the sarcophagus back into place, engulfing her; enclosing her; entombing her.

She tried to move her arm; tried to reach up to the lid, but her movements were sluggish. What good would it do, anyway?

She was trying to think of something when the first wave came. It felt as if she had been sucker-punched. The intensity of the pain made her retch and she cried out; hoarse sound that it was. She tried to curl her body up into a ball, into the fetal position, into safety; but the pain kept coming, like storm waves breaking on the shore, never giving her chance to catch her breath before the next one hit.

She was drowning, that's how it felt. She couldn't catch her breath, the pain wouldn't let her. She saw the black and white dots, heard the hollowness and ringing in her ears, felt the sheen of sweat break out across her skin, and succumbed to the blackness as it closed in.

Becca jolted awake. Blackness surrounded her. *Christ, it must still be the middle of the night*, she thought. She looked around her, but saw no chink of light. Strange. She didn't have black out blinds.

Synapses started firing in her head and images swam into her mind. Faces. His face. Antony Cardover.

Panic fuelled her and she sat up, cracking her head against something cold; something hard.

She stretched her fingers out to the side, only to be met with resistance. Flashes of memory flickered in her head, like a reel of an old home movie.

She placed her palms flat on the surface beneath her – stone. She moved her palms to the sides – stone. She reached her palms above her – stone.

The movie was becoming clearer; the images less flickering. She saw his face, his eyes. She felt his grip, his teeth. She experienced the longing, the pain. Becca opened her eyes wide and spread her palms against the stone once more. Nothing. Didn't stone used to feel cold to her touch?

The memory flooding back, Becca screamed and pounded her fists as hard as she could against the lid of the sarcophagus, Antony's sarcophagus.

CHAPTER 1

Becca screamed, beating her fists against the shroud of darkness. She kicked, screamed and pounded as hard as she could. Finally, she broke through. Finally, there was light. Harsh light. Glaring light. Morning light.

'Morning, Spook,' she said as her gaze followed the journey of her quilt to the floor and to the two pools of orange that stared at her.

Becca flopped back against her damp pillows and rested the back of her hands on her forehead. Drenched. Jeez, she couldn't keep having the same nightmare. It was killing her. She was exhausted. It was too real, too vivid, too…she didn't want to think about it anymore.

She kicked the remaining covers off her and lay there, naked, allowing the coolness of the early morning air, drifting through the open window, to sooth the fever of her dream, of her nightmare.

A weight landed on the bed next to her and Becca felt the softness brush her skin, causing her to curl into a ball, giggling.

'Okay, okay, buddy. Don't you worry that I've not had any sleep, hey? All you care about is your tummy!' She ruffled the huge fluffy grey cat behind his ears, to be rewarded with an affirmative purr.

She sat up and swung her legs off the side of the bed before standing up and stretching, massaging the back of her head where it had struck the bottom of the sarcophagus. Her other hand went to touch the marks on her neck, as was her morning ritual, just to be sure.

'Okay, let's get this show on the road. We've got a party to get to.'

What a day, Becca thought as she flopped down onto the squashy brown leather sofa and slipped her feet out of the unfamiliar strappy sandals. She looked down at the soft floaty fabric swathing her limbs and smiled. She had to hand it to Jan, the pale lilac suited her to perfection and the baby-doll cut of the dress hadn't been as uncomfortable as she'd expected. In fact, she'd had many a compliment and offer of a date during the course of the day, something she certainly didn't get in her usual attire.

'It's still me, buddy,' Becca said as she looked up and saw Spook appraising her from the doorway, his head cocked to one side, his orange eyes narrowed as he stared at her.

She leaned forward and rubbed her fingers together, a gesture that usually brought him running over. This time, however, he stayed where he was, adjusting his gaze from her face to her hair, a low growl emanating from within him.

'Ah, it's this you don't like,' she said and reached up to pull the lilac blossom adorned tiara out of her raven hair, holding it in front of her. 'Me neither, but sometimes you have to wear what you're told, especially when it's the bride doing the telling,' she said and stared at the flora laden head-piece before putting it on the coffee table and massaging her temples.

She watched as Spook meandered over to her, giving the head-piece a stern look as he circumnavigated the table before jumping up onto the sofa and nuzzling against Becca, careful not to lay a paw on the dress.

'Still smarting from your last scolding are you, buddy?' Becca said, as she rubbed Spook behind the ears; remembering Jan screeching when she'd walked in to find Spook asleep on top of Becca's bridesmaid dress. She'd never seen him exit a room so fast.

'C'mon then, let me change out of my girlie gear and we can have a proper cuddle.'

As if in agreement, Spook jumped off the sofa and raced out of the room.

A couple of hours later, her fleecy pyjamas on, a mug of hot chocolate clasped in her hands and Spook curled up contentedly in her lap, Becca allowed herself to sit back and relax.

What a day it had been, but in a good way or, better yet, a fantastic way; boy had they all needed it after the traumatic time they'd been through. Becca shuddered as she remembered what Antony Cardover had done to her and her family, and what he had almost done to Jakes. She squeezed her eyes shut to block out the thought, and to try and stop the hollow feeling she felt when she dwelled on the fact she could have lost Jakes.

Frank Jakes, a man she had never heard of a year before, was now the most important person in her life and the closest thing she had to a father, so much so that she had been honoured to be a bridesmaid at their wedding today, even consenting to wear a floaty dress for Jan.

Ah Jan. Becca smiled, as she thought of her and saw her walking down the aisle towards Jakes, stunning in the simple ivory satin gown she'd chosen, which set off her complexion and auburn hair, laced with baby's breath, perfectly. Jan had been a rock since Becca had lost her mother; since Becca had killed her mother. She'd been there to hold Becca as she'd shouted and screamed, and to soothe her as she'd cried. Jan had known exactly what Becca had needed when Jakes had run dry and, between them, they had helped Becca heal, both physically, from the injuries Antony had inflicted, and emotionally, from the trauma of having to kill her own mother and the fight against Antony for her life.

Without them, Becca dreaded to think where she'd be. They were her family now and she loved them dearly. She'd been so proud to stand with them today and bear witness to their marriage, a marriage Becca had no doubt would go the distance.

Her gaze drifted to the clock on the mantelpiece; she felt her chest tighten. It was time to go to bed. She leant her head back against the sofa and sighed. She wanted to go to bed, but she didn't know if it would happen again. It didn't happen every night, but it had happened last night and it would continue to happen, for the time being at least.

Becca lay in bed, Spook curled up closely beside her as she stared around her childhood room. She couldn't get used to being back here, in the house she grew up in, but she couldn't go back to the apartment, not after what had happened there. She marvelled at how her mother had left it untouched, after all their years of estrangement. Had she hoped that one day they would reconcile? Becca would never know.

She hadn't decided what she was going to do with the house yet. She wasn't sure she could afford to keep it, but part of her didn't want to let it go. She had a short while left to decide, as the bank had agreed to suspend the mortgage payments until her mother's estate was settled. That had taken some of the pressure off at least.

She still had to go through all her mother's things though and she'd decided that Jakes' wedding would be her last day of wallowing. From tomorrow, she would start to piece her life back together.

That thought soothed her and she switched off the light, deciding to let the happy memories of the day lull her to sleep for a change, rather than the horrors of the past.

CHAPTER 2

'Becca? Becca, are you back here?'

'Yeah, Frank. Having my caffeine shot,' Becca called and pulled her robe more tightly around her, cursing herself for forgetting their arrangement.

'I rang the doorbell, but…sorry, am I too early?' Jakes said as he averted his gaze.

'No, no, don't worry. I forgot and I kind of hoped you'd listened to me and taken your lovely new wife on a well-deserved honeymoon.'

'We agreed we'd go when everything's okay here, with you, and we can relax and enjoy it.'

'I'm fine, Frank. Stop worrying about me. I just…'

'Well, you don't look fine. It happened again, didn't it?'

'Oh yeah. Two nights in a row now. In high definition too. Frank, it was so real I…' Her voice broke off and she looked down into the bowels of her coffee cup.

'Exactly why we're postponing the honeymoon.' Jakes held up his hand to stop her protest. 'I'm worried about you, Becca. We both are. So, let's drop the honeymoon conversation and concentrate on you, shall we?'

'You really should go and talk to someone,' he said, forgetting his earlier embarrassment and coming to sit down next to her on the step, pulling her towards him.

Becca rested her head on his shoulder, allowing herself to release some of the load, if only for a moment.

'No. What I need to do, is get on with finding a cure for him. Then we will both be free,' she said and pulled out of Jakes' embrace.

'And if you can't?'

'I have to. I can't contemplate the alternative.'

She stood up and helped Jakes to his feet.

'Hey, no stick!'

'Yep, first day. About time I gave it up. I never thought I would, to be honest, not after what Antony did, especially at my age, but I've been lucky.'

'You've worked hard you mean,' Becca said, smiling at him.

'That too.'

'Well, you might be in need of it again after helping me today,' Becca said and opened the back door. 'Oh, after you, buddy.' She stepped back to avoid getting entangled with Spook, as he made a beeline for his morning hunting ground.

'I don't know. Not even a nod. What is the world coming to?' Jakes said, as the grey cat shot passed him, not stopping for his customary fuss.

'Don't take it personally. He's far too interested in exploring his new home.'

'So, you've decided to stay then?'

Becca shrugged. 'I don't know. I don't think I can afford to, but I don't know until I sit down and work it out. And I can't even think about that at the minute.'

They walked into the kitchen.

'Right, there's the coffee. I'm going to make myself decent. No idea where to start, so take your pick and I'll come and find you.'

CHAPTER 3

'Jesus Becca, how much painting did your mother do? There are hundreds,' Jakes said as Becca walked into her mother's studio, to find Jakes in the centre of what could only be described as chaos.

'Is this the only room you've been in?' she said, laughing, feeling better after a hot shower. She had thrown on her work clothes – tatty jeans and paint spattered t-shirt.

'Well, yes. I thought, being her studio and all…'

'Mum didn't confine her paintings to one room. They are all over the house.'

'I did see the hallway was a bit jammed. What are you going to do with them?'

'No idea, to be honest,' she said, staring at one of her mother's splashes of colour; mesmerised. 'Some of them are pretty good.'

'I'll say,' Jakes said. 'Look. I don't know if you're interested, but I know a gallery owner. Maybe you could sell some of them? It would help out financially.'

'You know a gallery owner? Wow, you are a bit of a dark horse, Frank Jakes. Didn't think you were into art!'

'I'm not and I don't know the owner directly, but she's the best friend of one of my protégées, Ellie Lawrence. The gallery is The Victoria Stephens Gallery.'

'In Scotsford? Really? Wow. I've seen her work and she is amazing. Bit of a recluse though, isn't she?'

'That's one way of putting it. I could get in touch with Ellie if you're interested?'

'Sure, why not. Give's a bit of focus to the clear out now, doesn't it?' Becca laughed.

They worked side by side for the rest of the day, speaking only to decide which paintings to keep, which to sell and which to get rid of.

Every painting they looked at seemed to bring back memories for Becca, even though a large number were done during her estrangement from her mother.

Despite this, she saw her mother in every canvas – the paint smeared smock and paintbrush speared hair. She smelt her in every brushstroke – oils and paint thinners. She heard her in every colour – the songs hummed, dependent on the colour; the colour dependent on her mood.

'I can't do this anymore, Frank,' she said at about seven o'clock. 'Enough is enough for one day. I just feel…' But what did she feel? Sad? Scared? Alone? Abandoned? In truth, it was all of these things.

'Well, we've pretty much finished anyway,' Jakes said, patting her hunched shoulders as she knelt in front of a stack of paintings she'd spent the last hour staring at, but not touching.

'Ha, I wish,' she said, looking up at him and wiping away a stray tear.

'Do you want to come and stay with Jan and I tonight?'

'No, I'll be fine, thanks.'

'Come for dinner at least. Jan is concerned you're not eating and after seeing you today, I…'

'Honestly Frank, I'll be fine. And I promise I'll eat something,' she said, giving him a hug. 'Thank you for today.'

'You don't have to thank me. Same time tomorrow?'

'I'd kind of like to go through the rest myself. I have to.'

'Well, you know where I am, Becca.'

'I do and thanks again,' she said as she opened the front door, allowing the balmy evening air to permeate the stuffy house.

'Anytime, anytime. I'll give Ellie a call about the paintings and let you know.'

'That would be great. Thanks, Frank,' she said, giving him a peck on the cheek. 'Thank Jan for loaning you out today,' she called after him and he turned and waved.

Becca shut the door and leaned back against it, closing her eyes. What a day. She opened them again and looked down at Spook, sitting expectantly by the kitchen door.

'What would I do without you to remind me about meal times, hey buddy?'

She picked him up and nuzzled her face into his thick grey fur, feeling the soothing effect he always had immediately take hold.

'How about we share the rest of this chicken?' she said to him as she pulled half a roast chicken out of the fridge. Spook licked his lips and his purring grew louder in response.

CHAPTER 4

Becca spent the rest of the week alone going through the house - systematically and methodically. It helped to calm her, helped to sooth her, helped her start to heal.

She wanted to do this alone. She needed to do this alone and so every time Jakes or Jan, or sometimes both of them, called or came over, she didn't answer. She always found food and coffee on the doorstep and felt a pang of guilt for shutting them out.

They were her family now, but she just wasn't ready. She hoped they'd understand. She was sure they would. Spook's reproachful looks when she hid each time the doorbell rang, didn't help.

Maybe it was the guilt or maybe it really was because she was starting to heal. Whatever it was, Becca found herself devouring the food that was left. Little by little she found her strength returning. Gradually, the spark was beginning to ignite and the desire to fulfil her promise was filling her waking thoughts.

Her dreams, however, were a different matter. They weren't dreams, nor could they really be described as nightmares. They were visions; warnings of what was to come. They varied little in content, but their intensity, their vividness and their effect on her, grew. Becca knew they wouldn't stop; not until she fulfilled her promise. After all, they didn't start until after she'd made it - the night of her mother's funeral. Someone or something didn't want her to forget and they certainly wanted to remind her how dangerous it was going to be.

As anxious as she was to be rid of the nightmares, to be able to sleep again, she needed to purge. Clearing her mother's house enabled her to do just that. All the anger, all the resentment, all the anxiety, all the sadness and all the love she had for her mother, was coming to the surface and she was having to face it, having to deal with it and having to move passed it.

Every object that Becca picked up, every painting she sorted, every photograph she flipped through, all of it brought back a myriad of emotions for her. Emotions she had no choice but to let wash over her. Emotions she had no choice but to give in to. It was exhausting, but it was cathartic.

After a week, though, Becca didn't think she had anything left, until she opened the door to her mother's bedroom; a room she hadn't set foot in for over a decade.

'Well, here goes, buddy,' she said to Spook who was, as usual, poised and ready to shoot into a new place to explore.

Taking a deep breath, Becca grasped the brass door knob and turned. She pushed open the door with a little help from Spook, who was trying to force his ample form through the too slowly to expand gap.

She let the door swing open and watched as Spook dashed in and immediately started sniffing and rubbing his cheeks around everything, in a rather random pattern, marking his turf. His task completed, he jumped on the bed and settled himself down to watch Becca.

Despite Spook's amber eyes almost willing her forward, she couldn't bring herself to cross the threshold; the memories were too intense, causing her heart to constrict and her breath to catch. Nothing had changed. Every piece of furniture, every fabric, it was all as it had been the day she'd left.

She closed her eyes and inhaled the scent of lavender, mixed with oils and paint thinners, so typical of her mother. She smiled as she saw herself running into the bedroom and jumping on the bed, excitedly shouting for

Ginnie to wake up because Santa had been and had brought Becca lots of paints. She chuckled as she remembered the ensuing disaster of spilling said paints all over her mother and the beautiful Egyptian cotton linen she'd always had on the bed. From that day forward, a threadbare patchwork throw had always protected those precious sheets.

Becca opened her eyes and brushed away a stray tear. Taking another deep breath, she walked into the room. She felt a chill run through her as she did so and shuddered. It was as if her mother was still present.

The room was quite sparse; the bed being the most lavishly adorned. The dressing table bore only a hairbrush and some moisturiser, her mother never having had any use for make-up.

Becca picked up the pearl handled hairbrush and pulled at the wisps of red hair caught in the bristles. Maybe she should keep it?

'No!' she shouted, dislodging Spook from his comfy perch. She couldn't keep stuff. She had photos. She had paintings. That was enough. She didn't need the rest. No one did. Closing her eyes again briefly, she dropped the hairbrush into a bin bag.

Her resolve restored, Becca focused on the task, her mind elsewhere, on the attic. A room which she really didn't want to tackle alone.

She sorted her mother's clothes into bags for charity, cleared the rubbish and stripped the bed, much to Spook's disgust. She decided to keep the sheets, just to see what her mother had raved about.

Once the room was empty, she did what she'd done with all the other rooms, she scrubbed it from top to bottom, cleaning it to the point she wasn't sure there would be anything left. Maybe, that was the point.

Spent, Becca left the room, leaving the door open now; her mother's essence, her mother's spirit, no longer present. She had wiped the room clean, as she had with all the others.

She piled the bags of clothing with the rest and made a mental note to ring the charity shop to see if they would collect it.

As she grabbed the last two bags and turned to make her way back downstairs, she stopped at the foot of the attic stairs. She wasn't sure why, but her heart felt heavy. She looked up the winding staircase and sighed. Her past was up there - her history, her heritage - and, more importantly, the key to helping Antony was somewhere to be found in what resided in the eaves. Yet, why was she so afraid? After all, helping Antony was what she promised to do, what she wanted to do.

As she pondered this, the doorbell rang and, for the first time in a week, she didn't hide.

CHAPTER 5

'Hey, Frank,' Becca said as she opened the door, to see another bag of food on the doorstep and Jakes hastily scribbling a message on the back of a crumpled receipt.

'Becca! Thank God,' Jakes said, dropping pen and paper and pulling her into a bear hug.

'Okay, you can let me go now,' she said, struggling to catch her breath.

Jakes released her and pushed passed her into the house.

'Come on in,' she said and picked up the bag of food, before following Jakes into the living room.

'Why the hell haven't you returned any of our calls? Jan and I have been worried sick about you,' Jakes said. Becca stepped back at the ferocity of his words and out of range of the finger he was gesticulating in her direction.

'Steady on, Frank. You know where I've been.'

'But we didn't know whether you were alive or dead,' he said, his hands now on his hips, his face red; perspiration beading his forehead.

'Oh come on. You know I've just been going through mum's stuff. It's hardly life threatening,' she said and turned to leave to take the food into the kitchen, but Jakes grabbed hold of her arm and swung her around.

'How the hell can you say that after everything we've been through?' His grip was so tight on her arm that he was cutting off her circulation. She looked up, into his eyes, and could see the war of emotions there – anger, pain, relief. Becca felt the hard-faced attitude leave her and her shoulders slumped. This was Frank, the man who had helped her stop Antony, the man who had saved her life, the man who was the closest thing she had to family now.

'Oh, Frank, I'm so sorry. I've just been caught up in all this and…oh, God, I honestly didn't think you'd miss me.'

'Don't be ridiculous. Of course we do. Christ, Becca, we've been frantic. Why else do you think we've been stalking you? My next move was going to be to kick the door down.'

'Good job I opened it then, wasn't it?' she said and they both laughed, breaking the tension.

'So, what's on the menu tonight then? Want to share?'

'Don't get too excited, it's take out. Jan's working late, so I picked it up on the off chance you might let me in.'

'Come on then. Let's go and eat before it goes cold. I'm ravenous.'

'That's good,' Frank said and followed her into the kitchen. 'What's with all the black bags?'

'Oh, that's for the charity shop. Stuff I don't want to keep.'

'There's an awful lot of it, Becca. Are you keeping anything?'

'A few bits.' She kept her back to him and busied herself with dishing out the take away, not wanting him to see the tears pricking her eyes. 'I'm going to see if they'll pick it up, as there is so much of it.'

'Are you sure? You don't have to get rid of it straight away, you know. You can wait a while. Maybe put it in one of the spare rooms and see how you feel in a couple of months?'

'No!' Becca said, slamming her hand on the counter. 'I'm sorry,' she said, turning to face Jakes. 'I've made up my mind. I want it gone. I can't afford to dwell on the past. I don't want to. I have things I need to do.'

'We all dwell on the past,' Jakes said as he took the plates off Becca and set them down on the table.

'You know what I mean,' she said and swept aside the paraphernalia cluttering the table, to give them more room.

'It wasn't your fault, Becca. You know that, right?'

'I know, but if I hadn't come here, he wouldn't have found her and…'

'Yes, he would. Maybe not as quickly as he did, but he would've found her. You can't go on blaming yourself. You have to move on.'

'And that's exactly what I'm doing, hence the bags,' Becca said and stuck her tongue out at him.

'Okay. Touché. I'll stop going on about it. So, how far have you got?'

'I'm done,' Becca said between mouthfuls.

'Good grief, Becca. Slow down. You'll get indigestion! That's good, that you've finished, right?'

Becca shrugged, continuing to fork food into her mouth as if she hadn't seen food in weeks. 'When I say "finished", I mean everything but the attic.'

'Okay.'

They lapsed into silence for a while as they ate.

'Really not sure I want to tackle it on my own,' she said.

'Why?'

She shrugged. 'Dunno really. I mean, when mum was alive I went up there. But things are different now. The answer may be up there…'

'And isn't that what you're anxious to find, so you can free Antony?'

'But what if it isn't, Frank? What if I can't help him?'

'Hey, less of that! I'm the doubting Thomas, remember. Look, I'll help you. Tomorrow we'll make a start, okay?' Jakes said and patted her hand.

'Thanks, Frank,' Becca said, fighting back tears again. Christ, what was wrong with her?

'Right. I best be off. Jan will be home and she'll be anxious to hear about you.' Becca felt the colour rushing to her cheeks, as she thought of what she had put them both through.

'Frank. I am sorry. Tell Jan I…'

'It's fine, Becca. You're fine and that's all that matters. Goodnight and I'll see you bright and early in the morning.' He winked at her and she groaned.

'Still on police time, I see,' she said and hugged him.

'Always,' he said, waving as he walked down the path.

'Ah, Frank. What was the note you were scribbling when you arrived?'

'Ah, yes,' he said, retracing his steps. 'The gallery I told you about. They'd like to see your mother's paintings.'

'Really?'

'Yes. Leon, the manager, was quite excited at the mention of your mother's name.'

'I didn't realise she was that well known. When do I need to take them in?'

'You don't. He'll come to you. Tomorrow afternoon, I think he said. I'll check and let you know in the morning. Goodnight Becca.'

'Night Frank,' she said and closed the door behind him, her gaze coming to rest on a stack of her mother's paintings.

'What else don't I know, Mum?' she muttered and wandered into the kitchen to clear up.

CHAPTER 6

'Blimey, Becca, you could keep a car boot sale going for months with this lot,' Jakes said, his mouth agape, coffee and a bag of goodies still clutched in his hands, staring round at the rammed attic.

'I know,' Becca said as she stepped passed him, grabbing the bag and perching on one of the many trunks. She opened the bag and peered inside. 'Oh, yummy, croissants,' she said and dived in, thrusting the buttery pastry into her mouth before handing the bag back to Jakes.

'Good to see your appetite coming back. Get some meat on those bones.'

Becca pulled a face at him.

'So, where do you want to start?' Jakes said, handing Becca her favourite latte.

Becca inhaled the delicious aroma through the hole in the lid and shrugged.

'It depresses me to look at it all, to be honest. I thought I'd gone through it all. But, then again, I did wonder where a lot of her crap was and now I know.' Becca pushed herself off the trunk and stretched. 'Any more pastries?'

Jakes handed the bag to her and Becca feasted on the remaining croissant.

'Do you want to keep any more of your mother's stuff or even go through it?'

'Not really, if I'm honest. If it's up here, it didn't mean that much to her. She always kept what she considered most precious close by.'

'Okay, well, let's get that done and out of the way. It'll give us space, if nothing else,' he said as he tried to negotiate the mountain of belongings.

'What about the trunks?'

Becca felt her heart lurch at the mention of the trunks and she reached out to run her finger along the lid of one.

'They were my grandmother's. I have no idea what's in them. I…' Her voice cracked at this point and a tear plopped onto the dusty lid, revealing the cracked leather surface, for the first time in years.

'We'll get to them,' Jakes said, squeezing her shoulder. 'Let's start with the easy stuff. What's underneath those sheets against the wall?'

'No idea,' Becca said, taking a deep breath to compose herself.

Jakes set his coffee down and picked his way through the debris, almost losing his footing on more than one occasion, to reach the back wall of the attic. He reached out and grasped the dust laden sheet and tugged. The sheet slipped away, revealing its secret. Becca felt her heart constrict as she stared.

'When was that painted?' Jakes said.

'I…don't…know. Where..? Bottom left corner,' Becca said as she stared into the haunting eyes of the man who walked the realms of her dreams. Or, that's who it looked like, but there was something different in his coal black eyes; something softer. Sadness? Love? She couldn't put her finger on it.

'There's no date, just a message.'

'What does it say?'

'Just a sec,' Jakes said as he struggled to bend down, his injured leg hindering his progress.

'I'm sorry, Frank, I'll look,' Becca said and started forward, but Jakes held his hand up to stop her.

'I've got it. It says, "Becca's something friend. Imagery. Imaginary. Becca's imaginary friend".'

'Oh my God,' Becca said, coming to stand in front of the life sized painting.

'Do you remember him?'

'Not from then, no,' she said and reached out to trace her fingers along the oiled lines of his jaw.

'He looks so different,' she whispered, her heart starting to ache for the man Antony used to be.

'Yes, he does,' Jakes said. 'And I'll bet he broke a few hearts in his time, looking the way he does.'

'Mmmm,' Becca said, dropping down to her haunches, her attention caught by the smaller canvasses stacked behind the full sized one of Antony.

'Look at these,' she said, passing them to Jakes.

'Looks like you spent a lot of time with him, doesn't it?'

'Why can't I remember any of it? Remember him? Even when I saw him when all this started, I didn't recognise him.' She marvelled at the various paintings of herself and Antony. He was pushing her on the swings, helping her climb a tree, carrying her on his shoulders.

'I don't know, Becca. A psychologist would probably say we forget. When did your father leave?'

Becca shrugged. 'I'm not sure. Mum would never talk about him. I don't remember him.'

'These paintings beg to differ, I suggest.'

'But Antony isn't my father.'

'No, but he's doing fatherly things in these paintings.'

'But how can I have imagined him?'

'Well, the church has been derelict for many years. Maybe the spells started to weaken a long time ago.'

'Maybe.'

'Do you want to put these with the others for Leon to go through?'

'Mmmm. What? No…these are…I don't know…too personal to share, I think.'

'Right, well let's get a shift on, shall we?' Jakes said, covering the paintings back up so they didn't get covered in dust. 'Let's go, missy,' he said, throwing a roll of black bags at her and knocking her off balance.

'Hey!' Becca said, grabbing the roll and hurling it back at him. It hit him in the stomach, causing him to double over and Becca burst out laughing.

'Unfair. Old man here,' he said, pulling out a handkerchief and waving it in surrender.

'Okay, old man, you hold the bags and I'll do the heavy lifting.'

Within two hours, they cleared the attic of everything except the paintings and the trunks; trunks Becca remembered her grandmother guarding as if they contained the crown jewels.

'Where do you want to start?' Jakes said as Becca stood staring at them.

'Who knows? They all look the same, so I guess it doesn't matter.'

Jakes stepped towards the smallest one and reached out to open it.

'Not that one. I know what's in there.'

'Really?'

'Yeah, it's the one I was given on my sixteenth birthday. Nothing much in it of interest, except the Grimoire, which you would love.'

'Can I see it?'

'Later. Let's check out the rest first, otherwise I'll never get you to help.'

'Fair point.'

'Okay, here goes,' Becca said and, taking a deep breath, she lifted the lid on one of the remaining trunks.

CHAPTER 7

The lid creaked and sighed as Becca opened it, releasing long held air. A musty scent permeated the space and both Becca and Jakes looked down to see a cloth, intricately embroidered with Wiccan symbols.

Becca reached down and plucked the edge of the cloth and lifted it up.

'Books,' she said and dropped it back down.

'What kind of books?' Jakes said, stepping forward and lifting the cloth.

'Does it matter to you, Mr Bookworm? Probably spell books, knowing grandma. She had hundreds,' she said, moving on to the next trunk.

'They're not spell books, Becca,' he said, plucking one out of the top of the trunk.

'Mmmm,' she said, fiddling with the rusted catch on the next trunk. It didn't want to give up its cargo.

'Bloody hell, they're journals.'

'Really? Whose?' Becca said, her attention drawn. 'I don't remember grandma keeping a journal. She walked back over to Jakes and peered over his shoulder at the leather-bound book.

'This is Anna's,' he said as he looked at the inscription on the front sheet. 'And, by the looks of it, it is one of many.' He indicated the dates in the bottom corner of the page.

Becca dropped to her knees and pulled the cloth out of the way.

'There are hundreds,' she said as she ran her fingers down the edge of the assortment of bindings. 'They can't all be Anna's, can they?' She started to pluck volumes at random from the trunk's ancient contents.

'Possibly,' Jakes said.

'Anna…Anna…Anna…Anna…oh, wait a minute. This one's different.' She held it out to Jakes and he squinted at the handwriting.

'This is Carla's,' he said. 'I'd know that handwriting anywhere.' He traced his finger over the childish scrawl. 'How many are there?'

'A jam-packed trunk full, as you can see,' Becca said, trying to guide Jakes' gaze to the contents, but he was lost.

'I mean of Carla's. How many of Carla's?'

'I don't know until we empty the trunk. They're not exactly indexed and filed in chronological order, you know,' she said and plucked the journal Jakes was lost in from his grasp and dropped it back in the trunk.

'Hey! That might be important,' he said, his bottom lip coming out like that of a petulant child.

'And how might that be?'

'Well, it seemed to be one written later, when she was older. When Rebecca had grown and…'

'And one written a long time after Antony was entombed and even longer after he was cursed and so of little immediate use, wouldn't you agree?'

'I know, but I want to know what happened to her. I need to know she had a good life, Becca.'

'I know, Frank, and I promise you can devour Carla's journals to your heart's content after we've found something that will point me towards helping Antony. Deal?'

'Deal.'

'So, by rights, anything pertaining to the curse and to Ebenezer is likely to be in Anna's journals, wouldn't you say?'

'Mmmm,' Jakes mumbled and started reading one of Anna's journals.

'Not now. We've got those other trunks to go through,' Becca said, laughing, as she removed yet another journal from his grasp and closed the lid on the trunk. That seemed to bring his attention back to the task.

'Sorry. Got lost in the past.'

'Easily done, Frank. Don't worry. Right, can you see if you can get that one open and I'll go through the others.' Becca indicated the largest of the trunks; the one she had been fighting with a few minutes before.'

'Do you have any WD40?'

'No idea. Possibly in the kitchen. I haven't seen any, though.'

'Could the trunk be locked?'

'I never thought of that, but, yes, I guess it might. Bit strange, though, given none of the others seem to be.'

'Key?'

'Er, no.'

'Hairgrips?'

'Now, those I do have, thanks to mum. I'll just…'

'I'll go. I need to get some air anyway. Where are they?'

'In a pot on the dressing table in mum's room.'

'Okie dokie. Do you want coffee while I'm down there?'

'What? Yes, that would be great, thanks.'

'Won't be long.'

Becca rested for a moment on the closed lid of the trunk and tried to process what they had already found.

Seeing the painting of Antony had shaken her to the core and had stirred something inside her, something she had given up hope of ever being awakened again after Pete. This had alarmed her more than the realisation that Antony had been her childhood companion. This man wanted her dead and had very nearly succeeded too. Yet, those eyes, they bore through her and caused butterflies to awaken inside her.

Could this be why she promised to help him? Did her subconscious remember the special place he held in her heart once?

And then there were the journals. Her ancestry, her heritage, her roots, all documented and saved through four centuries. Had her grandmother read them? Had her mother read them? No, she couldn't have. Surely, her mother would have told Becca if she'd known of their existence, wouldn't she?

If her mother had read the journals, if her grandmother had read them, then they'd know if there was a cure for Antony. Why hadn't they helped him? Her grandmother had said it wasn't his fault, so why leave him there?

Becca had felt a flicker of hope when she'd seen Anna's journals, but maybe there was nothing in them after all. This thought made her sad, for if the answer, or at least a clue, wasn't in the trunks, then she really didn't know how she was going to help.

She pushed herself off her resting place and eased open the lids of the remaining trunks. The smell of mould and age greeting her as her ancestors possessions met her gaze.

She knelt down and rummaged through the trunks, finding clothes of all shapes and sizes, woven baskets, wooden bowls, pots, dried flowers, a wooden stool and what she took to be children's toys – intricately carved wooden animals.

She was running her fingers over one of the carvings, familiarity plucking at her mind, when Jakes reappeared.

'What've you got there?' he said as he set a cup of coffee down on the floor beside her.

'Something I found in the trunks,' she said, holding it out to him. Jakes took the animal and turned it over in his hands.

'Is there anything else in there?'

'Loads of stuff – clothes, pots, more animals and a wooden stool, of all things, why?'

'A stool? Really? Let me see.'

Becca pulled the small stool out of the trunk and passed it to Jakes.

'Well, I'll be… I bet it is, you know.'

'Bet it is what?'

'You remember me telling you what I'd found in Carla's journal?' Becca nodded.

'Well, I'm not sure if I told you about these.'

'What about them?'

'These animals were made by Antony, for Carla, and this stool, well, Carla made it, with Antony's help.'

'Seriously?'

'Seriously,' Jakes said, placing the objects back in the trunk.

'So, these trunks probably contain the contents of Anna's house.'

'Maybe.'

'So, all the spell books etc. must be in that last trunk, as there is nothing pertaining to the Craft in any of the others. And we know there were some, as Anna's letter to Carla said they were under the floorboards.'

'There's only one way to find out. Are you ready?' Jakes said.

'Ready as I'll ever be,' Becca said, her fingers absently massaging one of Antony's wooden carvings.

CHAPTER 8

With care, Jakes lifted the lid of the final trunk. It creaked and groaned at first, but then relinquished its hold.

Becca kept her distance, stepping from one foot to the other, letting Jakes take stock of the contents.

'Well, what's in there?' she said after Jakes had been standing staring into the trunk for what seemed an eternity.

'Hmmm? Oh, sorry, Becca. Pretty much what we said…spell books…jars…'

'Jars? Jars of what?' Her interest now greater than her nervousness, she approached the trunk and peered inside.

One end was full of books – spell books – as Jakes had said, while the back of the trunk held a variety of jars, all different shapes and sizes and labelled with the same handwriting Becca recognised from Anna's letter to Carla.

Becca extracted a few of the jars.

'Looks like herbs and stuff to me. I don't recognise some of the names though and this looks like…urghh…gross,' she said replacing the jars.

'What is it?'

'Desiccated frog by the looks of it,' she said, wrinkling her nose. 'They'll all be ingredients needed for the spells I expect, although after all this time would they even work?'

'You could always try.'

'Hmmm…maybe. Hey, look at these. Corn dollies,' Becca said, holding up differing shapes and creations, made out of various crops. 'Grandma used to make these every year at harvest time.'

'Bet hers weren't ploughed back into the land in the spring though,' Jakes said.

'Hark, listen to you. Been swatting up on paganism have you?' Becca laughed and threw one of the dollies at Jakes.

'Whoa, what on earth are these?' Carefully, Becca lifted out what looked like a handful of twigs, but as she straightened them out, the twigs transformed into miniature puppets – their arms and legs moveable.

'Poppets,' Jakes said as he reached out to take the stick man from Becca. 'How many are there?'

'Poppets? What's a poppet? Becca said as she looked in the trunk. 'There seem to be a few more.'

'Have you heard of voodoo dolls?'

'Of course I have.'

'Well, poppets are the pagan version. Any actions performed on the poppet would be transferred to the person it was an effigy of. They were used for casting spells on people or helping that person.'

'Interesting,' Becca said. 'I wonder who they were used on. Hang on a minute, there's something else in here.' She knelt down in front of the trunk and had to use both hands to dislodge the metal object she'd touched.

'What is it?'

'Not sure as it's stuck under these bloody books. Ah, got it,' she said and lost her balance as she gave it one last tug. She fell backwards on the dusty floor, the metal object clattering to the floor next to her. Jakes bent down to retrieve it, as Becca dusted herself off.

'What is it?' she said, as she stood up and tried to get a look at the object in Jakes' hand.

'It looks like some sort of medallion,' he said, walking over to the window in the roof to get a better look. He held it up by the chain and watched the sun glint off it.

'Wow, look at the colour of the stone in the middle. I've never seen anything so blue. It's not sapphire is it?'

'Unlikely, given whose it was. I am guessing it is more likely to be lapis lazuli.'

'Never heard of it,' Becca said. 'It's a bit creepy though. It almost looks like an eye in the centre of that silver. It's a bit unwieldy to be jewellery isn't it?'

'It was probably used in some sort of ritual, given the size of it. An amulet to ward off evil or something.'

'How do we find out?'

'No idea, Becca. Maybe the journals or spell books will mention something.'

Becca groaned. 'All that reading. It's going to take us forever.'

'Well, we best start soon then, hadn't we, if you want to find this cure.'

'If there even is one,' Becca muttered. 'Shall we drag the trunk down?'

'Er, have you felt the weight of that thing?'

'Okay, let's just grab an armful of…was that the doorbell?'

'I didn't hear anything. What time is it?'

Becca glanced at her watch. 'Just after three.'

'It'll be Leon.'

'Who?'

'From the gallery. About the paintings. We'd better get down there. He doesn't like to be kept waiting.'

CHAPTER 9

By the time she got downstairs, the bell was sounding non-stop and Becca could feel her anger building.

'Who the hell does this guy think he is?'

'Just keep calm, Becca,' Jakes called as he hobbled down after her.

'What the hell do you think you're playing at?' Becca said as she yanked open the front door. Jakes groaned.

'Ms Martin? Leon Crowther from the Victoria Stephens Gallery. Sorry I'm a little late. Traffic was an absolute beast.' Leon extended his hand towards Becca, but she kept hers planted on her hip, the other on the door.

'You have some paintings of your mother's for me to look at, I believe?' he said and stepped into the hallway. 'Where are they?'

'Come in, why don't you,' Becca said and folded her arms across her chest, looking down at the smaller man, whose presence was far bigger than his stature.

'Look, Ms Martin, do you or don't you want me to look at these paintings? It's your decision. I'd love to see them and the gallery would be honoured to show them, but I'm not going to beg you. I have hundreds of up and coming artists clambering for gallery space. So, if you're not interested, I'll be on my way.'

Becca stood with her mouth agape as the dapper man, with an umbrella hooked over his arm, swept passed her and back out of the front door.

'Mr Crowther, wait,' Jakes said and pushed passed Becca. 'Of course she wants you to look at the paintings. It's just been a rather stressful time and…'

'I'm not being spoken to…' Becca let the sentence lapse as she caught Jakes' withering look. 'Yes, Mr Crowther, I would like you to review the paintings,' she said and stood aside to let him back in.

'Excellent. And do call me Leon,' he said, clapping his hands as he waltzed back into the hallway.

'Exquisite. Absolutely exquisite!' Leon said as he took the cup of Earl Grey tea from Becca. 'I can't tell you how excited I was when Ellie told me about the paintings. I mean, Ginnie Martin. Gallery owners tried for years to get her to show her work, but she always refused.'

'That was mum all over,' Becca said. 'Who's Ellie?'

'Ellie Lawrence. She's Vicki's best friend and I believe she knows you, Mr Jakes.'

'Ellie's the one I told you about. My mentee, so to speak.'

'Ah, yes, I remember. So, what's your verdict then, Mr Crow…Leon?' Becca said, glancing at her watch.

'I'll take the lot!' Leon said and let out a high pitched laugh, which made Becca wince. 'Well, I would if I could and I still may; I just need to do a little planning. The gallery isn't big enough to show them all, but if there are certain themes then I could run different shows. I need time to study each one and then I can decide. So, can I send over some crates tomorrow and take them all away?'

Becca turned to Jakes, but he just shrugged.

'Don't worry, they'll all be receipted and they are all insured, although I'm sure you'll agree that art is irreplaceable.'

Becca didn't answer.

'Okay then, I'll be on my way. Good day Ms Martin, Mr Jakes.' Leon said and Becca waited for him to tip his non-existent trilby.

'Thanks for coming, Leon,' Jakes said. 'And tomorrow is fine.'

Leon just nodded, glanced at Becca, and left.

CHAPTER 10

'Wow, this looks amazing,' Becca said as she stepped through the doors of the Victoria Stephens Gallery.

'Frank was right, Becca, your mother was a very talented woman,' Jan said, squeezing Becca's hand and giving her a kiss on the forehead.

'Look at all these people, though,' Becca continued. 'I can't believe all these people have heard of her. I still can't believe anyone has heard of her. I…'

'Come on, Becca. You're blocking the door,' Jakes said and propelled Becca into the gallery and towards Leon, who was looking at his watch and tapping his foot.

'Looks like we're in trouble already,' Jakes said under his breath as Leon finally saw them.

'I thought you were going to be a no show,' Leon said, looking pointedly at Becca, who was staring around the gallery at her mother's works; arranged to show them at their best. She stared at the people huddled around each one and at the red "sold" signs that already decorated many of the paintings.

'I can't…' Becca started and tears filled her eyes.

'I had no doubt she would be a success and I'm delighted you approve, Ms Martin,' Leon said, his stiff veneer crumbling, briefly, at Becca's reaction.

'I don't know what to say. Thank you seems so small and please, call me Becca.'

'I think it is Mr Jakes you should be thanking or maybe even Ellie, because it was her, not me, who persuaded Vicki.'

'All of you. Thank you,' Becca said and gave Leon a hug, much to her own surprise.

Flustered, Leon excused himself and went to attend to some customers who were getting into a heated debate over a painting.

'Is Ellie here, Frank? I'd like to meet her.'

'I'm sure she's here somewhere. Let's go and get some drinks and have a wander, shall we?'

'Becca, this is Ellie.' Becca turned at the sound of Jakes' voice, away from the last painting her mother had ever painted; the one she'd been working on the day Becca went to see her; the one that, for Becca, represented the chaos that was going on in her life.

'Sorry, Frank, I was lost in the chaos again,' she said and smiled at his tall, blonde, attractive companion.

'This is Ellie.'

'Hi Becca, Frank's told me all about you,' Ellie said, stepping forward and giving Becca a hug. 'I feel like I know you already.'

'Hope he hasn't told you everything,' Becca said, not returning the hug. 'Have you, Frank?'

'Yeah, pretty much.' Jakes said. 'Have you seen Jan?'

'Yeah, she's being escorted around by Leon. He's taken a bit of a shine to her.' Becca smiled at the look of panic that crossed Jakes' face.

'Don't worry, Frank, Jan's not his type, if that's what's worrying you,' Ellie said, rubbing Jakes' shoulder.

Becca felt a flair of heat deep inside her at the intimacy of Ellie's touch.

'Why, what's wrong with her?' Frank said, as he twisted and turned, clearly trying to find his new wife.

'I think Ellie means "women" aren't his type. Not that you have anything to worry about anyway,' Becca said and gave him a hug, separating Ellie from him.

'I'm going to go and find her, just in case.' With that, he disappeared into the crowd.

Becca stood next to Ellie, staring at the floor, feeling very small in more ways than just the physical. How could she know "all" about Becca when she, Becca, had only just heard Ellie's name?

'Your mother was an extremely talented lady. Vicki was over the moon when we told her about the find,' Ellie said, grabbing two glasses of wine from a passing waiter and handing one to Becca.

'No thanks. Bourbon's more my thing.'

'Thank God! Mine too. Shall we go set up camp at the bar then?'

Becca couldn't help but smile as Ellie stashed the glasses behind a strategically placed plant.

'I don't know why I've just done that given it will be me clearing up tomorrow,' she said and ordered two Johnny Walker, Black Labels, from the bar.

'I thought you worked at the station?' Becca said, accepting the dark liquid.

'I do. In Scotsford.'

'So, how do you know Frank then?'

'I worked on a case with him over here. He took me under his wing. Defended me from all the abuse.'

'Abuse? Is it still that bad for a woman joining the police?'

'Hah! If only it was "standard" abuse. No, it was far different to that.'

'Different how?' Becca put her bourbon down; her interest piqued.

Ellie turned and looked at Becca and Becca felt a shiver run up her spine at the intensity in Ellie's sapphire eyes.

'How much has Frank told you about me, Becca?'

'Ummm, nothing, if I'm being perfectly honest. The first he's mentioned you to me was about the paintings.' Becca looked down at her hands, a little embarrassed by her lack of knowledge. Ellie laughed and took a sip of her drink.

'Good old Frank. He always could keep a secret when asked.'

Ellie lapsed into silence and though Becca wanted to know what the secret was, she didn't know Ellie well enough to prod further.

'Well, if you ever want to talk about it…' Becca drifted off, cringing at the lameness of what she'd said.

Ellie just smiled at her and signalled the barman for another drink.

'Ah, here you ladies are,' Jakes said as he and Jan wandered over. 'Everything okay?'

'Everything is fine, Frank,' Becca said. 'Ellie and I were just chatting.'

'Have you asked her then?' Jakes said to Ellie.

'No, Frank, for goodness sake!'

'Asked me what?' Becca said, after draining her glass and ordering another.

'Ellie is looking for a place to live and I…'

'Frank!' Ellie said and Becca could swear she heard Ellie growl.

'…thought she could rent one of your rooms. You know, help you out with the mortgage.'

'Frank, leave it,' Ellie said and this time, Becca definitely heard the underlying growl. She saw Jan move closer to Jakes and gently rub his arm.

'So, what do you think?' Jakes said.

'Don't listen to him, Becca, I…'

'Er…to be honest, I hadn't really thought that far ahead,' Becca said. She looked up at the faces before her; at the frustration in Jakes' expression; at the sympathy in Jan's; and at the disappointment in Ellie's, though she was trying hard to hide it. 'I haven't decided if I'm even going to keep the place yet, but…'

'Please, Becca, it's fine. I'm sorry for Frank's bluntness,' Ellie said.

'Hey, I'm used to that and, seriously, if I decide to keep the house, a lodger would be a great idea. The thought of rattling around in that big house on my own, even with Spook, is not too appealing.'

'Spook?'

'Spook is Becca's cat,' Jan said. 'A huge grey bundle of fur with orange eyes and an attitude.'

'Yes, he's definitely got one of those,' Becca said and smiled.

'Ah, cats aren't really that fond of me,' Ellie said.

'Don't worry about it,' Becca said. 'Spook isn't fond of many people.'

'Yeah, he even went off Becca for a while,' Jakes said.

The group lapsed into silence at that point, a silence soon broken by Leon's arrival.

'That's it. We've done it. A complete sell out! Becca, your mother's paintings have sold faster than anything we've ever shown before. Even Vicki's,' he said, the last point muttered under his breath.

'Really?' Becca said.

'Really,' Leon confirmed. 'And I have reserves put on some pieces from the later shows too. So, all in all, Ms Becca Martin, your mother has left you quite a legacy!'

CHAPTER 11

'So, what did they say?' Jakes said as Becca put the phone down and lapsed into silence. 'Becca?' he prompted after a few minutes.

'What? Oh sorry, Frank, er, well, it would seem I am now the proud "mortgage free" owner of this house and have a sizeable nest egg too…a very sizeable one…a "I'm never going to have to work again" one. All thanks to mum.' Becca's voice broke and tears pricked at her eyes as she thought of the decade long estrangement from her mother, about the uncomfortable reunion and about her mother's death.

Becca hadn't realised she was sobbing until Jakes came and sat down next to her and pulled her into his arms.

'It's okay, Becca, let it all out.'

'Oh God, Frank, I was so awful to her and…'

'It's what she would have wanted.'

'But I don't deserve all this. I…'

'Of course you do and I'm sure she'd approve of what you've done.'

'Not so sure about that,' Becca said and sniffed, wiping her nose with the back of her hand. 'There must be a reason she never sold more.'

'Maybe they were your inheritance all along?'

'I just can't believe it, though. I never have to worry about money again, yet she scrimped and saved. I just don't get it.'

'Believe it and embrace the opportunity it has afforded you. You can do whatever you want now, Becca.'

'After I've helped Antony.'

'Well, yes…or you could forget about helping him and get on with living your life. Get yourself a boyfriend, some friends…'

'What is it with you and me getting a boyfriend?'

'I just want you to be happy, Becca. I want you to have someone special in your life.'

'I do. I have you and Jan, and I have Spook.'

'You know what I mean.'

'Well, I can't. Not yet. I have to help Antony. I want to help Antony.'

'Becca, you don't…'

'Frank! I made a promise and, besides, he deserves the chance at a life too, doesn't he?'

'I just can't forget what he did to you, what he could do to you again; what he will do to you again.'

'You don't know that.'

'Yes, I do. Whatever you believe he may have been, he is a monster now and you are the only thing keeping him that way.'

'He's not a monster, Frank. Not deep down.'

'For God's sake, Becca, wake up!' Jakes said, jumping up from the sofa and pacing the room. 'Don't you remember what he did to you, what he did to your mother?'

'Of course I do,' Becca said, her anger igniting inside her. 'I remember very clearly having to kill my own mother and I will never forget being strung up and tortured.'

'Well, why risk getting hurt again?' Jakes said, placing a hand on Becca's shoulder, a gesture that always seemed to calm her down.

'Because I made a promise and I want to help him. You read Anna's letter. None of this was his fault, Frank. He doesn't deserve to be left in that sarcophagus.'

'I know. I know. I just don't want you to get hurt again.'

'I won't. I promise.'

'You can't promise that.'

'I can. I started reading through some of the books we found and I can use one of the poppets to control him.'

'And if that doesn't work?'

'It will.'

'If it doesn't?'

Becca shrugged and looked down at her hands.

'Have you thought any more about a lodger?' Jakes said, deciding to change the subject.

'Not really. I probably should though as I don't want to be living here on my own.'

'So, you've decided to keep the house then?'

'Yeah, I think so. I can feel mum here, and grandma. Somehow I think it's what they would have wanted. Besides, I can't bear to be in my apartment now, not after everything that happened.'

'Do you think you'll be able to sell it?'

'Oh yeah, I've already had notes shoved through the door with some pretty good offers on. Some people are just weird.'

'Sick more like,' Jakes said.

'Who cares, as long as I can sell it, hey?'

'True. So, how about Ellie?'

'How about Ellie what?'

'As a lodger?'

' Hmmm, maybe. What's her story anyway?'

'You mean she didn't tell you?'

'No, she clammed up. She was surprised and I think a little relieved that you hadn't told me.'

'Well, I think she should be the one to tell you, but suffice it to say, she's experienced something like what you've just been through, but it's rather more permanent and rather more personal.'

'Are you telling me Ellie is a vampire?'

'No, not a vampire.'

'Then what?'

'I think it best she tell you. I will vouch for her though. You have nothing to be afraid of and she would be a great person to have around right now. I'd feel better knowing you weren't alone, at least.'

'Okay, Frank. For you. Ellie can move in, but on a trial basis.'

'Excellent! I'll get her to give you a call. Right, shall we make a start on these journals then?'

'That is why you came round. Where do you want to start?'

'How about I take Carla's and you take Anna's?'

'This is going to take forever.'

'Not if we speed read,' Jakes said and winked at Becca. 'Try not to get too involved.'

But it was too late, Becca was already lost; lost in the early journals of Anna Harris Martindale.

CHAPTER 12

'Stop, stop, we can't do this, John. It's not right,' Anna said as they broke the cover of the trees and followed Tom into the clearing.

'Don't you want to know what's inside his house then?' John said, twisting his arm out of Anna's vice like grip.

'Of course I do, but…'

'Well, we know he's not there, so what better opportunity than now?'

'But what if he's put some sort of spell on the house?' Anna said, grabbing John by both arms and spinning him around to face her. 'He's dangerous, John, you know that; we all know that. I just don't think this is a good idea.'

'You did an hour ago. In fact, it was you who started all this. You who wanted to see if he really does have poppets of the villagers, if he really does have a dead human head on a spike next to the fireplace.'

'I know, but…'

'But nothing. A dare is a dare and, sobered up or not, we are going through with it.' With that, John shrugged out of her grasp and followed Tom to the house.

Anna stayed where she was, rooted to the spot on the edge of the copse. What had seemed like a good idea not so long ago, when she had had a couple of ales, now seemed like utter folly.

He was not a man to be trifled with. He was not a man at all; not really. He was a man feared by the villagers of Breccan, Carlford and beyond. He was a man who could turn your world upside down on a whim and frequently did so.

Yes, he did what he wanted, to whom he wanted, whenever he wanted. All anyone could do was pray they wouldn't come to his notice.

So, what were they doing breaking into his home? Of all the things to do to bring yourself to his attention, this had to be at the top of the list.

Why, oh why, had she suggested it?

Sure, as kids they'd all stood, pretty much where she was now, and wondered what horrors he kept hidden in there. They'd all whispered and debated the existence of souls he'd captured, in trade for something else. They'd all imagined those tortured souls roaming around inside his home, awaiting the day the debt would be paid and they would be returned to their rightful owner.

But, what they'd never done was stray beyond the edge of the woods. They'd never set foot in the clearing that housed his ramshackle home and they'd certainly never even contemplated going up to the cottage and breaking in.

What had they been thinking? What had she been thinking? He may not be there, but he'd know, she was sure of that. The knot in her stomach had tightened and she stepped forward.

'John! Tom! Don't!' Anna said and ran towards them, but it was too late. As she called out to them, she heard the splintering sound as one of the windows was broken. 'Stop, please. We shouldn't do this,' she called, but they both ignored her and she watched in horror as John climbed in through the broken window.

Anna stopped, ten feet from the cottage, and held her breath. *Please be okay, please be okay*, she prayed and almost fainted as the front door opened and John took a bow, indicating for Tom and herself to come in. Tom didn't hesitate.

'Come on, Anna,' John said. 'You'll love it in here.'

'No, John. It's wrong. He'll know and then…'

'Then we've nothing to lose, have we? We might as well make it worth the punishment he's going to dole out, hadn't we, my love?' John said and extended his hand to her.

Anna looked at it and then up into the face of the man she loved so fiercely, that she'd agreed to be his wife. Placing her belief and her trust in this man, Anna reached out and took his hand and then stepped over the threshold into the home of Ebenezer Lightwoller.

CHAPTER 13

'There's nothing here,' Tom said as Anna entered the cottage. 'Nothing. The place looks more like an abandoned hovel. Are you sure this is the right place?'

'Of course it's the right place,' John said to him and caught Anna just as her legs gave out under her. 'Whoa, steady Anna. Are you okay?'

Anna grasped John's arm for support and then steadied herself against the wall. Her head was spinning, as if she'd been twirling around in circles as fast as she could and then stopped suddenly. She closed her eyes and dropped her chin to her chest, but that only served to make her feel nauseous.

'Anna, darling, are you okay?'

'Not…really, no,' she said. 'Could you get me a chair please?'

Tom grabbed a rickety chair from around the bench table and dragged it across the stone floor, the noise seeming unnecessarily loud for the apparent weight of the chair.

'Can you make any more noise, Tom,' John said. 'Just pick it up and stop being so lazy.'

'You pick it up. The damn thing weighs a tonne.'

'Don't be ridiculous. It's barely held together,' John said and yanked the chair out of Tom's grasp.

'What the hell is this thing made of,' John said, massaging his shoulder.

'I told you,' Tom muttered and proceeded to go around the parlour, picking up or trying to pick up and move the various mundane objects he came across. 'Everything is the same. It looks one way, but feels another.'

'That's because nothing in this house is what it appears to be,' Anna said, lifting her head up from between her knees, where she'd been resting to quell the nausea.

'What are you talking about?' Tom said with a snort. Anna swallowed and mopped her now clammy brow with the handkerchief she always carried. How do you explain to someone who doesn't have the gift what is actually in this house?

'What do you see, Anna?' John said.

'Everything,' she said and patted John's hand. He'd always been so good and understanding about her gift, unlike the rest of the village. Tom had too, of course, but it was John whom she'd fallen head over heels in love with several years ago and recently agreed to marry.

'Oh, how I wish you could see what I see,' Anna said, placing a hand on her heart to try to calm its ever increasing rhythm. 'Tell me what you see.'

'Nothing,' Tom said. 'It's just a dark empty room with a broken table and rickety chairs in front of an empty stone hearth.'

'And what about that in your hand?' Anna indicated the glittering jewel encrusted box in Tom's hand.

'See for yourself. It's just a wooden box with a broken hinge,' he said, lifting the lid. Anna turned her head away as the light of the window caught the mirrored surface inside the lid.

'No, it isn't,' she said. 'None of this is what it appears to be. Where you see a broken table, I see a solid oak, sturdy one, polished until it shines. Your bare hearth is alight with flames and a cauldron bubbling away. Can't you smell the delicious food?'

'You know we can't, Anna,' John said and rested his hand on her shoulder. 'Are you feeling any better?'

'No and I won't until I leave here,' she said. 'I think we should leave.

He'll be back soon.' She tried to get up, but the dizziness returned and sent her back down again.

'But why can't we see what's really here?' John said, his attention drawn to something hanging over the fireplace.

'Because he has placed a cloaking spell on the place, to deter thieves. Think about it. Think about your reaction to it. You saw nothing but junk in here and certainly nothing worth stealing. It's very clever.'

'What about this then?' John said, dangling what looked at first like a necklace from his hand.

'I can't see it properly from here. What is it?'

'Looks like some sort of medal or amulet or something. It's weird. It looks like an eye in the centre and it feels like it's looking right at us.' John shivered.

'Let me see,' Anna said, sitting upright and holding out her hand.

John passed the amulet to her and Anna shuddered as she stared into the eye at its centre; an eye of the brightest blue stone she had ever seen, surrounded by beaten iron, to form a diamond shape.

'We have to leave now,' she said and forced herself to stand up, reaching for the wall to stop herself falling.

'Why? What did you see?'

'Come on, let's go. Both of you. John, help me, please.'

'Not until you tell me what you've seen.'

'For God's sake, John,' Anna said, looking into the stubborn defiant eyes of her soon to be husband. 'Fine. This amulet is what keeps this cloaking spell in place. This amulet is a way for Ebenezer to keep watch over all that is his. This amulet is how he finds out the things he does and then uses that knowledge against people, for his own gain. You want to know why it feels like you are being watched? Because you are. Put it back, John, please and let's go. God only knows what he will do to us for this.'

Anna handed John the amulet, but he dropped it in his pocket and nodded towards Tom.

'John, I said put it back. He'll…'

'Not be able to do anything to anyone again if he can't see them, will he?'

'Don't be so ridiculous,' Anna said as she was ushered out of the cottage, Tom and John on either side of her. 'Do you honestly think that is his only way?'

'No, but it's one less,' John said and frog marched Anna across the clearing to the cover of the trees.

As they moved away from the cottage, Anna swore she felt eyes boring into the back of her and, before following the others back through the woods, she turned to find Ebenezer standing in front of his home, his hands pointing to the ground, staring straight at her.

Anna felt a tightness around her heart as she turned away. Nothing would be the same again, of that she was sure. Now she would be forever looking over her shoulder, until the time when Ebenezer would eke his revenge.

CHAPTER 14

'You didn't see him, John,' Anna said, grabbing John by the arm and spinning him around.

'Oh, for goodness sake, Anna. What's he going to do, put a curse on us?' He shrugged out of her grasp and went back to chopping wood.

'That's exactly what he's going to do and you know it.' Anna paced back and forth, her arms crossed over her chest, her right hand up to her face, chewing her nails.

'You'll be able to stop him though, won't you, you being a witch and all?'

'No, John, I won't,' she said and John stopped what he was doing and looked at her.

'What do you mean, "no"? You said you'd be able to break any spell he cast. That's the only reason we went there.'

'Yes, break any spell he had put on the shack so we could get in, but that was it. I can't compete with his power, John. You've seen what he can do. The whole village has seen what he can do. I can't…' her voice broke and she collapsed to the ground and buried her head in her hands.

John dropped his axe and ran over to her and pulled her towards him.

'Oh, God, John, what have we done? It's all my fault. I should have been more clear.'

'No, no, no. It's not your fault. We all decided to go. We're all to blame.'

'But you didn't see him. It was me he looked at. It was me he blamed. It will be me he punishes. I felt it, when he looked at me. I felt it right here.'

Anna massaged her chest above her heart. 'He's going to take something from me, something I love. I know he is. Oh God, John, he's going to take you.' Anna burst into tears and clung to John.

'He's not going to take me, don't worry.'

'How do you know?'

'Because I won't let him, Anna, don't worry. I'm not going…'

'Do you really think you'll have a choice?' Anna said, infused with anger as she pushed John away from her and stood up. 'Do you really think you'll be able to stop him? Well…do you?'

Anna's eyes flashed and she clenched her fists. A rumble of thunder sounded in the distance and clouds blackened the sky.

'Anna, calm down. Look what you're doing,' John said, indicating the gathering storm as he approached her, but she just backed away.

'There's only one thing for it,' she said unclenching her fists. The sky brightened immediately.

'What?'

'Return the amulet.'

'No chance.'

'Why? If we return it then maybe, just maybe, he will be more lenient.'

'Do you honestly believe that?'

'I have to,' she said. 'It's the only thing we've got to give him.'

'Not the only thing, dearie.'

Anna screamed at the sound of his voice and whirled round to face Ebenezer. He started to walk towards her and she backed away until she could feel the warmth and comfort of John's arms around her. Not that they would protect her from Ebenezer's wrath.

'But it is a start. Now, where is it?'

'What?' Anna said.

'Oh, don't play the fool with me, dearie,' Ebenezer said, pointing his walking cane at her chest. She felt her heart constrict and she dropped to the floor, gasping for breath.

'Now, do I have to ask again?'

'I…don't…know where it is.'

'Oh, I think you do, dearie,' Ebenezer said and turned his wrist. Anna cried out as her heart was squeezed even tighter.

'Leave her alone, Lightwoller,' John said, putting himself between Anna and Ebenezer.

'Ah, the white knight. I was wondering how long it would be before you defended the woman whom you love.'

John's distraction was all that Anna needed. As she lay on the ground, she closed her eyes, reached out to touch John - to make the necessary connection - and then whispered as quietly as she could the protection spell. Just in time, she felt the familiar ripple through her body as the spell took hold.

'So, white knight, where is my amulet?' Ebenezer said and rammed his cane into John's chest. John didn't flinch.

'Somewhere you won't find it. Somewhere where you won't be able to see anymore.'

'Oh really? I know you want to look brave in front of your woman, but didn't you see what I did to her?'

John didn't say anything.

'What makes you think I won't do to you what I did to her? Only, I don't think you'll fare as well, as you're not as strong as she is.'

Ebenezer placed his cane on John's chest, directly over his heart and leaned against it, twisting it as he did so.

'One last chance, Martindale. Where is my amulet?'

'Somewhere where you can't use it to hurt others.'

'You are a very stupid man,' Ebenezer said and, without a word, raised his cane to the heavens and, chanting in a language Anna had never heard before, he whipped the cane down and aimed it at John's chest. Anna screamed as a bolt of lightning shot from the end of the cane and into John's chest.

John shuddered and then collapsed to the floor, twitching.

'John!' Anna screamed and threw herself over him, praying her spell would be enough. 'How could you?' Anna said, glaring up at Ebenezer.

'You're really asking me that, knowing what I do?' He laughed and rested both hands on the cane in front of him.

'Now, where were we? Ah, yes, my amulet. Where is it?'

'I've already told you, I don't know where it is.'

'That's too bad for you then, isn't it?' Ebenezer said. 'You've taken something precious from me and now it is my turn to return the favour.'

'What could you possibly take from me that you haven't done already?' she said, looking down at John.

'Don't mistake me for a fool, dearie. I know what you did. Whether it was strong enough, you'll just have to wait and see.'

'I don't have anything else.'

'No, but you will,' Ebenezer said and, dipping his chin down to his chest, he started to murmur and slowly raised his cane again.

Anna felt pains shoot through her abdomen and she collapsed to the floor, the breath squeezed out of her.

Bracing herself on her hands and knees, she looked up, ready to retaliate, but Ebenezer was gone.

CHAPTER 15

'I need a drink,' Becca said, twisting her neck from side to side to release the tension. 'What time is it?' she said, yawning and stretching; Anna's journal forgotten for now, in her lap.

'Almost seven,' Jakes said, glancing at his watch before returning to Carla's journal.

'Anything?' Becca said, intrigued by the intensity of his concentration.

'Mmmm,' Jakes said.

'Earth to Frank, come in Frank,' Becca said and threw a cushion across the room. It glanced off his shoulder, but did the trick.

'What? Sorry Becca. Did you say something?'

'Have you found out anything?'

'Yes, lots, but nothing pertaining to Antony. You?'

'Well, I've found out who the amulet belongs to.'

'Really? Who?' Jakes said, closing the journal he was reading and looking intently at Becca.

'Ebenezer Lightwoller.'

'The man who cursed Antony.'

'Exactly.'

'So, how did it come to be in Anna's possession?'

'It would appear that petty theft was a past time of my ancestor's and Ebenezer was none too pleased.'

'I'm not surprised. What does surprise me is that Anna lived to tell the tale, so to speak. Why didn't he punish her?'

'I'm not sure that he didn't…yet,' Becca said and yawned. 'Drink?'

'No, thanks. I need to be off, really. I promised to take Jan to dinner.'

'Lucky Jan,' Becca said and smiled at Frank.

'You're welcome to join us, you know.'

'I'm sure Jan has a more intimate dinner in mind,' she said and winked. She laughed when she saw colour flood Jakes' cheeks. 'Besides, Ellie will be here shortly to look at the room.'

'Ah, yes, I'd forgotten. Right, well, I'll leave you to it. Do you mind if I take this with me?'

'Knock yourself out. We've got plenty to get through, though I think we're more likely to find what we're looking for in Anna's journals, don't you?' Becca could see she was talking to herself.

'Frank!'

'Sorry, what? Did you say something, Becca?'

'How about you put Carla's journals to one side, just for now,' she said as Jakes was about to protest. 'What we need is more likely to be in Anna's journals. Why don't you take these?' She thrust a pile of journals into Jakes' arms. 'They are earlier than the ones I'm looking at and so may well have some useful information on Ebenezer in them.'

'What makes you so sure?'

'I'm not, but it is more likely to be in those than in Carla's, don't you agree?'

'Point taken,' Jakes said. 'Right, best be off.'

'Have a lovely evening,' she said and kissed him on the cheek as she saw him out. She closed the door behind him and rested her back against it for a moment.

'Now for that drink, buddy,' she said to Spook as he sauntered into the hallway, bleary eyed from his afternoon of sleeping, while she and Jakes read. As she pushed away from the door, her stomach rumbled and Spook stopped his march to the kitchen and turned around to look at her. 'And perhaps some food,' she said.

Spook's ears perked up at the word "food" and he dashed to his bowl, his sleepiness suddenly forgotten as his second favourite past-time took over.

The ringing of the doorbell jolted Becca awake, just over an hour later. It took her a few minutes to come round and realise where she was.

She'd picked Anna's journal up after she'd eaten and had become so engrossed in Anna's life that she'd been dreaming about it, a little too vividly if she was honest.

Becca glanced at the clock on the mantelpiece and saw it was eight thirty. She stretched, the journal sliding from her lap as she did so. One down, she thought as she bent to pick it up and the doorbell sounded again.

'Okay, okay, I'm coming,' she mumbled and pushed herself out of the armchair. She went to open the front door, loosening her neck and shoulders as she did so.

'Ellie,' she said as she opened the door.

'Hi, Becca. Sorry I'm late. I got stuck at the station,' Ellie said and shrugged her shoulders.

'Hey, no worries. Come on in,' Becca said and stood aside to let Ellie in.

'Look, thanks for this,' Ellie said and turned to face Becca. Becca had to look up to make eye contact and she felt her tired neck muscles grumble.

'I hope Frank didn't force you into this?'

'No, don't be daft. You'll soon find out no one forces me into doing something I don't want to do. Coffee?'

'That would be great, thanks,' Ellie said and followed Becca into the kitchen.

'Wow, I haven't seen a kitchen like this in, well…'

'Never,' Becca finished and started laughing. 'Yep, unfortunately, though functional, most of the house is in serious need of updating.'

'Hey, I love the original features,' Ellie said as she took the mug of coffee from Becca.

'Ha! You won't be saying that when you've experienced the original shower,' Becca said and winked. 'Still fancy the tour?'

'Yep.'

'So, what do you think? Still interested?' Becca said as she and Ellie sat in the living room, sipping a glass of Chianti.

'Definitely,' Ellie said. 'It has a wonderful sense of home that I've never had before.'

Becca noticed this reference to a home again. It was something Ellie had kept referring to as they went round, but when Becca had asked about it, Ellie had clammed up. Becca decided to let it go this time. Ellie would tell her if and when she was ready.

'Is that why you've decided to keep it?' Ellie said.

'Sorry, keep what?'

'The house. Because it reminds you of your childhood; your home?'

'God no,' Becca said and snorted. 'I certainly don't want to be reminded of my childhood.'

'Why?'

'Well, let's just say, witches didn't exactly make for acceptable friend material,' Becca said and her eyes clouded over.

'And we're supposed to be a less prejudiced society nowadays,' Ellie said, the sarcasm not lost on Becca.

'Yeah, well there are certain things people will never accept, unless they want something of course. But then, acceptance is only temporary.'

'Tell me about it,' Elle said and they both lapsed into silence for a while, each lost in her own thoughts.

'So, what won't people accept about you?' Becca said, deciding the direct approach as the best option.

'Oh, just what I am,' Ellie said.

'And what are you?' Becca said, holding her breath, sure she was about to find out Ellie's secret.

'A superhero,' Ellie said. 'No one likes superheroes, not really. It's the jealousy thing,' she continued and burst out laughing. 'Right, I'd better hit the road and get some sleep. Early shift tomorrow.'

Becca opened her mouth, intent on pressing Ellie for the truth, but something told her to leave it. This same feeling told her she would find out soon enough.

'When do you want to move in?' she said instead.

'Well, I've got a couple of days off next week. Would it be okay if I did it then?'

'Yep, no problem. It gives me time to get your room ready before you move in.'

'Don't worry about that,' Ellie said. 'Right, I best be off. Thanks again for this, Becca. I really appreciate it.'

Becca waved away her thanks and spotted two orange eyes watching them from the hallway.

'C'mon buddy and meet Ellie,' Becca said to Spook and clicked her fingers, but the big grey cat didn't move. His gaze flicked from Becca to Ellie.

'Sorry about this. His curiosity usually overwhelms him and he can't resist seeing what's going on,' Becca said and went out into the hallway. Spook tried to back away from her, but hit the wall instead.

'Don't worry. Like I said, cats aren't that fond of me anyway. I guess I'm more of a dog person.'

'Well, he needs to learn, don't you buddy?' Becca said and carried him into the living room towards Ellie.

Becca felt him stiffen as they approached and as they got to within a few feet, he started to growl.

'Spook! Be nice,' Becca said, hugging him to her as she brought him up close to Ellie. But Spook was having none of it. He hissed at Ellie, his hackles raised and, before Becca could stop him, he lashed out. Ellie dodged out of his way, as if she'd been expecting it.

Becca was so shocked by his behaviour that she didn't try to stop him as he fought his way out of her arms.

'I'm so sorry about that. He doesn't normally…'

'It's okay, Becca, but if me being here is going to be an issue for him, then…'

'Absolutely not,' Becca said. 'He'll get used to you. He'll have to.'

CHAPTER 16

Becca spent a frustrating week reading through Anna's journals. Whilst she enjoyed learning about the life of her ancestor, an insight that few, if any, get a chance to see, it wasn't giving her what she wanted – answers. She needed to find a way to break the curse, to give Antony his life back, without it costing hers to do so.

By the time moving day came she was grateful for the distraction and walked away from the journals to help Ellie move in.

Spook, quite un-Spook like, decided to abstain from his usual cardboard box fetish and spent the day in the garden, watching from behind the veil of the laburnum tree.

'Does he always hide there?' Ellie said as she stopped next to Becca on the landing, where Becca was watching Spook.

'No, not really, but we haven't been here long enough for him to have developed any real habits. Is that the last?' Becca said, a twinge of concern for Spook tugging at her heartstrings.

'Yep, all done,' Ellie said and continued along the hall to Becca's mother's room, now her room.

'Blimey, you didn't have much to move,' Becca said, leaning on the door-jam and crossing her arms as she observed the sparse collection of boxes.

'Not really had the opportunity to accumulate anything,' Ellie said and shrugged.

'How come?' Becca said before she could stop herself.

Again, Ellie shrugged, but didn't offer any comment.

'Do you have any furniture?'

'Just a couple of bookcases. I was hoping I could make use of this,' Ellie said, gesturing to Ginnie's furniture.

'Of course,' Becca said. 'I've cleared the bathroom next door for you too. It's all yours.'

'Are you sure?'

'Yep, I've got an en suite in my room, so I don't use it really.'

'Wow, thanks, Becca.'

'Hey, don't thank me until you've sampled the plumbing. Like the rest of the house, it is rather dated,' Becca said and went to leave.

'Still, thank you. I appreciate you letting me stay,' Ellie said, touching Becca's arm. Becca jumped and whirled round; how the hell had Ellie moved so quickly?

'Sure,' Becca said, shaking a little. 'Are you hungry? I'm going to make an omelette if you're interested?'

'Thanks, but I need to get to work. I've been called in to cover tonight.'

'No problem. I'll leave you to it.'

Becca wandered downstairs and into the kitchen. She leaned against the sink and stared out of the window at Spook, who was now curled up asleep, a safe distance from the house.

Little flickers of alarm were trying to ignite inside her and her mind kept flicking between two incidents – the growling at the gallery and the speed and silence in which she'd moved just then. Who was Ellie Lawrence? Or, to be more precise, what was Ellie Lawrence?

Becca shivered as her thoughts shifted to Antony, but she dismissed that thought. Ellie moved around during the day, so she couldn't be a vampire.

'Right, I'm off. I'll try not to wake you when I come in,' Ellie said, popping her head around the kitchen door.

'What? Oh, don't worry. I don't sleep very well, anyway,' Becca said, trying to settle her heart rate after Ellie's appearance had made her jump.

'Okay, well, have a good evening.'

'You too.'

Becca heard the front door slam and within minutes, the cat flap sounded and Spook meowed at her feet. Becca bent down and picked him up, nuzzling her face into his soft fur.

'What have I done, buddy? Who on earth have I just allowed into our lives?'

CHAPTER 17

Unable to sleep, the subject of Ellie playing on her mind, Becca decided to return to Anna's journals. Instead of carrying on from where she left off, she decided to flick through them until an entry caught her attention.

After two hours of nothing, Becca was about to call it a day when a smudged page stopped her. At first, she thought someone must have spilt water on it and then tried to wipe it off, but on closer inspection, she noticed the damage was in patches. Tears, Becca thought, curious to know what had upset the person Becca had grown to believe to be the strongest woman she had ever had the privilege to know; she read on, having to piece together some entries as the damage had obscured a number of words.

'I won't go through it again, John. I just can't,' Anna sobbed as John pulled her into his arms.

'It'll be okay, Anna. It's just asleep, that's all. Try not to fret too much,' John said, resting his chin on his wife's head and squeezing his eyes shut tight, a tear escaping and plopping into Anna's auburn hair.

'But it's been days. It hasn't moved for days, just like the others,' Anna said and looked down as her swollen belly, her hands keeping up a steady massage in the hope of rousing the baby.

'It's not like the others, Anna. You know that. You're almost there now. The others were…well…a lot sooner.'

'It's still the same. It's still the same feeling, John. I know. The baby is dead. Again.'

John pulled her tighter towards him, silent, for he had no words to soothe the anguish. There were none.

'It's just a matter of time now. Time to wait for my body to understand what I know in my heart,' Anna said, her voice calm now, resolute, resigned. She pulled away from her husband of five years and went back to stir the broth she'd been making.

The pain came out of the blue, so swiftly that Anna could have sworn someone had just thrust a red hot poker through her abdomen. She cried out and collapsed to the floor, the ladle clattering against the stone. She vaguely heard John as he ran towards her, but the pains, relentless in their punishment, were too much and Anna's vision receded into blackness.

When she came to, she was in her own bed and the pain had gone. Disorientated, she reached her hands out and felt the swell of her belly. Had she dreamed it? She tried to sit up and a searing pain shot up from between her legs and seemed to pierce her heart.

Anna cried out as the pain radiated through her body, sucking the air out of her.

The door to the bedroom banged open and John came crashing through, arms laden with sheets, a look of terror on his face.

Anna tried to reach out to him, but the pain shot through her again, causing her to clutch her belly and roll over. She tried to curl up, to cradle against the pain, but her body wouldn't allow it.

'Hold her down, John. Don't just stand there!' Anna heard her mother's voice and felt John's bear like hands gently pull her onto her back again.

'Mama?' Anna murmured.

'There, there, pet. It will soon be over,' her mother said. Anna looked into her mother's eyes and saw tears of sorrow and concern.

'No, mama! Not again. I thought this time…' her voice broke as the pain seared through her again, her body having caught up and wanting to purge itself as soon as possible.

'I know pet, I know. But we have to get this baby out of you before it kills you.'

'Noooooo,' Anna wailed and John leaned in close to her.

'There'll be others, Anna. We'll have a baby…one day,' he said.

'No, there won't. This will happen again and again. He did this to us. He killed our four babies…' Anna screamed; the room spun around her and she felt her eyes roll back in her head. She was dying. This time she wouldn't survive.

She could make out her mother's voice issuing orders to John and felt herself being held down. Her legs were dragged open and she felt pressure on her belly as her mother pushed against the baby Anna so desperately wanted, trying to push it out of her.

'No!' Anna screamed again and slapped her mother's hands away.

'Listen to me, Anna,' her mother said, grasping her wrists and holding them tightly. 'You cannot keep this baby. It will kill you. You have to let it go.'

'Noooooo,' Anna wailed again, tears flowing freely now.

'You have to let it go, my girl. Now push.'

'Nev…' But she didn't get to finish as her body took over and the waves of pain crashed down, forcing her dead child out of her. Anna had no choice. Gathering all the strength she had, she pushed and felt the still form of her fourth child, as it slid out of her.

She held her breath, she couldn't help it, waiting for the cry she knew would never come.

'What did you mean "he did this to us"?' John said, as he and Anna stood at the foot of the tiny grave in the cemetery of St Martin's church. Edward's grave, for that's what they'd named him, was flanked by those of his sisters and brother.

'Mmmm,' Anna said, staring transfixed at the name carved into the wooden cross. *Just one more month and you would have been in my arms*, she thought and squeezed her eyes shut. A tear ran down her cheek, which surprised her because she didn't think she had anything left.

'Anna, what did you mean?' John said again and gently shook his wife.

'Ebenezer did this to us,' she said, her gaze remaining on the graves of her four stillborn children.

'What? How? We haven't seen him or heard of him in years,' John said and forced Anna to turn and face him.

'It doesn't matter,' she said, not looking at him. 'He cursed us that night, John.'

'Which night? What are you talking about?' John said and hooked his finger under Anna's chin, tilting her head upwards, forcing her to look at him.

'The night he almost killed you. That night…that night he said he'd take something precious from us…and he has…again and again…' With that she turned away and headed back towards the house.

CHAPTER 18

'Stop, Anna, wait,' John said and grabbed her by the arm.

'Wait for what? Him to take another baby from me?' Anna snapped and yanked her arm from John's grasp. She glared at her husband, feeling sad at the pain and the sadness she saw etched across his handsome features.

'Anna, please, don't.'

'Why not, John? Why?' She couldn't contain her anger anymore and she lashed out at him, pummelling his broad chest. He tried to pull her into his arms, but she fought against him.

'What are you going to do, Anna?'

'Speak to him. Reason with him. Offer him something he wants.'

'You can't reason with someone like him, Anna. He doesn't care about you or what he's done.' John strode behind her as she ran through the woods.

'I can try,' Anna said and burst through the woods into the clearing. 'Noooooo!' she said and John quickened his pace, breaking cover just in time to catch his wife as she collapsed to her knees, her head in her hands and burst into tears.

Anna leant against her husband and slowly raised her head, staring disbelieving at the scene before her.

Gone was the dwelling that she, John and Tom had broken into years before and, in its place, was a tiny broken down shack with boarded up windows and the front door hanging from its frame.

'No, this can't be,' she muttered, almost to herself. 'He has to be here.

He has to.' She pushed away from John and stood up. Haltingly, she made her way across the clearing to the shack.

'Anna, where are you going? He's not there,' John called after her.

'He has to be,' she muttered and stumbled forward. She pushed open the broken door and stepped into a room which, a few years ago, was alive with the treasures it contained. This time, however, she saw nothing, nothing except a broken table, a couple of rickety chairs and an empty hearth.

'Ebenezer!' she said, turning around on the spot, her face raised to the heavens, her palms outstretched. 'Ebenezer Lightwoller, I summon you to come before me.'

Nothing. She looked around her for an object, something that was his and again tried to call him, but again there was nothing.

'He's gone, Anna. He left a long time ago,' John said from the doorway.

'He isn't gone,' she said. 'I just need to find the right object to make him come.'

'Okay, what do you want me to look for?'

'The amulet.' Silence hung between them for a while. Anna stared at John, but he just looked at the floor.

'I can't.'

'Why not?'

'Because it would put at risk too many lives, Anna. You know that.'

'And what about our lives? What about the lives of our children? Haven't we suffered enough?'

'Of course we have, but you don't know he will stop.'

'No, you're right. I don't, but I have to try. Now, go and get the amulet. Please John,' Anna said and walked over to him, taking him by the hands and looking up into his soft brown eyes. 'For our children.'

John sighed and pulled Anna towards him.

'I never could refuse you anything,' he said and kissed the top of her head before turning and leaving her in the doorway of the tumbledown shack.

Anna didn't know how long she'd been sitting there, rocking back and forth, thoughts of her dead babies filling her head. It was the snap of a twig that brought her back to reality and she noticed the sun setting, casting the clearing into a pale shade of orange. She looked up and saw John ambling towards her, his shoulders sagging, his step heavy. In his hand he held a small cloth sack.

Anna tried to stand, but her legs had gone numb and it took a while for the feeling to come back to them.

John handed her the sack without a word and sat down with his back to the outside of the shack and rested his head on his arms.

'I'm sorry, John, but I have to,' she said and rested her hand on his as she passed him. He grasped it for a moment and squeezed it before releasing her.

Anna walked back inside the shack and placed the amulet above the fireplace where it had once hung. Standing before it, her gaze fixed on the central eye, Anna angled her palms to the ground and started to chant the summoning spell she had learned. Over and over she chanted, focusing her mind on one single image – that of Ebenezer Lightwoller – but nothing happened. The amulet didn't glow, the earth didn't shift, the air didn't flinch. It was as if any power that Ebenezer had imbibed the amulet with was dead; a useless trinket.

Anna slumped to the floor, buried her head in her hands and cried, loud wracking sobs; sobs that shook her whole body and brought John rushing into the shack.

'What, Anna? What happened?'

'Nothing.'

'Then what's wrong?'

'Nothing happened, John. Nothing! That's what's wrong. Nothing happened! The amulet is powerless. You might as well just get rid of it.'

'Oh Anna, I'm so sorry,' John said and went to put his arms around her, but she pushed him away.

'Are you, John? Are you sorry?'

'Of course I am. How can you..?'

'Because you didn't want me to summon him in the first place.'

'Yes, but…'

'But nothing. You must be very pleased I have failed.'

'Anna, please. Don't be like that.'

Anna ignored him and walked out of the shack.

'What about the amulet?'

She didn't answer him, just shrugged and trudged away, shoulders sagging.

CHAPTER 19

Anna was sitting staring into the fire, lost in her own thoughts, when he came. She didn't hear the knock on the door; didn't hear it until the knock turned into an endless hammering. It was then that the cold hand of fear took hold. It was then she regretted sending John to get rid of the amulet – to destroy it, as it had destroyed her. For, it was then that she knew her call had been heard.

The fear soon changed as she pictured his smug expression, his self-righteous condemnation of her. Yes, the fear turned to hatred and then to anger as she remembered what she had lost, what this "man" had taken from her.

Taking a deep breath, Anna raised herself from her chair by the fire and, with steady measured steps, she moved to the door. With one pull, fuelled by her rage, she threw open the solid oak door and stood before him.

'You called, dearie?' Ebenezer said and extended his palms in a questioning gesture.

'Three days ago,' Anna said through gritted teeth.

'Well, I'm a busy man, dearie. I can't jump just when you decide you want to return what's mine.'

'Never!'

'I thought you might say that so it's a good thing I don't really want it anymore isn't it.'

'Then why did you come?'

'You really have to ask?'

'What?'

'What? You think that just because you haven't seen me, I haven't been around?'

'Where?'

'Oh, I've been around, dearie; around to collect what's owed to me. Shame about that broth you wasted, but I couldn't resist watching your reaction as I took that poker to your belly. It was worth it.'

'You did what?' Anna couldn't control herself any longer. She flew at him, clawing at his face with her nails, tearing into his flesh, hitting him, kicking him, screaming at him. All the time her pain and hatred were coming out, Ebenezer laughed at her, fuelling her, coercing her.

When she felt she had no fight left, she felt strong hands grasp her around the waist and pulling her away, into a strong embrace, her head cradled against a powerful chest, while she sobbed.

'Good timing, Martindale. I thought I was going to have to cage your animal myself.'

'What do you want, Lightwoller?'

'Oh, it's not what I want, it's what you want. It was your wife who called me, after all, wasn't it! Or at least I hope she's your wife, otherwise you should be thanking me for sparing you so much shame.'

Ebenezer barely flinched as John threw a punch at him, only to be pulled back by Anna.

'Stop it! Just stop it!' she cried.

'Listen to your wife, Martindale. She's finally talking sense.'

'I'm not talking to him; I'm talking to you!' Anna said and rounded on Ebenezer once more. 'Leave us alone.'

'Why, dearie, you know I can't do that.'

'Why not? Haven't you taken enough from us?'

'Not nearly enough, dearie. You should know that a debt to me is rarely, if ever, repaid.'

'How much more pain can you cause us?' Anna said, her voice breaking.

'Do you really need to ask, dearie?'

'You can have the amulet back. I don't care about..,'

'No, he can't,' John said.

'Yes, he can!' Anna said, a look silencing John, literally. For when he tried to object again, no sound came out.

'Oh dear, someone's made the witch angry.'

'What do you want from us?' Anna said through gritted teeth, her power pulsating in her palms, barely contained, but still no match for him.

'The same as I did all those years ago. To take from you what you took from me – something precious.'

'You can have it back. I don't want it. I don't care what you do with it. I don't care who you hurt. I just want you to stop hurting us.'

'Ah, Anna, you know that's not true. You would rather yourself be in pain than others.'

'No, no, not anymore. Not like this. I…'

'Ah, but you would, dearie. It's written in your aura. It always has been and it always will be. You are one of life's healers, not harmers, Anna. You would never forgive yourself if you gave me back that amulet and I destroyed someone's life with it – which you know I will.'

'Noooooo, I just want to have a child. Please let me have a child. There must be something you'd take in return?'

Anna was on her knees now, all anger and pride having left her as she clasped her palms together and raised them up to the man before her.

'Please, I beg you. Tell me what I have to do and I'll do it.' Tears ran freely down her cheeks as she looked into his dark eyes – dead eyes – with brows raised in amusement at her behaviour.

'There is nothing you can do,' he said and dropped his arm from where his chin had been resting on it and turned to leave.

'No!' Anna said and threw herself after him, catching hold of his britches. 'There must be something you want.'

Ebenezer turned just as John ran to his wife and unclasped her fingers from the warlock, before wrapping her protectively in his arms and placing himself as a barrier between the two. Still unable to speak, he gestured for Ebenezer to leave, but the warlock merely smiled and walked around until he was standing in front of Anna once again.

'There is something, dearie,' he said. Anna's head snapped up and her heart filled with hope.

'What?' she said.

'I'll take him instead,' Ebenezer said, nodding towards John.

'What?' Anna said, fear clutching at her chest as she snuggled deeper against John.

'It's very simple, dearie. If you want a child so badly, you must give up the only other thing that matters to you – your husband.'

'Never!'

'Now, now. Don't be too hasty. Think about it. You know where to find me.' With that, he swept out of the cottage.

CHAPTER 20

'Absolutely not. It's not even an option,' Anna said and slammed the dough onto the table.

'But it's the only solution, Anna. It's the only way for you to get the child you crave so much,' John said and took hold of his wife's shoulders and kissed the top of her head.

'It is not a solution, John. How many times do we need to have this conversation? I am not going to lose you. I love you too much to make that sacrifice.' She leaned back against him and clasped his hand with one of her doughy ones, the other massaging her swollen belly.

'So, you're willing to keep putting yourself through this, through this pain, through this heartbreak?'

'If I have to, yes,' she said, her chin jutting out defiantly.

'He won't forget, you know. You heard him. Our debt will never be repaid. We will never have a child, not one who lives.'

'We might. If it can survive the birth…'

'Oh, Anna, you know it doesn't matter how long it survives, he will find a way to take it away from us, unless I go to him.'

'No, John. I won't hear of it and I don't want to talk about it anymore.' She shrugged out of his grasp and went back to her bread making.

John sighed and trudged out of the cottage. A few minutes later, Anna heard him chopping wood. She closed her eyes and a tear seeped out from one corner. She was trapped. No matter which way she turned she lost out.

She couldn't bear the thought of losing John, the love of her life, and yet she couldn't bear the idea of never being a mother; of never having the chance to love and nurture a little soul.

Ebenezer had been very clever with his curse. He knew she had no choice in what she did. It had taken her longer to work it out, but she couldn't bring herself to make that decision.

Anna had an obligation, an obligation passed down through the generations from grandmother to grand-daughter, an obligation to protect the people of Breccan and Carlford from the evil such that Ebenezer Lightwoller possessed. But to fulfil her obligation, she needed to have a daughter and that daughter needed to have a daughter.

Yes, Anna was trapped. To fulfil the obligation of her bloodline, she had to sacrifice the only man she would ever love.

Anna sighed, the flutter in her belly bringing a brief respite to the anguish she was feeling.

John didn't come in for dinner that night. Anna ate alone, her heart heavy as her mind flicked between the unborn baby and her husband.

She edged outside after supper and looked around for him, but he was nowhere to be found. She presumed he had gone into the village, to the tavern for a drink, something he often did when they had a disagreement. Some ale and some male company usually lightened his spirits and he would return, happy and jovial once more, their disagreement forgotten.

That didn't happen that night. Anna sat up and waited, all the while staring into the fire as she massaged her belly, greeted every few minutes by an angry kick. As the last embers died down, Anna shivered and pulled her shawl around her shoulders. Slowly, she eased out of her chair and shuffled into the bedroom alone; the first night she had done so in all the years they had been married.

She slept fitfully, her dreams plagued with images that vanished with the morning light. As she opened her eyes, the bright sunshine streamed in through the bedroom window. By the rays dancing across the walls she could tell it was late. She never slept late.

She reached her hand out, but the bed was empty. John must already be up and going about his day. Strange that he hadn't woken her. But, when she rolled her bulk over to face his side of the bed, Anna saw that it hadn't been slept in. He hadn't come home last night or…

Fear clutched at her heart and she levered herself, as quickly as she could, out of bed. Not bothering to dress, something uncommon for her, she pulled her shawl over her nightgown and rushed into the living room area of the house. All was still, all was calm, exactly as she'd left it.

Panicked now, she rushed outside, nearly losing her footing on the steps, but catching herself just in time. She called out for him, she searched for him, she even went into the woods, but to no avail. He was nowhere to be found.

Exhausted and distraught, Anna went back into the cottage and slumped into a kitchen chair. Just as she was about to drop her head into her hands she saw it, leaning against the milk jug. Anna reached out and pulled the piece of paper towards her. As she did so, the amulet slid out from between the folds and came to rest noisily on the table in front of her, its eye looking up at her; mocking her.

Her heart heavy, her movements unsteady, her mind numb, her tears now withheld, Anna unfolded the paper and recognised John's stilted, almost childlike, handwriting.

My dearest Anna,

I cannot tell you how sorry I am for choosing to do what I have done in the way I have done it, to not face you and stand firm in my decision, to not hold you once more in my arms, to not kiss you one last time.

Please, Anna, please do not think of me as a coward for not facing you. Instead, think of me as the one strong enough to make the decision you couldn't make. Yes, Anna, I know of your duty. Your mother told me and I'm glad she did, for now I understand even better the agony you have been facing all this time. And, my love, I understand that my decision is the right one.

Ah, Anna, my dearest darling Anna. I cannot begin to tell you how happy and fulfilled you've made my life and how much I love you. And I do love you, Anna, more than anything and anyone in the world. It is for this reason – because of my love for you – that I must do this, must give you the one thing I know you want more than anything (maybe even me) and the one thing I know you have to do.

My final gift to you, Anna my love, is the gift of a child. Please know that I do this for you with a heart full of love and gratitude for all you have given me.

Don't be angry with me, Anna, for you know that if I'd stood before you to say these things, you would have talked me out of it, for I never could deny you anything. But, we both know we would have only been delaying the inevitable.

So, as my final act, let me not deny you that child. Let me give you this gift and may you love her (yes, it is a girl) with all your soul. You will be a wonderful mother, Anna, just as you are a wonderful wife.

Goodbye my love, my life. Know that I will never stop loving you.

John

Anna let the letter drop to the table and then she cried. Through the numbness and through the pain, she cried. She cried for the man she had loved and lost, she cried for the fate of her unborn child and she cried for the burden she was placing on her and all her descendants. A curse in itself.

'Why the tears, dearie? I thought you'd be happy now you'll get what you want.' Through the veil of pain, his voice sparked an anger deep inside her and she raised her head out of her hands.

'How could you?' she screamed at him and balls of light shot out of her palms straight at Ebenezer, but he deflected them with barely a movement.

'Now, now dearie, there's no need for that. A simple "thank you" would suffice.'

'You've ruined my life!'

'On the contrary. I think you'll find that I've saved your life and that of your kind.'

Anna didn't say anything, just stared at him, her fists clenching and unclenching.

'What do you want?' she said eventually.

'Ah, yes. That child you are carrying. Be warned. She will destroy you.'

'What? What is that supposed to mean?'

'Exactly what I said, dearie. Goodbye.'

Before Anna could react, Ebenezer disappeared.

Isabella Martindale was born two weeks later.

CHAPTER 21

'Jesus,' Becca said as she leaned back into the armchair, allowing the journal to come to a rest on her lap. Spook, who had been waiting patiently for his turn, wasted no time in jumping onto her lap. Becca rubbed the soft grey fur behind his ears as she stared at the fireplace, watching as dawn spread its tendrils of light slowly up the stonework, coming to rest on the amulet Becca had placed there, the sunlight reflecting off the stone causing it to look like it was winking at her; mocking her.

'Ebenezer Lightwoller, you complete bastard,' she said and thumped the arm of the chair, causing Spook to scatter.

She couldn't believe what she had just read, couldn't believe the pain and anguish Anna had had to endure, couldn't understand how anyone could be so cruel to someone else, especially someone so gentle as Anna. Any doubts Becca may have had over the severity of the curse placed on Antony had just been blown to pieces.

Someone must have done a real number on him for him to be so cruel, Becca thought, or at least, she hoped that was the cause of his evil nature, for the alternative was a bit too much for her to accept.

The front door slammed, making her jump, and Spook immediately disappeared around the back of the sofa.

'Hi Ellie. In here,' Becca said and stretched, feeling her aching muscles sigh as she loosened them up after hours spent sitting and reading.

'Hey, Becca. You hungry? I grabbed some breakfast on the way home and there's plenty for two,' Ellie said, popping her head around the door, on her way to the kitchen.

'Perfect,' said Becca and eased herself out of the chair and yawned. She really needed to quit these all night reading sessions. Her gaze alighted on the pile of journals still to read and she winced. It would have been bigger if she hadn't been able to pry Jakes away from Carla's journals.

Becca shuffled into the kitchen, her hand in front of her face to stifle yet another yawn, and was greeted by the aroma of coffee, pastries and, her favourite, blueberry muffins.

'Hmmm, it seems you deliberately bought enough breakfast for two,' Becca said, eying the two Venti lattes on the Formica table.

'Guilty as charged,' Ellie said and held up her hands in mock surrender. 'I took a punt at you pulling another all-nighter. Although, by the looks of you, you should make it your last.'

'If only it was so simple,' Becca said. 'These all-nighters keep the nightmares away.'

'But you can't do without sleep three nights in a row, Becca.'

'I know, I'll have a sleep later. How was work?' Becca said, changing the subject before she sank her teeth into a blueberry muffin.

'Really good,' Ellie said, crumbs falling from her mouth as she spoke. 'We got the rapist we've been after for a while.'

'Oh, that's brilliant news.'

'Tell me about it. Shame they won't let me in a room alone with him. I'll teach him a lesson,' she said and Becca swore she saw something dark flit across Ellie's eyes. 'How about you? Any progress?'

'Depends what you mean by progress,' Becca said, leaning back in the chair and nursing her latte.

'Go on,' Ellie said after Becca had been silent for a while.

'Well, I'm getting through the journals and I'm finding so much out about Anna and her life, which is fantastic, don't get me wrong, but I'm not sure I'm getting any closer to finding out how I can help Antony.'

'Okay, well, tell me what you've got so far,' Ellie said, settling back in her chair.

'I dunno, that's just it. My head is so full of stuff.'

'How about the amulet?'

'What about it?'

'Well, have you found out what it is, what it does et cetera?'

'It was Ebenezer's. He's the warlock that cursed Antony. He used it to spy on people, from what I can gather, and then punish them for whatever it was they did.'

'Okay, so how is it that you have it?'

'Anna and a couple of others stole it.'

'That must have pissed him off!'

'I'll say,' Becca said and lapsed into silence again.

'Did Ebenezer not try to get it back?'

'He did at first, but then said he didn't need it.'

'Really?'

'Yeah. He said he had other ways, which I have no doubt he did.'

'So, he just let them get away with it?'

'God no. He held Anna fully responsible and punished her by killing her unborn children. Four in all.'

'Jesus, what a bastard! But she must have repaid her crime because she did have a child?'

'Yes, but he took Anna's husband instead.'

'Poor woman,' Ellie said and stared down into her coffee.

'I know. She even summoned him to try to reason with him, offer him something in return for leaving them alone.'

'Hang on a minute. Did you say she summoned him?'

'Yep.'

'How?'

'Some sort of spell…oh, and the amulet.'

'The amulet, hey. I take it, it must have worked – the summoning?'

'It did, but not straight away. It took him several days before he appeared and that's when he told Anna he had no use for the amulet anymore.'

'No, he may not have, but obviously the amulet is, or was, still connected to him in some way. Do you know what spell Anna used?'

'No, the journal just mentioned a summoning spell.'

'Would it be in the Grimoire or one of the other spell books?'

'It might be. Why?'

'Okay, missy, you really do need to get some shut eye as it's glaringly obvious to me that you've hit the jackpot.'

Becca stared at her, the caffeine not succeeding in its usual manner to fire up her synapses.

'Okay, let me spell it out for your sleep deprived brain shall I? You have an amulet that has been used to summon Ebenezer, the very man who placed the curse on Antony and who will, most certainly, know how to break it.'

'Yes, but it might not work now, after all this time.'

'But it might.'

'And even if it did, why on earth would he help? From what I've learned, he doesn't seem to be in the business of helping people.'

'People change. Maybe he will. Maybe he won't. You won't know unless you try.'

'But what if I then end up under his focus?'

'I guess that's a risk you need to decide if you're willing to take.'

'Anyway, Anna went to his house to summon him. She didn't do it from home.'

'And?'

'I have absolutely no idea where his house was.'

'Yes, you do.'

'I do?'

'Honestly, Becca, anyone would think you didn't want to find the answers.'

'Not at all!' Becca said, jumping up and spilling her coffee. 'Of course I want to help Antony. If, for no other reason than to make these nightmares stop.'

'Okay, Becca, calm down. I wasn't having a go. I'm just trying to help you pull out the information you need.'

'I know, I'm sorry. I guess I am overtired. Maybe I should just go to bed and clear my head.'

'Good idea, for both of us. But, before you do, think about what you gleaned from the journals about Ebenezer's home.'

Becca sat back once more, her gaze resting on the crumbs from her muffin as she played with them. She honestly couldn't remember anything useful.

'All I know is it was in the woods, in the clearing.'

'Exactly.'

'But this was four hundred years ago. The place was covered in woods. Now, we only have the park.'

'And the forest between here and Scotsford.'

'Okay, but how am I going to pinpoint the location?'

'The library must have some maps. Maybe we can narrow it down from there?'

'We?'

'Yeah. I'd like to help you if you want me to?' Ellie said and smiled.

'That would be great. Thank you, Ellie.'

'No problem. That's what friends are for, isn't it?'

‘I wouldn’t know,’ Becca said.

‘Well, you do now. Right, sleep, for both of us.’ Ellie stood up and clapped her hands.

Becca didn’t need any more encouragement than that.

CHAPTER 22

Becca awoke with a start, a sheen of sweat covering her skin, her heart racing, her senses on high alert. What the hell had just woken her?

She lay inert, not daring to move. Then she heard it again. A low guttural animalistic growl, a growl that was close by, too close, in fact. Squeezing her eyes shut tight, she reached her hand out and flicked on the bedside light. Slowly, she opened her eyes. Her room was empty.

The growling continued. Becca could make out another, lower pitched growl and recognised it immediately as Spook's.

Panic fuelled her body and she bolted out of bed, only to check herself at the door. She had no idea what was out there and, given recent history, it could be dangerous.

Resisting the maternal urge she had to go and rescue Spook, whatever the cost, Becca squeezed her fists tight and took a deep breath to try to calm herself down.

Her panic under wraps for now, she twisted the door knob and prayed hers wasn't one of the many doors she hadn't got around to oiling yet.

She squealed as the door opened without a sound and quickly clamped a hand over her mouth. Had it heard? Becca held her breath and listened. The growling continued, but Spook's had gone up a notch now and he was practically screeching at whatever was torturing him.

It sounded like a dog, but how on earth had it got in? She never left the door open, unless…Ellie. Maybe she had? But Becca remembered Ellie was home early and there'd been no sign of a dog all evening. So, what the hell was it?

Becca peered out of the gap from the open door. She could see the top of the stairs and she could see Spook on the top step. She could not see his assailant.

Spook was crouched down, paws braced against the floor, hackles raised, ears back and flattened against his head, teeth bared. Every few seconds he spat and lashed out at whatever was causing his distress.

Tears pricked at Becca's eyes as she watched. She needed to save him, but she also needed to see what was frightening him; to see what she was up against.

Easing the door open and hoping that Spook wouldn't give her away, Becca crept out of her bedroom onto the landing. She needn't have worried though, as Spook was fully occupied.

Becca crossed the landing and flattened herself against the wall before slowly and quietly sliding herself along until she reached the top of the stairs. Still Spook ignored her presence.

Her heart thundering in her chest once more, she rested her head against the wall and closed her eyes. She willed her breathing to slow down, willed her nerves to still. Without thinking about it anymore, she peered around the edge of the wall and down the stairs.

The scream was out of her mouth before she could stop it and she bent down and grabbed Spook, before running back to her room and slamming the door.

She threw Spook on her bed and then proceeded to drag the nearest bookcase, books and all, across the doorway, reinforcing the flimsy door.

Only then did she notice herself trembling, tears running down her cheeks and an unmistakable smell of ammonia. She turned, her vision blinded by her tears, and fumbled for her mobile phone.

'Becca? Do you know what time it is?'

'Frank, You…need…to…come…over,' she sobbed into the phone.

'Becca? What's wrong?'

'There's…an…animal…in…the…house.'

'What kind of animal?'

'I…don't…know. Just come!' Becca disconnected the call and slumped to the floor in the corner of her room, away from the door, out of sight of the door, and hugged her knees to her.

Spook emerged from his hiding place under the bed and forced his way into Becca's arms. She could feel him shaking and hugged him to her. It was there that she stayed, stroking Spook, her gaze fixed on the doorway, waiting.

CHAPTER 23

Becca didn't know how long she'd been sitting there when she heard the gentle tap on the door.

'Becca. It's me. Can I come in?' Jakes' voice sounded through the door.

'Has it gone?' No answer. 'Has it gone, Frank?'

'Yes, Becca, it's gone,' Jakes sighed. 'Now, can I come in?'

The door handle twisted and the door banged against the bookcase wedged behind it.

'Hang on a minute,' Becca said, pushing herself up off the floor and sending Spook to his hiding place under the bed, once more.

Becca moved the bookcase out of the way and opened the door, falling into Jakes' embrace.

'Are you okay?'

'I'm fine, just scared to death. What was that thing? Did you see it?'

'Come downstairs into the living room. Ellie's downstairs.'

'Oh my God, Ellie! I completely forgot about Ellie. Is she okay?' Becca said, her hand flying to her mouth, her face flushing in shame.

'She's fine, Becca. A little shaken and upset, but she's fine.'

'Did it hurt her? Did she see it?'

'I think you should just come downstairs.'

Alarm bells were firing in Becca's brain at how calm and sad Jakes was.

'Frank? What's going on?' she said and stopped at the top of the stairs, shrugging out of his embrace.

'Nothing's going on, Becca. I just need you to come downstairs.'

'Why? What's downstairs?'

'Nothing, just Ellie.'

'So, why the urgency to get me down there. Spook and I have just been traumatised by some hulking wild animal, the likes of which I've never seen…' Becca let the sentence lapse as she stood and looked at Jakes, who fidgeted from one foot to the other.

'How long has Ellie been downstairs?'

'What? I don't know. She was on the doorstep when I arrived, in floods of tears.'

'I didn't see her when all this was going on, nor did she appear, and it wasn't exactly quiet!'

'Becca, please, just come downstairs and…'

'That was her, wasn't it? That thing, that creature was Ellie, wasn't it?'

'Becca…'

'Wasn't it?' Becca said and stamped her foot. Jakes looked at her and his shoulders sagged.

'I had hoped she'd have told you by now. She is mortified by what has happened.'

'Mortified? She nearly scared Spook and I to death. What the hell is she, Frank?'

'Isn't it obvious?'

'Not to me it isn't. So, it's probably best you just spell it out.' Becca was in no mood to play games. Even though she knew what he was going to say – she'd seen the movies – she needed to hear him say it.

'She's a werewolf, Becca.'

CHAPTER 24

'Oh God, Becca, I'm so sorry. I never meant to scare you. I thought you were out, at your class. I would never have…'

'Never would have what? Tortured my cat if you thought I was here?'

'Now, Becca…'

'Stay out of this, Frank,' Becca said and thrust her palm towards him, a ball of light shooting from it and hitting him in the chest, knocking him off his feet.

'Frank!' Ellie said and lunged forward to try to break his fall, but Becca stepped between them, the power pulsating through her, clouding the reality of exactly what she was facing.

'I'm okay, Ellie,' Frank said, the breath clearly having been knocked out of him. 'Becca…'

'I'm sorry, Frank. I didn't mean to hurt you, but this is between Ellie and I,' Becca said, keeping her gaze fixed on Ellie, the guilt at hurting him pulling at her heart.

'Becca…'

'No, Frank. I've told you to stay out of it.' This time she did turn around and zipped her hand through the air, silencing Jakes.

'Now,' she said, rounding on Ellie, who sat hunched on the floor. 'Just what exactly were you doing to Spook?'

'Nothing, Becca, I swear,' Ellie said, edging herself backwards, away from Becca.

'It didn't sound like nothing to me,' Becca said, flexing her palms, the static crackling as she did so. 'It sounded like you were threatening him.'

'No…no…no,'

'Like you were going to attack him,' Becca took a step forward and raised her right hand, aiming her palm at Ellie.

'No, Becca,' Ellie said, her back slamming against the wall as she got as far away as she could.

'Like you were going to rip him to shreds.'

'Absolutely not!' Ellie growled.

Becca saw Ellie's eyes flash red, saw the rippling across her skin as the anger started to take hold, watched as her face started to morph.

'Just like it looks like you're planning to do to me,' Becca said and raised her hand and launched a ball of light at Ellie. In a flash, Ellie was across the room, the ball hitting the wall leaving a charred crater in its wake.

Becca whirled round, ready to launch another shot. The sight before her, however, took all the wind out of her sails. Ellie sat huddled by the fireplace, sobbing into Jakes' shoulder. Jakes was staring daggers at Becca, who slumped into a chair, deflated by his withering look. She released the spell on him, but immediately wished she hadn't.

'What the hell has got into you, Becca?' he said.

'Oh, like she couldn't kill me if she wanted to, just like she was going to kill Spook,' Becca said, cringing at how petulant she sounded.

'She wasn't trying to kill Spook, for Christ's sake.'

'Then what the hell was she doing?'

'I…was…trying…to…make…friends…with…him.'

'Yeah, right,' Becca snorted. 'What, by scaring the crap out of him?'

'I was just trying to get him used to me, get him used to what I am. I thought that if he saw me, then…'

'What? That he'd go "oh yeah, she's a werewolf, that's cool"! He's scared of the Yorkie next door for goodness sake.'

'I'm…sorry,' Ellie said, her shoulders sagging and a sob escaping from her throat.

Becca felt a pang of guilt for being so hard on her.

'Why didn't you just tell me?'

'I have to say, El, I'm with Becca on this. I told you to tell her before you moved in.'

'I don't know,' Ellie said, shrugging. 'I guess part of me just wanted to be normal, just wanted to be treated normally.'

'Ha! No one's normal around here,' Becca said.

'I really am sorry, Becca. I was hoping to make friends with Spook and then I wouldn't have to tell you.'

'Well, that didn't work out too well, did it?'

'Becca,' Jakes said, a warning tone in his voice.

'I'm not starting anything, Frank. Don't worry.'

'Sorry, Ellie, I need to get up. My leg is killing me,' Jakes said and pulled himself to his feet, using the fireplace.

Ellie jumped up after him and helped him to the sofa, then went to sit in the other armchair.

'How long have you been an ummm..?'

'A werewolf? It's okay, you can say it. It's a fact of my life. Hmmm, since I was about six.'

'Wow, how did it happen?'

'Safari park. I wandered off and got lost.'

'And your parents?'

'Becca, that's enough.'

'Not really, Frank. I mean, she's moved into my house, threatened my cat. I think I have a right to know.'

'I vouched for her and I still do. You have…'

'It's okay, Frank,' Ellie said. 'My parents put me in an institution. That's the last I ever saw of them.'

'Oh God, Ellie, I'm sorry. I…'

Becca let the sentence fall, feeling herself go red at her own obstinacy.

'Look, Becca, you really don't have anything to worry about with Ellie. She has her demons under control, don't you?' Jakes said and looked at Ellie, who gave a half smile and nodded.

'I thought it would be good for you to have her around…for protection…'

'I don't need protecting,' Becca said, folding her arms over her chest and thrusting her chin out.

'You will if you continue on this ridiculous path of freeing Antony.'

'It isn't ridiculous. I made a promise.'

'So did I,' Jakes said. 'I promised myself I wouldn't let anything happen to you again.'

'So, does werewolf trump vampire, in the supernatural stakes then?' Becca said, uncomfortable and warmed by Jakes' words.

'Not exactly,' Ellie said, 'but werewolf venom is poisonous to vampires.'

'Venom?'

'A werewolf bite is the beginning of the end for a vampire and it is a very slow and painful death.'

'What, you mean there's no cure?'

'Oh, there's a cure. The blood of the same werewolf that inflicted the bite, but few want to cure the enemy,' Ellie said.

'And you know this how?'

'It's part of what you learn when you are indoctrinated into a pack.'

'Pack?'

'Yes, every werewolf is part of a pack. We get together every so often, but especially around the time of the full moon.'

'Of course you do,' Becca said.

'Coffee anyone?' Jakes said, breaking the tension in the room.

'No thanks Frank,' Becca said and yawned. 'I think I need to go and assimilate my once fictional world with my real one.'

'Okay, sleep well. Spook will be fine,' Jakes said as Becca bent to kiss him goodnight.

'Goodnight, Becca,' Ellie said. 'I would like to help you in any way I can.'

'Goodnight,' Becca said without acknowledging the offer.

CHAPTER 25

Becca was sitting at the kitchen table the next morning, Spook curled up on her lap, journals laid in front of her, a steaming mug of coffee just under her nose, when Ellie walked in. Spook didn't flinch.

'Morning,' Ellie said.

'Oh hi, Ellie,' Becca said. 'Sleep okay?'

'Yes, you?'

'Not too bad.'

'Are we good after last night?'

Becca was quiet for a while, as she massaged Spook behind the ear. He sat up, yawned, arched his back in a stretch and then sat down looking at Ellie.

'Well, if Spook can forgive you, then I guess it's only fair I should too. Coffee?' Becca said, holding out the cafetiere.

'That would be great, thanks,' Ellie said. As she sat down and proffered her mug for filling, Becca noticed Ellie's hands shaking and felt a pang of guilt.

'I am sorry about last night, El. It's just that Spook means the world to me and I would kill anyone who harmed him.'

'I know. I understand and I'm sorry too.' They lapsed into silence. 'What're you doing?' Ellie said, eventually.

'Oh, I was lying awake all night thinking about Ebenezer's cottage and where it might have been. I just thought I'd reread the journals and see if I missed anything.'

'And did you?'

'Nope,' Becca said and dropped one of the journals back on the table and leaned back, picking up her coffee. 'It's still at the edge of a clearing. Trouble is where?'

'Maybe go to the library and see if they've got any old maps?'

'Yeah, that's kind of the conclusion I'd come to.'

'Let me know how you get on. I've got to get to work now, but maybe I can help you narrow it down later.'

'Okay, thanks. Have a good day.'

'You too,' Ellie said and then she was gone. Becca felt herself relax slightly, as did Spook. *So, there was still some apprehension there*, she thought, as she stood up, dislodging Spook, and stretched.

'Time to go trawl through the archives, buddy,' she said, but Spook had already left the building.

CHAPTER 26

'Can I help you?' a clipped female voiced asked, as Becca stood in the library entrance, staring around her.

Becca looked up at the middle aged woman in front of her, glasses perched on her nose, grey hair pulled back in a bun. Her name badge identified her as "Marion".

'You're the one who helped Frank.'

'I'm sorry,' Marion said. 'Do I know you?'

'No, not me, but you do know a friend of mine – Frank Jakes.'

'No, sorry, I don't recall anyone by that name.'

'He used to be a detective and you leant him an old journal, about six months ago?'

'Ah, yes, Detective Inspector Jakes,' Marion said, folding her arms across her chest and pursing her lips. 'Would you mind reminding Mr Jakes that he has yet to return that journal?'

'I'm sorry, I thought he had. It's probably my fault. You see, it came from my grandmother; it is part of my family history and maybe he thought…'

'It was donated to the library and is a historical part of the town's history.'

'Yes, okay. Anyway, I need to get on,' Becca said, trying to dodge around Marion.

'What is it you're looking for? Maybe I can help, save you some time?'

'Hmmm, you're probably right. I'm looking for any maps you have of the town.'

'From when?'

'I'm sorry?'

'What time period are you looking for? We have hundreds of maps. Things change so quickly and new maps are always required.'

'Around the late sixteen hundreds. I'm not sure exactly.'

'Okay, yes, I think we've got them dating back that far, but I'm afraid, due to their age and delicate nature, I can't allow you to touch them…'

'Then what is the point in having them available?'

'Well, if you'd let me finish, young lady, I'll tell you,' Marion said, looking at Becca over the top of her glasses, making Becca feel like she was back at school again. 'I will have to handle it for you. You are free to take a look and take photographs, without a flash of course, but the maps are quite fragile.'

'I understand. Thank you.'

'Are there any others you need?'

'Just the most recent ones too.'

'May I ask what it is you are looking for?'

'Oh, nothing much. I'm just interested in seeing how the landscape has changed since the time of the journal Frank has.'

'Hmmm…borrowed. Right, give me fifteen minutes to get some cover and locate the maps, and then I'll come and find you.'

'Okay, thanks.'

'There's a café now, through the science section. I can come and find you in there.'

Before Becca could respond, Marion was gone.

'There are hundreds,' Becca said, her shoulders slumping as she stared down at the map Marion had carefully laid out in front of her.

'Hundreds of what?' Marion said.

'Clearings.'

'Well, yes, there would be. The clearings would have been where dwellings were. The larger the clearing, the larger the population density.'

'So, the smaller clearings would have housed just one house?'

'Possibly, but not necessarily. They may not have had any dwellings. They may simply have been natural clearings.'

'Great, it's like looking for a needle in a haystack.'

'May I ask what it is you're actually looking for?'

'A particular residence. So, unless your records show the exact location of homes and who owned them, I doubt you could help.'

'You could always ask,' Marion said and started to roll up the map.

'Hang on a minute, could I just take some photos before you put it away?'

'Yes, of course. No flash, remember.'

Becca nodded.

'So, whose dwelling are you looking for?'

'Ebenezer Lightwoller,' Becca said as she tried to make sure she didn't miss any bits of the map.

'The warlock?'

'Yes, do you know where he lived?' Becca said, hope surging through her.

'Unfortunately not,' Marion said. 'I've read about him and the atrocious things he did, but I've never seen a home referred to anywhere.'

'Typical.'

'Why are you looking for his home?'

'No reason,' Becca said, trying to keep her voice casual. 'I'm just curious about him, that's all.'

'Hmmm, well, just be careful. He wasn't a very nice man and if folklore is to be believed, he is still out there, somewhere.'

'Folklore?'

'Yes, if you look him up in the local history books, as well as learning of the atrocities he committed, you'll also learn that he was believed to be indestructible. Of course, I don't believe in any of this nonsense. Like vampires and werewolves, it is just a story invented to scare people.'

'Of course,' Becca said, suppressing a smile. *Oh to be ignorant of the supernatural*, she thought. 'Well, thank you for your help, Marion. Do you have an up to date map I could look at?'

'Yes, they're for sale upstairs on reception,' Marion said and disappeared out of the door, leaving Becca to see herself out.

CHAPTER 27

'It's going to take forever,' Becca said, pacing up and down the kitchen as Jakes poured over the Sellotaped A4 sheets, which formed the old map, and compared it to the new map; more than seventy five per cent of which had now been built on.

'And the journals you've got don't give any clues as to where it might be?'

'Nope, and before you ask, they don't give any clues to where Anna lived either. How about you? Anything in the ones you took?' Becca said and slumped down into a chair, the force causing some of the stuffing to blow out of a hole in the seat.

'Not so far,' Jakes said. 'Look, Anna was in walking distance of the main village, which must have been a sizeable place.'

'Already thought of that, but there are several sizeable locations and all the clearings except about three or four are in what I consider to be walking distance.'

'True. I guess if you're so hell bent on this, you're going to have to visit all the locations and try the locator spell. Speaking of which, have you found it yet?'

'No. I was hoping this would be more straightforward.'

'You still need the spell.'

'I know. I also know who would know where Ebenezer's shack was.'

'Who?' Jakes said as he stood up, stretching his back out.

'Antony,' Becca said and held her breath, waiting for the eruption. It didn't take long.

'Absolutely not! Are you out of your mind? You have no way of helping him and no way of controlling him, but you want to dig him up and ask him where the shack is? Unbelievable!' Jakes slammed his fist onto the counter, causing the crockery in the cupboards to rattle.

'What on earth is going on in here?' Ellie said as she came in, dumping the takeaway bags on the counter.

'Try to talk some sense into her, will you, because she's not going to listen to me,' Jakes said, glaring at Becca.

'Well, it's true,' Becca said. 'He is the only one who knows and so there is no other option.'

'Yes there is. Forget about it.'

'Frank. I'm not going over this again,' Becca said and got up to help Ellie dish out the food.

'Will someone fill me in, please? I leave you pouring over a map, trying to work out the best way to locate the shack and I come back to find you at each other's throats.'

'Genius here wants to release Antony, as he is the only one who knows where the shack is.'

'Makes sense,' said Ellie, emptying Frank's favourite vindaloo onto a plate and turning to give it to him.

'Ah, it doesn't look like you'll be needing this to make you red in the face, does it?' Ellie nudged Becca, who turned to see Jakes a dangerous shade of red.

'Frank, I'm not going to do it tonight. I'll make sure I can protect myself.'

'For God's sake, Becca. You can't protect yourself from him.'

'I can. I have the poppets. I can use one of those.'

'They are used to control humans, not supernatural creatures. What the hell are you going to do if it doesn't work?'

'I'll be there with her,' Ellie said and placed the curry in front of Jakes. 'I'll protect her, Frank, I promise,' she said and patted his shoulder.

'I'm not going to win this, am I?' Jakes said, stabbing his fork into the middle of his curry.

'Not really. Not against the two of us. I'd say you were out voted, old man,' Becca said, sitting down next to Frank and mouthing a thank you to Ellie.

'Hey, less of the "old man",' Jakes said. 'I have one more question for you though Becca and it's something I think you need to think long and hard about.'

'Okay, shoot,' Becca said, tucking into her food and not looking up at him.

'What on earth makes you think Antony will help you find Ebenezer, when his quickest and easiest route to freedom is killing you?'

The kitchen was silent for a while, as no one ate or spoke. Becca pondered Jakes' question, not sure how to answer him, because, in reality, she had no idea.

'I'll have to convince him,' Becca said.

'And how are you going to do that?'

'I'll think of something,' she said. 'Now, eat before it gets cold.'

CHAPTER 28

'Still no luck?' Ellie said as Becca flung her bag on the floor and slammed the front door.

'Nope,' Becca said and slumped into a kitchen chair, tapping her keys on the counter.

'Are you going to carry on?' Ellie stirred the pan on the stove and then lifted the spoon out and tasted it. 'Here, taste this,' she said, proffering the spoon to Becca, her hand cupped underneath to catch any drips.

'Mmmm, lovely. What is it?' Becca said before slumping back at the table and resting her chin on her arms.

'Just a risotto I knocked together.'

'Who are you trying to impress?'

'No one. I just thought it would make a change from takeaways.'

'I'm not going to find it without his help, you know.'

'You don't know that. You've barely started.'

'I've been at it over a week and I haven't covered even a third of the clearings on the map.'

'That's what I mean, you've barely even started.'

'And it could take months and what if I have been at the right place, but not exactly the right spot? Antony would know.'

'Yes, he would and he'd also kill you.'

'You've changed your tune. I thought you were on my side?'

'I'm not on anyone's side, Becca. I can see it from both sides. Whilst I understand your promise and your desire to help Antony, he is a cold-blooded killer whose desire to end your life to regain his own, will not have gone away.'

'But there is another way.'

'Is there? Do you know this for sure?'

'There has to be.'

'Maybe there isn't and if you free him and there isn't another cure, then what are you going to do?'

'I'll put him back.'

'You really think it will be that easy a second time? For goodness sake, Becca, he won't be fooled again.'

'Then I'll just have to convince him to help me find Ebenezer and find a cure so both of us can live.'

'Becca. Which part of "he's a cold-blooded killer" do you not get? He is not going to listen to anything you have to say. He will just want to achieve what he failed to do last time and as quickly as possible.'

'He was human once, you know, and from what Jakes has said, he appeared to be a decent guy.'

'Yes, but he's not human now,' Ellie said and turned the heat off from under the risotto. 'Right, that's ready if you're hungry now? I'll take mine with me.'

'Mmmm,' Becca said. She was still sitting, lost in thought, when Ellie left.

CHAPTER 29

'This is my only option,' Becca said as she stuffed a rucksack with gear she doubted she would need. 'My best option at least, isn't it?' She said and looked up into the watchful eyes of her audience.

Spook, however, did not look convinced. Nor did he try to stop her. He just stared down his nose at Becca.

'Don't give me that look, buddy. You know I have to do this. Anyway, I have this,' she said and held up the poppet she had chosen and "bound" to Antony, using the wooden animals she'd found in the trunks, as the link. Spook recoiled from the stick like object and turned his attention towards the doorway and then looked back at Becca. He repeated this cycle.

'Ellie's not here, Spook. And if she was, I think she'd try to talk me out of it.' At this, Spook turned his orange stare onto Becca again.

'I'm doing it, buddy, so stop looking at me like that.' She glanced at her watch and cursed. 'Gotta go. See you later,' she said and blew Spook a kiss. He meowed in response, something he never did, and it stopped Becca in her tracks.

'I have to do this. Please understand.' She turned and left. Spook nestled down in her bed, burying his face under his paws.

CHAPTER 30

'I'm so sorry I'm late,' Becca said as she ran up to the group of men, bunched together at the back of the cemetery.

'Yeah, well, another minute and we'd have gone. But yer 'ere now. Where's the cash?' The man who'd spoken – she didn't know his name – shifted from foot to foot, sniffing every so often and wiping his nose.

'I'm not sure what…'

'Look, lady, we don't care. I'm just interested in the cash. Don't give a rat's arse what yer paying us to do. Now where's this grave you want robbing?'

Becca was a little startled by his nonchalance, but also pleased. The less explaining she had to do, the better.

'Er, over there at the back. Under the oak tree.'

'Right lads. Let's get this done. The sooner we finish, the sooner we can blow this dough.' This caused muttering of ascent from his crew, but no one moved.

'It's over there by…'

'Cash first. Work second,' the man said and held his hand out. Becca looked down at his grimy palm and then reached into her rucksack and handed him the wad of money. He flicked through it and nodded. His crew got to work.

Becca stood by and watched, pacing up and down, her stomach doing somersaults, the words of the spells bouncing around in her head and, most importantly, the poppet clutched in her hand.

'Right, almost done. Are yer sure yer want this lifted out? I mean, how are yer gonna put it back? No offense, love, but yer ain't gonna be able to do it yerself.'

'Yes, yes. The pulleys will hold it, won't they?'

'Course, what do yer take me for?' Becca glanced at the dishevelled man she'd found in the wanted ads and questioned her judgment.

'Yer ain't gonna be able to operate them yerself though, love. That thing weighs a tonne.'

'It's fine, I've got it covered, thank you.'

'For a bit extra, me and the lads could 'ang around and…'

'No, no, it's probably best if you don't.'

'Why, what yer gonna do?'

'I'm sorry?'

'Well, I know yer paid us not to ask questions, but this is just weird and way beyond anything we've done before.'

'I paid you what you asked, now it would be wise for you to leave.' Becca's palms were starting to sweat and she was beginning to regret coming here alone.

'Yeah, but I'm thinking we might just 'ang around and see what yer up to, just in case it's something illegal.'

Becca couldn't help herself; she burst out laughing.

'What's so funny?' the man said.

'You acting like you've never broken the law before.'

'Don't get lippy wi' me, love,' he said, advancing towards Becca.

'I'm not; I'm just being honest. Look, stay if you really want to, but I'd advise you to keep back – hidden – for your own safety.'

'Why? What yer gonna do?' Becca couldn't help a smug smile at the shift in power. Confidence really did work.

'You won't believe me if I told you and neither will anyone else for that matter.'

Becca walked towards the gravesite and was satisfied to see the men she'd hired retreating and hopefully leaving altogether.

As she neared the casket though, all thoughts of anyone and anything else left her mind. All she could think about was Antony and what he had done to her. Instinctively, she reached up to touch the scars on her neck. Still scars she was pleased to note.

The wood of the pulleys creaked under the weight of the sarcophagus and Becca hoped they would hold out long enough for her to do what she needed to.

She stepped forward and placed her hand on the stone. Nothing. The spells still held in this consecrated place.

Becca dropped her rucksack on the ground and laid the poppet gently on top of it, within easy reach. She planted her feet firmly, allowed her chin to drop down to her chest and closed her eyes.

'By my Goddess and by my God, I call upon the power of the four elements. Of earth,' she said and turned her palms to the ground, feeling it shudder as she did so, and drew the power up into her body.

'Of air' Becca whipped her hands around and the rush of wind almost knocked her off her feet. The crashing thunder resonated deep in her soul.

'Of fire' she said and directed her power fingers towards the sky to meet the bolt of lightning; the connection leaving a charcoal taste in her mouth.

'And of water.' She clapped her hands together three times. The heavens opened and the dry ground soon muddied.

Becca struggled to hold her balance as the elemental powers surged through her and she felt them buzzing in the centre of her palms.

She stepped towards the sarcophagus once more and placed her hands against the seal. Without stopping to allow rational thoughts to enter her head, she said the Spell O' Manumission. As she finished, lightning shot down through her body and out through her palms, sending a ray of light around the seal of the casket. Once its circuit was complete, it pulsated three times and then went out.

Becca reached into her rucksack for her Maglite and shone it on the seal. It was broken.

Now for the hard part. She had never practiced on something so heavy before.

Firming her stance once more, Becca rubbed her palms together to gather the energy. Then, focusing her attention on the lid of the sarcophagus, she held her palms over it.

She could feel the energy she had summoned coursing through her body and out of her palms. Shafts of light erupted and swathed the lid, but for the longest time nothing happened. Then, just as she was about to give up, Becca saw the ancient stone shift, just a fraction.

Remembering what her grandmother had taught her all those years ago, she suppressed the bubble of excitement and instead closed her eyes and focused her mind on her task. Soon she was rewarded by the sound of stone grating against stone. She visualised the lid slowly sliding down the sarcophagus and, when it had reached halfway, she dropped her palms and opened her eyes.

Before her stood the open casket. Nothing stood between her and her nemesis, except one final spell.

It's not too late to change your mind, a voice sounded in the rational part of her mind.

'I've come too far to back out now,' she muttered and stepped forward, leaning tentatively over the lip of the sarcophagus.

There, bound in vines – immobile – lay Antony Cardover.

Becca flexed her hands and felt the energy pulsate. She placed her hands over Antony's vine covered form, closed her eyes and began to chant the Spell O' Unbinding. As she did so, she moved her hands along Antony's body and towards the ground, in a rhythmic motion. Slowly, the vines loosened and began to unwrap themselves and disappear back into the earth from whence they'd come.

As the last vine slipped away, Becca turned her palms heavenwards. The rain ceased, the thunder silenced and the lightning withdrew. The elements were calm.

She gave her thanks to her Goddess and her God, and then allowed herself to look down.

Her heart skipped a beat as her gaze rested on his ruggedly handsome face, calm and serene in repose. A face so different from the angry, hate filled one she was so familiar with, a face reminiscent of the painting in her mother's attic, a painting depicting a carefree handsome man, a man Becca played with as a child, a man she was now certain she wanted to help get back.

'Hello, Rebecca,' Antony said as he opened his eyes and grabbed her by the throat, his face changing in an instant. 'Why, pray tell, have you decided to free me after you almost killed yourself putting me in here?'

Antony stood up in the sarcophagus, lifting Becca off her feet as he did so. She kicked her legs out trying to get a foothold on the edge of the casket, but couldn't; his reach was too long. All she succeeded in doing was restricting her airflow.

She gripped his hand and tried to prize his fingers away.

'What are you trying to do?' he said, laughing. 'Ah, you thought I would be weak, didn't you? Well, my dear, I hate to ruin your dreams, but it takes several hundred years to desiccate my body.' As if to emphasise his strength, he squeezed a little harder and Becca could hear the blood pounding in her head and the dizziness start to form, due to lack of oxygen.

'I am a little hungry though,' he said, pulling Becca towards him. Panic fuelled her now and she kicked and punched with all her strength.

'Oi, mate, let 'er go,' a voice sounded.

'What's this? A knight in shining armour come to protect his princess?' Antony said and jumped down from the sarcophagus, dropping Becca to the ground.

Antony advanced towards the swarthy man who had led the excavation of his casket.

'I have to say though, Rebecca, I thought you'd have better taste.'

Becca crouched on the ground on her hands and knees, trying to regulate the air that was fighting to get inside her lungs. She looked up to see Antony closing in on the man.

'Leave him alone,' she said, but all that came out was a croak.

She looked beyond them and saw her bag with the poppet lying on top of it. If she could just get to it.

'So, my good man, what was it you said to me?'

'I said, leave 'er alone,' the man said and stepped towards Antony.

'And if I don't?'

'You'll 'av us to deal with.'

'Us? Forgive me, but I don't see anyone here but you.'

The man snapped his fingers and the rest of his crew emerged from the shadows and came to stand behind him.

'Ah, excellent. This will be a much fairer fight now,' Antony said.

Becca held her breath as she watched confusion appear on the men's faces.

As Antony lunged for one of the men, Becca made her move. She grabbed the poppet and whirled round, brandishing it in front of her, but it was already too late.

All she could do was watch as Antony finished tearing the head off one of the men, dropping the body to the ground next to the other four.

The last man, the one Becca had dealt with, was running. She watched as Antony laughed, straightened his rotting clothing and then went after him.

She started to mutter the incantation to activate the poppet, but Antony was too quick. The man didn't stand a chance.

Whilst he had been quick and callous with the others, he took his time with this one. She couldn't watch as Antony played with the man, like a cat did with a mouse – worrying it, biting it, throwing it up in the air, before finally putting it out of its misery and ending its life.

She stared as Antony drained the man of life and then dropped him to the ground. She continued to chant as Antony turned towards her and she held the poppet out in front of her as he approached.

'Now, what have we here?' he said as he looked at the stick figure clutched in Becca's hand.

'It's a poppet.'

'I know what it is, Rebecca. I'm just curious to know what you think you're going to do with it?'

She didn't answer. She chanted the incantation one last time and then picked up the poppet's arm and started moving it around. She looked at Antony, but he remained, immobile. She tried the other arm, but still nothing. She shook the figure, but only succeeded in making Antony laugh.

'Please tell me you didn't think that would work on me?'

'I…I…'

'I'm not human, Rebecca. Those things can only be used by the supernatural to control humans, not each other. Surely Anna's instructions made that clear?'

Becca felt herself flush, much to her horror.

'Ah, only read the bits you wanted to? Well, you'll know for next time. Oh, no you won't, because there isn't going to be a next time for you. Not this time.'

Antony lunged for her, snatched the poppet out of her hand and crushed it to dust, before throwing her to the ground and straddling her.

'I had hoped you'd put up a bit more of a fight; to get the blood pumping. It tastes so much better that way.'

He pinned her hands above her head with one hand and then, using the nail of his index finger, he sliced through her clothing and pushed it out of the way.

Becca fought against him, to cover herself, to free herself, but it was hopeless. He didn't so much as flinch at her efforts.

'Get off me!'

'Now, we both know that's not going to happen, don't we?'

Antony caressed her exposed breasts with his fingertips and Becca was mortified to find her nipples hardening in response.

'Mmmm, you like this do you?' Antony said and bent his head, his tongue flicking against her erect nipples.

'Noooooo! Get off me,' Becca screamed, but her protests only served to make Antony's attention more intense, more focused, until she felt his teeth puncture her chest.

It was like the air had been sucked out of her. The pressure on her chest was so intense she gasped for breath, incapable of drawing anything in. She couldn't scream; she couldn't fight; she couldn't do anything.

How stupid had she been to come here alone and unarmed?

As this thought crossed her mind, the weight suddenly left her and air rushed back into her lungs. She lay still and waited for the roaring in her head to quieten. It took her a while to realise that the noise wasn't coming from inside her at all.

She eased herself up onto her elbows, suppressing a scream as pain shot through her chest. Forgetting the noise for now, Becca looked down at the open would in the centre left of her chest and the blood that oozed out with every heartbeat. She pulled off her clothes and making a pad with her bra, she used her shirt to secure it over the wound and tied it as tight as she could.

The grunts and growls soon drew her attention, however, and Becca squinted into the semi-darkness. Not too far away, she could make out Antony fighting with what looked like a huge dog.

'Ellie,' Becca muttered. Oh God, her friend was going to get hurt because of her own impetuousness.

'Ellie,' Becca called, but her voice was barely a whisper. She pushed herself up to her feet and as she stood, the dizziness took over and sent her straight back down to the ground.

She heard a yelp through the fogginess of her mind and then a roar and then nothing.

'Ellie,' Becca croaked again, trying to push herself up.

'Shhhhhh, I'm here. Don't try to get up,' Ellie's voice sounded.

'Ellie, you're okay,' Becca said and managed what she hoped was a smile.

'Now, hold still, while I take a look at this wound,' Ellie said and untied the shirt from Becca's chest.

'Where's Antony?' Becca said and flinched as she felt a rough tongue licking her chest wound.

'Hey, what the hell! Get off,' Becca said and pushed against the furry head of the wolf, but Ellie didn't budge until she had finished. 'What the hell was that?' Becca said, finally able to disengage and push herself out of reach.

'It will help you heal,' Ellie said, human again and reaching for the clothes she'd discarded.

'We couldn't have just gone to a hospital?'

'And told them what, exactly? How on earth were you going to explain that wound?'

Becca said nothing as she glanced down at her chest. An angry red scar had replaced the wound Antony had inflicted. Becca shuddered.

'Here, take my jacket,' Ellie said; Becca took it gratefully.

'Where's Antony?'

'Gone.'

'What do you mean "gone"? Gone where? He can't be…'

'Don't worry, he'll be back.'

'How do you know?'

'Well, there's the obvious point of you being the key to his freedom and there's the other point of me having wounded him.'

'Wounded him?'

'Yes, I bit him on the shoulder and that's going to start hurting like a bitch real soon.'

'But that will kill him,' Becca said, her stomach flipping.

'Eventually it will, yes. But I know how to cure him, don't forget, which I will do "if" he helps you find Ebenezer.'

'And if he doesn't?'

'Then he's a fool,' Ellie said. 'Now, we need to clean up this mess before the caretakers arrive.'

'Aren't you going to..?'

'I know why and I know what, Becca. I just wish you'd waited for me. I said I'd help you and you wouldn't have needed to involve anyone else.'

'We'd still have needed the muscle.'

'No, we wouldn't. Remember what I am. It does have its benefits.'

Becca looked down at the ground to hide the tears that had sprung up. Six men had lost their lives tonight, all because of her impatience.

'Come on, give me a hand with them.'

'What are we going to do with them?'

'Put them in the sarcophagus, as many as we can at least. The rest will just have to go in the hole.'

'Why would you do this? Why would you cover this up?'

'Because I know what it's like to be different and I know what it's like to take a life without meaning to. Now, come on.'

They worked in silence, managing to get three men into the sarcophagus. The others they pushed into the hole before Ellie lowered the casket on top of them. Between the two of them, they filled in the hole and Ellie stowed all the gear in her 4X4.

'It's a good job this patch doesn't have grass or anything growing on it. I doubt anyone will notice the disturbance.'

'I hope not,' Becca said as she leaned against Ellie and they walked back to their cars.

CHAPTER 31

Becca closed the door after them and leant back against it, closing her eyes and willing her heart to calm down. She was exhausted.

All the way home she had been waiting for Antony to jump out in front of her car, waiting for that thud on the roof. Every traffic light she had to stop at, she felt her heart contract. Every face she saw was his face.

She opened her eyes and sighed, her gaze drawn to the top of the stairs and the judgment she found there.

Spook looked down at her from between the bannisters, his eyes narrow, his head high. Reproach? Disappointment? Becca wasn't sure, but he certainly wasn't making her feel any better about her decision.

'At least we'll be safe here,' she said as she followed Ellie into the kitchen. 'What're you doing?'

'Calling Frank.'

'No, don't! Ellie, please. He'll kill me,' Becca said and tried to grab the phone out of Ellie's hand.

'And rightly so. What the hell were you thinking, Becca?' Ellie said and disconnected.

'Oh, God, I don't know,' Becca said, slumping into a chair and burying her face in her hands. 'I just thought that with the poppet, I'd be okay, that I'd be able to control him.'

'And those men?'

'I just found an ad in the paper. No names, no details. Cash job.

No questions asked.'

'Why didn't they go?'

'I thought they had. He did threaten to hang around to see what I was up to. Tried to extract more money out of me to keep quiet. I told them they might not like what they saw and…'

'And now six men are dead. Someone will miss them eventually.'

'Oh God, Ellie, what are we going to do?'

'About what? The dead men or Antony?'

'Both I guess.'

'Well, let's wait and see if anyone misses the men. I'll keep my ear out at the station. As for Antony, I have no idea. All I know, as I said, is that the wound will draw him back to you, if nothing else.'

'We're okay in here. He can't come in without an invite and that's not going to happen.'

'I feel so much calmer now,' Ellie said.

'I said I was sorry.'

'I know, but you should have waited until you had a firm plan. Not this. He's out there killing goodness knows how many innocent people. All because you couldn't wait.'

Becca didn't know what to say. In a way, Ellie was right, but would having had her and Jakes around to start with have made any difference? She doubted it.

'I don't know what to say,' Becca said and sighed.

A hammering on the door stopped Ellie's response. Becca felt her heart lurch and they both looked at each other.

'Who the hell is that?' Ellie said.

Becca didn't answer, for, deep down she knew very well who was banging on her door in the early hours of the morning.

CHAPTER 32

'Who is it?' Becca said as she stood a good distance from the door.

'Oh, I think you know who it is, Rebecca,' Antony's gruff voice sounded through the oak.

'What do we do?' Ellie whispered as she stood behind Becca.

'I don't know, but we can't let him leave.' Becca stared at the floor, her brain frantically trying to think of a solution. 'Can you keep him talking?' she said, slowly and deliberately.

'What? Why?'

'I'm going to go through Anna's spell book, to see if there is anything in there that will help us…I don't know…trap him or something.'

'Are you out of your mind?'

'What choice do we have? We can't let him go, can we? As you said, God knows how many innocent people he's killed already.' Without waiting for a response, Becca turned back and started to climb the stairs.

'Are you going to let me in, Rebecca, or am I going to have to force my way in?'

Full of bravado, Becca turned and walked a few steps towards the front door.

'You can't come in; you haven't been invited.'

'Oh yes I have.'

The sound of splintering wood made them both jump.

'Run, Becca,' Ellie said and Becca turned and ran.

How the hell..? And then the sickening feeling started in the pit of her stomach. There really was no other explanation. Her mother must have invited him in and as the deeds still hadn't been transferred to her name, there was nothing to keep him out.

'Not yet, anyway,' Becca muttered and headed for the attic, the sound of furniture breaking following in her wake, Spook having vanished to his chosen hidey hole.

Becca threw open the lids of the trunks until she found the one with the Grimoire in. She huddled behind the largest trunk, the sounds of the fight below making her agitated, and started flicking through the ancient pages. She'd seen it somewhere and she swore it was in here.

In her haste, she tore some of the pages and had to force herself to slow down before the whole thing fell apart in her hands.

She was nearing the end of the book, a sinking feeling settling in the pit of her stomach, as the only other book it could be in was downstairs, when she turned the last page and there it was – the spell to revoke Antony's invitation. It was scribbled in the corner of the back page, almost as if it were an afterthought. Becca struggled to read the looping script in the light from her Maglite.

A yelp sounded from below, followed by shattering glass and then silence. Becca held her breath and listened. Above the increasing pace of her thudding heart, she could hear the thump of heavy footsteps coming up the stairs.

'Shit,' she muttered and focused back on the revocation spell. There was one word she couldn't quite make out. It could be one of two words.

As the door to the attic banged open and the footsteps sounded on the steps, Becca prayed her gut instincts would be right.

Taking a deep breath, she stood up and, as Antony rounded the corner at the top of the stairs, she hit him with the full force of her power and the Spell O' Revocation.

Nothing happened. Becca's heart sank. She'd been wrong. Antony laughed out loud.

'You go to so much effort to free me and then so much again to keep me away. Make your mind up, Rebecca,' he said and went to step forward, but couldn't. He tried again. Nothing. He stepped backwards, towards the stairs, and then tried to move forwards again, but was held fast in his new position.

Becca felt a little leap of hope inside her and, buoyed by Antony's lack of progress, she repeated the spell and took a step towards Antony. He was forced backwards a step. Each step she took forced Antony to step back.

Becca increased the speed of her chanting and her steps, sending Antony flying down the stairs at such a speed that a slip stream was left in his wake.

Becca ran down the rest of the stairs and stopped in the doorway, looking out into the inky night. She couldn't see him, but that didn't mean he wasn't there.

A groan caught her attention and Becca looked to her left to see Ellie lying in the flower beds under the now absent living room window, Spook looking down on her from his perch on the sill.

'Ellie, are you okay? Can you move?' Becca heard a door slam across the road and saw one of her neighbours hurrying across.

'Yeah, I'll be fine. Just a bit sore,' Ellie said and pushed herself up to sit.

'Well, you need to get inside quick and we need a story fast.'

'What?'

'Incoming nosey neighbour,' Becca said and hauled Ellie to her feet and helped her inside.

'Go and find your clothes, I'll handle this,' Becca said and pushed Ellie out of sight as Mr Smethurst hurried up the drive.

'Are you girls okay? I heard a commotion and could see your front door open. I was about to come over when I heard the glass break, so I thought I'd call the police. They should be here soon. Are you okay, Becca?'

'Yeah, I'm fine. We're fine. No need to have called the police. I'll just go and call and tell them it's a false alarm.'

'Already covered,' Ellie said as she came up to them, not a scratch on her.

'But the window, the commotion? It sounded like someone was fighting…'

'Nothing so dramatic, I'm afraid,' Ellie said. 'Just proves that rounders is a game for outdoors only.'

'But why would you…'

'Thank you for your concern, Mr S., but we're okay. I promise. Now, it's late and don't you have to be up early?' Becca said.

'Well, yes I do, but…'

'But nothing. Now, go on. Honestly, we're fine.'

'He doesn't look convinced,' Ellie said as Mr Smethurst made his way back home, turning every so often. Becca waved at him the last time and he waved back before disappearing inside. The curtains twitched in one of the upstairs rooms. Mrs Smethurst will be itching for all the gossip.

'What on earth did you tell the police?' Becca said as they went back inside and Becca pushed the front door as closed as it would go.

'Exactly what I told our friendly neighbour.'

'And they believed you?'

'Why wouldn't they? I'm one of them,' Ellie said and smiled. She picked up her mobile and started dialling.

'Who are you calling?'

'Someone to come and replace the window and door.'

'At this hour?'

'Working for the police does have its advantages sometimes, you know. Oh hi, yes…' Ellie wandered off into the kitchen to organise repairs while Becca stood in the hallway, reeling from the events of the night.

How did Ellie maintain such calm? Becca wandered into the bomb site that was now her living room and shivered. She turned to look out of the open window, sure that someone was watching her. She moved closer and rested her hand on the window frame and squinted into the darkness, Spook brushing against her hand.

Becca reached down and picked up the huge grey cat, hugging him close as she continued to watch for any sign of movement.

In the shadows cast by the street lamps, Becca could swear she saw a figure standing there. Was it Antony? She closed her eyes and rubbed them, trying to massage the dryness away. When she opened them again, the figure was gone and her senses were calm again.

Spook, however, seemed to disagree, as he meowed for the second time that night; a high-pitched meow; his distress call.

CHAPTER 33

'What the hell has been going on here?' Jakes said as he stepped around the workman who was hanging a new front door.

'What are you doing here?' Becca said as she walked out of the kitchen with a tray of cups of coffee.

'The station called to say there had been a 999 call at this address.'

'Why would they call you?'

'Because the operator is a friend and knows my connection…anyway, that's beside the point. What happened here?'

'Ummm.' Becca looked down at the tray, unsure how to best word the events of the night. Did it matter? He would go ballistic anyway.

'Well?'

'Nutshell. Becca decided to go and free Antony by herself, armed with only a poppet, which, as predicted, didn't work. I arrived just as he was about to reclaim his freedom. I managed to wound him and he ran off, but turned up here. Apparently, he already had an invitation so Becca had to revoke it, hence the mess,' Ellie said and took the tray from Becca and went to deliver the now lukewarm coffee.

'You did what?' Jakes said walking towards Becca. Alarmed by the colour his face was turning and the ferocity of his voice, Becca backed away and into the kitchen. Jakes followed and closed the door behind him.

'Are you out of your mind? Didn't you hear anything I said to you? Anything we said to you?'

'Don't, okay,' Becca said. 'I've already had all this from Ellie. What's done is done! I've just got to figure out a way to fix it before anyone else dies.'

'Why, who's died.'

'The men I paid to raise the sarcophagus. They didn't leave like I asked them to. They wanted to see, wanted to…'

'And you let them?'

'I didn't exactly have a choice, okay. There were six of them. Besides, I honestly thought they'd left.'

'And their bodies? Where are they?'

'Ellie and I buried them in Antony's grave with the sarcophagus.'

'Jesus! I can't believe you've been complicit in all this,' Jakes said, rounding on Ellie as she came into the kitchen.

'What choice did I have? We can't let this get out. It was hard enough trying to cover it all up last time, remember.'

Jakes didn't respond and Ellie leant against the sink, arms folded across her chest.

Becca, sitting at the table, felt as if she was in front of the firing squad. As if sensing her vulnerability, Spook jumped up onto her lap and faced Ellie and Jakes. An ally.

'Where is he?'

'I don't know,' Becca said and sighed.

'We need to find him.'

'I'm well aware of that, but how?'

'I suggest you go through the Grimoire and other books with a fine-tooth comb. There must be some kind of locator or tracker spell.'

Becca nodded. 'I will; I just need to get some sleep.'

'I hardly think sleep would be top of your list of priorities at the moment.'

'It's almost dawn. It's not like he will be going anywhere for a while…'

'Okay, okay, you two. Enough!' Ellie said. 'Remember I said I'd wounded him? Well, that venom will be necrosing his body as we speak.'

'So?' Jakes said.

'So, he will probably be back here when the sun sets, wanting to know how to stop the pain.'

'We better make sure we're ready for him then, hadn't we?'

CHAPTER 34

'What if he doesn't come?' Becca said, twisting her watch around her wrist and moving from window to window, looking out into the darkness.

'Oh, he'll come,' Ellie said and went back to the book she was reading.

'How the hell do you know?' Becca snapped, whirling round to face Ellie, 'and how the hell can you stay so calm?'

Ellie sighed and put her book down. 'Becca, he can't come in until you invite him.'

'But what if he goes to the back door?'

'Then we lure him round to the front.'

'But won't he be suspicious of me inviting him in after I expelled him last night?'

'Maybe, but even if he is, he will be in too much pain to care.'

'Are you sure?'

'Positive. The burning he should be feeling through his veins will be driving him to distraction by now.'

Becca slumped down into the armchair and rested her head back. 'Do you think Frank is still mad?'

'Probably,' Ellie said. 'But he'll get over it. He knows it makes sense. Having him around is just one too many targets for Antony. Do you think it will hold him?' Ellie said, following Becca's gaze to the pentagram decorating the hallway floor, just inside the front door.

'It should, providing that dress was Isabella's. Besides, it'll have to as I haven't regenerated enough blood yet,' Becca laughed, but it sounded hollow, even to her. 'All we can do is wait and see.'

Antony gritted his teeth and squeezed his eyes shut tight, leaning back against the tree for support. He rubbed his arm viciously, trying to stop the burning, trying to stop the itching, trying to stop the throbbing.

What the hell had that bitch done to him? Sweat swathed his skin and his clothes were ringing wet. He hadn't felt heat in over four hundred years. He had forgotten how excruciating it was.

He leaned around the tree and stared across the road. He could see Rebecca pacing back and forth, occasionally moving the nets and peering out. He couldn't see the other one though, couldn't see the one who had done this to him, the one who had somehow turned into a beast.

The shock of seeing her transform had caught him off guard. That's the only reason she had been able to bite him, he told himself.

He couldn't remember the exact name for what she was – lycan something or other, he thought it was. He'd only half listened when Anna used to talk about such things, chuckling to himself at Carla's wide staring eyes. The poor child had hung on to every word.

He'd been told the same tales as he'd been growing up, but he'd never obeyed the rules and he'd never come across a lycanthrope. That was it – lycanthrope. Well, he hadn't come across one until now.

Antony looked across the road again. Rebecca was gone.

Was she alone in the house or was the lycanthrope in there too? Either way, it was a win-win situation for him, providing he could get in, or get one of them to come out.

Antony cried out and the dilemma was driven from his mind as the burning sensation stepped up a notch, crushing all sense of reason.

He flew across the road towards the front door, his weight causing the newly fitted door to buckle, but it held.

Becca jolted awake at the crash, her heart hammering in her chest. She looked across at Ellie, her book now in a heap on the floor.

'It's time,' Ellie said and Becca nodded.

Taking a deep breath, Becca stood up and walked into the hallway. The front door was bent away from its hinges and, with every hammer like thud, it bent a little more.

'Rebecca! Open this door.' Her breath caught in her throat as she heard his voice, heard the anger in it, heard the pain in it.

She felt Ellie's presence behind her and reached up to touch her hand as Ellie squeezed Becca's shoulder.

Becca closed her eyes for a moment, clenched her fists and focused her mind. She felt the elements with her as the energy pulsated in her palms.

'Have you got the chains, just in case?' Becca said and Ellie nodded.

Becca took another deep breath, stepped forward and opened the door.

CHAPTER 35

'What the hell have you done to me, bitch?' Antony said, clutching his arm.

Becca took a step back, despite knowing he couldn't get at her; the look in his eyes filling her with terror.

'Where is she? Where's the bitch that did this to me?' He jumped forward, causing Becca to step back again, and braced himself across the doorway. No sooner had he done so, he withdrew again, clutching his arm.

Becca could see the sheen of sweat across his forehead and the fever in his eyes. It was now or never. She turned to look at Ellie and Ellie nodded.

Becca stepped back, out of the pentagram, and Ellie stepped forward into Antony's line of sight.

'You!' Antony said and launched himself towards her.

Becca muttered under her breath as Antony came forward, praying the counter-spell would work.

Antony braced himself for the impact. Seeing her so close, he'd momentarily forgotten about the spell and had just lunged.

The impact never came, though, and he landed in the hallway in front of the lycanthrope.

He looked around him, wondering how he'd managed to get in. What does it matter? He now had them where he wanted them. His only dilemma was which one first? His gaze rested on Rebecca.

'What did you want to know?' He turned his gaze away from his nemesis and towards the lycanthrope.

'What have you done to me?' he said and lunged towards her. She didn't flinch. He couldn't reach her. 'What in God's name?' he said and turned in Rebecca's direction and tried to grab her. She shrank away from him, but she needn't have bothered, he couldn't reach her either.

He looked down and saw the markings on the floor. He stepped back to get a better look, twisting his head back and forth and then he saw the symbol.

'Well done, Rebecca,' he said, clapping his hands. 'It would seem you have put our time apart to good use.'

It was the lycanthrope who spoke first and Antony walked to the edge of the pentagram to get a better look at her. She was fair, like young Carla had been, but she had strength and she had confidence. A worthwhile adversary.

He gritted his teeth as a burning wave swept through his body, adding more fuel to the fire building in his veins.

'That's werewolf venom,' the blonde lycanthrope said. 'It is gradually killing you. I'd say you had a month, tops, before your insides completely burn up and turn you into a pile of ash.'

Antony stared at her, his growing anger outweighing the pain.

'What is the meaning of this? What is a werewolf?' he said, his teeth bared.

'I am a werewolf, a lycanthrope,' the blonde said. 'As to what it is about, I'll let Becca explain.'

Becca steeled herself as Antony slowly turned and walked towards her. Even though she knew he couldn't cross her bloodline, she stepped a little further back.

She stared into the deep, dark pools of his eyes and shuddered at the hate she saw there. What the hell had possessed her to want to help him? Why had she thought he'd be a willing participant?

Just as she felt her resolve fading, her grandmother's words floated into her mind. *This isn't Antony's fault*, she reminded herself.

'I want to help you,' Becca blurted out and then fell silent.

'Help me how, pray tell?'

'I…I…I want to find a cure for the curse. I…' she faltered then, clenching her fists and thumping them against her thighs in annoyance at her weakness. She felt the power pulsate. Why couldn't she have Ellie's confidence?

'But there is a cure. I kill you and I am cured. So, if you want to help me, come and join me,' Antony stepped back, inviting Becca into the pentagram, but she stayed where she was.

'There is a way of curing you, which doesn't involve me losing my life,' she said and watched his left eyebrow rise and a small smile play across his lips. He crossed one arm across his waist, rested his elbow on it and brought his hand up to stroke his chin. He walked towards Becca again, stopping at the edge of the pentagram.

'Oh really? And what might that be exactly?'

'Finding Ebenezer and asking him for another way to break the curse,' Becca said. Antony roared with laughter.

'Where to start,' he said as he brought his laughing under control. 'My dear, dear Rebecca, what, pray tell, makes you believe there is another way?'

'There has to be,' she said, pushing her chin out in defiance.

'Why?'

'Because every spell book I've seen has several ways to cast the same spell as well as break them, so why should a curse be any different?'

'Let's assume you are correct in your reasoning. My next question has to be why you think Ebenezer Lightwoller would want to tell you?'

'Because I have something he lost a long time ago.'

'And what might that be?' Becca didn't answer him. She wasn't sure whether she should tell him about the amulet.

'Hmmm, okay. I'll let that one go for now. So, how are you going to find Ebenezer? Oh, wait, let me guess, that's why I'm here? In order for you to help me, you need my help to find him? Am I right?'

Becca looked down at her feet, not enjoying the feeling of once again being at Antony's mercy. She willed herself to be strong and tried to remember the man Antony used to be; the man Carla had written about and the man Becca wanted him to be again.

'Yes, I need your help. Why else would I have dug you up without having a cure first?'

'Why indeed,' Antony said and began pacing around the circle.

CHAPTER 36

'And, let's face it, you don't really have a choice but to help Becca,' the blonde lycanthrope said. Antony stopped and turned around. He walked towards her and sniffed. No fear there at all. It amused him that she seemed to consider herself his equal.

'And why, pray tell, is that, Miss…?'

'My name is Ellie.'

'And why, pray tell, do I have to help young Rebecca here, rather than ripping her throat out and helping myself, just as the good curse intended?'

'Because, as I said before, you are dying and…'

'Ah yes, what was it? I'll burn up slowly from the inside until I am nothing more than a pile of ash. Yes, I remember.'

'So, you have to help us,' Rebecca said. Antony turned to face her, the shock of her resemblance to Isabella still raw. The myriad of emotions fought within him, until the anger and hatred regained its foothold. He smiled.

'Actually, I don't. If I remember rightly, a lycanthrope wound turns a human into a werewolf, so I'll be fine.'

'What, so you would swap one curse for another?' Becca said.

Antony watched as she stepped forward, dangerously close to the edge of the pentagram, but not quite crossing the boundary.

'Well, if that's the way you want to see it…'

'How else is there to see it? I thought you wanted your freedom, wanted your life back? Isn't that what this is all about?'

Antony didn't answer. He was focused on Rebecca. Her agitation was making her careless and he just needed that one small opportunity. She stepped forward again, her toe grazing the boundary and he made his move, but he wasn't quick enough. The lycanthrope dragged her to safety.

'For God's sake, Becca, be careful. He almost had you!'

'I can't believe he would do that. What would Anna think? What would Carla think? They both idolised him. They both believed him to be a good man. He was a good man.'

Antony felt an unfamiliar longing at the sound of Carla's name and memories flooded his mind. He hadn't thought about her in so long, hadn't wanted to remember the protectiveness he'd always felt for her.

He remembered the last time he'd seen her, remembered the look of betrayal in her eyes as he'd held Anna by the throat, remembered the shame he'd felt for what he had done to her.

Antony closed his eyes and pushed her face from his mind. He couldn't allow such weaknesses. He refocused on the two women in front of him. One dark and petite. One tall and blonde.

'Carla is dead. Anna is dead. So, what they think of me is of no concern or consequence.'

'But why would you even consider swapping one curse for another? I don't understand.'

'A curse without the need for blood is no curse at all,' Antony said and Ellie burst out laughing.

'Is that what you think?'

'It is true. You don't need blood to survive like I do. You are human. I am not.'

'I am not human. I am alive. There is a difference,' Ellie said. 'As for blood. I need blood to keep the wolf at bay. I just choose to be more discreet about it.'

The lycanthrope was nose to nose with him now. He could see the blackness in her soul, could feel the strength surging through her, could smell the animal, anxious to be set free.

'Besides,' she continued. 'You wouldn't become a werewolf. You would just die.' She continued to stare at him and it was a few minutes before what she said actually sank in.

'The laws of the supernatural are very clear on this, I think you'll find. A human bitten or wounded by a lycanthrope will, in turn, become a lycanthrope.'

'Very true. But you are not human.'

'But I will be, once young Rebecca here fulfils her promise to free me,' he said, gesturing towards a now open-mouthed Rebecca.

'But you weren't human when Ellie wounded you and so those rules don't apply,' Rebecca said.

'Exactly,' said Ellie.

'What?' said Antony.

'The curse of the werewolf applies only to the state you were in at the time you were wounded. It is not transferable,' Ellie said and placed her hands on her hips.

Antony whirled round at the sound of laughter, all too familiar to him – Isabella's laughter – to find Rebecca with a huge grin on her face, struggling to control her mirth.

'So, basically, you have no choice but to help me to help you,' Rebecca said.

Antony clenched his fists against the familiar rage that surged through him. Even the pain of his slowly disintegrating body couldn't subdue it. He stared at them both, all the hatred he still held channelled towards them.

'You will die if you don't,' Rebecca said.

CHAPTER 37

'I…don't…believe….you,' Antony said, his jaw clenched, his teeth bared.

'I don't think you have that choice,' Becca said, emboldened by this new information.

'Of course I have a choice. I always have a choice,' Antony snarled.

'Very true, you do,' Ellie said. 'You can choose to help Becca and, in turn, I will cure you or you can choose to die a very slow and painful death.'

Antony didn't respond; Becca watched him. She could see the battle going on inside him, reflected in the changing appearance of his face. The monster battling against the man he once was. She hoped with all her heart that the monster would not win. Oh, how she hoped the real Antony was still in there somewhere, rationalising the thought processes.

'So, what's it to be, Antony?' Becca said, the silence too much for her to bear.

'I believe you were right, Rebecca, there really is only one choice, isn't there?'

'I'm so glad you feel that way,' Becca said and clicked her fingers to release the spell.

'No, Becca, wait,' Ellie cried, but it was too late. Antony hadn't wasted the moment. He was outside of the pentagram and had Becca slammed against the wall by her throat before Ellie had chance to respond.

Becca stared into Antony's dark eyes once again, the hate as raw as it had ever been.

'But I thought..,' she said, her voice barely a whisper as he squeezed the air out of her and tears ran from the corners of her eyes.

'Well, you thought wrong didn't you, my dear?' Antony said and leaned towards Becca, the tip of his tongue caressing the pulsating artery at her throat.

Becca tried to withdraw, but there was nowhere for her to go.

'You see, I don't trust a word the lycanthrope says, but I do trust the old ways, as I have seen them in action. It's a shame I haven't got more time as I would truly have loved to make you suffer.'

Antony opened his mouth and exposed his fangs. Becca closed her eyes, resigned to her fate. She let her head loll to one side to make it easier for him; there was no point fighting it. As she did so, she heard a growl and she dropped to the floor.

'Get the chains,' Ellie's gruff voice sounded. Becca didn't respond at first, she simply sat slumped on the floor – dazed. 'Now, Becca, before I change my mind and kill this bastard.'

Becca looked up to see Ellie, half transformed, holding Antony in a headlock, struggling to keep her footing. Part of her wanted to let Ellie kill him; to be free of this promise she'd made, a promise she was no longer even sure she'd be able to keep. But, another part of her, the part that listened to her grandmother and was touched by Carla's tales of Antony, wanted to help him; to give him his chance at a full life again.

She pulled herself up and scrambled across the floor to grab the chains she had left there earlier - just in case.

'Quick, bind them around his wrists,' Ellie said, shifting her position to allow Becca access.

'Ouch, Jesus, Becca, be careful. Silver isn't my friend either,' Ellie said as the chains brushed against her arm as Becca moved into position.

'Sorry,' Becca said. As she laid the silver chain against Antony's skin, he howled in pain and fought against Ellie's hold. Startled, Becca dropped the chains, but picked them back up and bound Antony's wrists as quickly and as tightly as she could, turning her nose away to try to avoid the stench of burning flesh.

Once she was done, she placed both hands around the chains and murmured a binding spell to hold them more securely. She then stepped away. Ellie released Antony and he slumped to the floor, moaning like the wounded animal he was.

'It won't hurt as much if you stop fighting against it,' Becca said, a pang of guilt for the pain she was inflicting, pulling at her heart.

'Where did you leave the map?' Ellie said.

'On the kitchen table,' Becca called over her shoulder, already en route.

'Okay, let's go. No time to waste,' Ellie said and dragged Antony to his feet and pushed him towards the kitchen, in Becca's wake.

CHAPTER 38

'Sit down,' Elle said and shoved Antony into a chair, his weight almost costing the structure its existence.

'Ellie, no need to be so rough,' Becca said, seeing Antony grimace as the shift caused the chains to burn deeper.

'He needs to earn my compassion and yours, for God's sake.'

'This isn't his fault, Ellie,' Becca said through gritted teeth. As she looked up towards her friend, her gaze locked with Antony's and her heart jolted.

Was she mistaken? Was it just the pain affecting him or did she really just see a flicker of gratitude in his usually hate filled eyes? She looked away and then back to make sure, but Antony's gaze was now focused on the old map spread out on the Formica table.

'Do you recognise it?' Becca said, her voice gentle, touched by what she hoped she'd seen in his eyes.

'Of course I do,' he snapped, his eyes filled with hate again as he looked up at Becca. 'What is the meaning of this?'

Becca swallowed, trying to compose herself, trying to get her emotions under control, trying to focus.

'What do you see?' Becca said, countering his question.

'My village. My home Or, at least, what used to be my home,' he said through gritted teeth and Becca saw the pain flit across his eyes. 'What is the point of this, Rebecca?' he said and shook his hands in their chains, the look on his face indicating instant regret. 'Are you trying to torture me more? Trying to make me relive the past? Well, are you?' he spat across the table at Becca, causing her to jump out of her seat.

Becca walked toward the sink and leaned against it. She knew his gaze had followed her because the hairs on the back of her neck were standing on end. She shivered and then turned back towards Antony.

'I'm not trying to make you relive anything. I think what Isabella did to you was unforgivable and I feel the price that you have paid for that is deplorable.' She fell silent for a moment, her gaze locked with his. She thought she could see a softening deep inside him as the monster fought to retain its hold. 'This is why I want to help you. Through Anna and Carla, I have learned of the man you once were and neither of them would want to see you like this, would believe you'd want to stay like this…'

'I…' Becca held her hand up to silence him and, strangely, he obeyed.

'Neither of them would believe you would hurt someone to obtain your freedom, not if there was another way. And neither do I.' Becca fell silent again, but Antony never said a word, he just looked down at the map again. 'Come on. There's something I think you should see,' Becca said and pushed herself away from the sink.

She walked over to Antony and hooked her arm through his to help him up, trying not to disturb the chains too much.

'Becca, what are you doing?' Ellie said, standing in the kitchen doorway, every ounce of her being emanating her heightened concern.

'It's okay, Ellie. I think this may help.'

Ellie shrugged and stepped out of the way to let them pass.

'Wait there,' Becca said as she led Antony into the attic and positioned him in the little space there was.

She walked over to the stack of paintings that she'd kept and, taking a deep breath, she pulled the sheets off and stood back.

Not a sound could be heard in the attic until Ellie let out a low whistle.

'Wow,' she said.

Becca's gaze was fixed on Antony and the changing emotions she saw on his face, as his gaze moved over each of the paintings, coming back to the almost life sized one of himself.

'How?' he said and stepped forward, tripping over a box and crying out as the chains burned into his wrists. He fell to his knees in front of Becca. 'How?' he said again and as he looked up at her, Becca saw tears rimming his eyes.

'I don't know,' she said. 'All I know is that my mother painted these when I was a child, based on my stories of my imaginary friend.'

'Your what?'

'Imaginary friend. It's someone children make up, but who adults cannot see.'

'Like a ghost?'

'If you like, yes.'

'But that's me or, at least, it's who I used to be.'

'I know.'

'It's who I want to be again,' he said as he looked back at the painting.

'It's who I want to help you to be again,' Becca said and crouched down next to him, placing a hand on his shoulder. She saw Ellie jump to attention, but raised her palm to stop her. 'Let me help you find him again,' Becca said, gesturing to the painting. 'Trust me to help you.' She looked into Antony's eyes once more and reached out to wipe away a stray tear.

She shuddered at the coolness of his skin, but she held his gaze, her heart constricted by the fear and helplessness she saw there.

'Will you let me help you?'

Antony nodded.

'Do you trust me?'

He nodded again.

'Can I trust you?' Becca held her breath as Antony remained still. She could hear her heart thundering in her chest as she prayed she'd got through to him. It seemed like an age before, slowly and deliberately, Antony inclined his head.

'You can trust me,' he whispered and Becca let go of the breath she'd been holding.

'Stay still while I take these chains off.'

'Becca, no,' Ellie said, jumping forward. Antony growled and Becca placed a calming hand on his shoulder.

'It's okay, Ellie.'

'Are you mad? He could just be saying that to get free.'

'Yes, he could. And, if he is, you have my permission to finish what you started. But, until then, I'm going to give him the benefit of the doubt.' Becca placed her hands around the knot of chains and muttered under her breath. The chains released their hold on Antony and, as carefully as she could, she unwrapped them, freeing him once more.

Antony flexed his hands and stood up. Becca remained crouched down, butterflies dancing in her stomach as she waited.

The attack never came.

'Okay, Rebecca, where do we start?' Antony said and extended a hand to help her up.

CHAPTER 39

'So, you recognise this map, then?' Becca said, wanting to make sure.

'Yes,' Antony said, tracing his finger over a lone house on the bottom right of the map.

'Anna's house?' she ventured, but knew the answer without him saying, when she saw his face; the anger and hatred had returned.

'No, mine and Isa…hers,' he said. 'Anna lived here,' he continued, pointing to a house on the edge of the map; a barrier of trees shielding it from the village, or the other way around.

'Away from everyone?' Ellie said as she brought mugs of coffee to the table. Antony accepted his and wrinkled his nose at the smell.

'I'll bet it tastes better than anything you've had before,' she said.

'Hmmm, we'll see.'

'Why away from the village?' Ellie asked again.

'Because of what Anna was. The villagers may have sought her help all the time, but, as a witch, she would never be accepted in society. It's probably different now,' he said, his voice tinged with sadness as he spoke of Anna.

'Not entirely,' Becca and Ellie said at the same time.

'Society may be more accepting than back then, but it still doesn't readily accept those of us who are different,' Ellie continued and then fell silent.

Antony sipped the coffee Ellie had given him and swallowed it with a grimace.

'Nowhere near as tasty,' he said.

'Well, I'm afraid you'll have to get used to it if you want to live in our time,' she said. Anger flashed in Antony's eyes.

'Or, maybe we could find the recipe and make it your way one day?' Becca said, hoping to diffuse the tension. 'Is Ebenezer's shack on the map?'

'Yes,' Antony said, pointing to a tiny house Becca hadn't noticed before, on the top left of the map, surrounded by what looked like an impenetrable ring of trees. 'The same rules applied to him, not that he took any notice.'

'Blimey, I'd have been looking forever, El. I never noticed that, did you?'

Ellie squinted at the map. 'Nope, but now we know it's there, it's hard to believe we missed it.'

'Mmmm,' Becca said. 'It's almost like it has just appeared.' She looked down into her pocket where she carried the amulet, certain she'd just felt it pulsate, but it looked the same as it always did.

'Okay, watch out a minute,' Becca said and pulled a sheet of tracing paper from underneath the old map. On it she'd marked gridlines and map references, which were missing off the old map. She carefully laid it over the map and adjusted it until she had it in place. She then marked on the tracing paper the location of Ebenezer's house and, for some unknown reason, the location of both Anna's and Antony's houses. 'Right, let's see what we're up against,' she said and lifted up the sheet of tracing paper. 'El, can you lay out the current map please?'

'Sure, where is it?'

'Just behind you.'

Ellie turned and grabbed the rolled up map leaning against the wall. She spread it out on the table and weighted the corners with the now empty coffee cups.

Antony jumped up and spread his hands across the map.

'Where is the forest? This isn't the same village; it can't be. There should be more trees, more greenery.'

'Not anymore, there isn't,' Becca said. 'The population is too big to allow forests to continue as they did. What's left is there,' she said, pointing to Breccan's award winning green space. 'Our wood is huge by today's standards, believe me,' she said. Antony slumped down into the chair, shaking his head.

Becca laid the tracing paper over the map and clipped the edges together to hold it firm. Both she and Ellie squinted through the partially opaque paper at what lay beneath the former homes.

'We'll never find it,' Becca said and sat down with a sigh.

'Why, what is there?' Antony said, leaning over the map. 'What are all those little boxes?'

'Those little boxes are a housing estate,' Becca said, resting her head in her hands.

'A what?'

'A large number of homes built close together,' Ellie said. 'We can find it, Becca, we just need a more detailed view.'

'I guess,' said Becca, not convinced.

'Oh, for goodness sake, stop being such a pessimist! It'll take two minutes on the Internet.'

'The what?' Antony said.

'Becca can explain, while I go and narrow down our target location,' Ellie said and disappeared out of the room, leaving Becca and Antony in silence.

CHAPTER 40

'Think I've got it,' Ellie said, coming back into the kitchen. 'What're you doing?'

'Trying to show Antony how the Internet works,' Becca said, hiding the paper she'd crudely sketched on.

'Any the wiser?' Ellie said.

'Not really. It's a little much to take in.'

'So, where is it then?' Becca interrupted, not wanting to delay things any longer, given the night wouldn't last forever.

'I think it's somewhere in Scarsdale.'

'Nice,' Becca said, wrinkling her nose.

'What's Scarsdale?' Antony said.

'It's not a very nice part of town,' Becca said. 'But quite an apt location given who we're looking for. Shall we go? We've only got a couple of hours until dawn,' Becca said, getting up from the table and heading for the front door. Antony followed.

Ellie grabbed Becca's arm and pulled her to one side, allowing Antony to continue into the hallway.

'Where are you planning on stashing him during the day?' Ellie whispered.

Becca was silent for a moment, her mind running through the various options. 'The attic,' she finally said.

'You're not serious? Here? Frank will do his nut.'

'Where else am I supposed to hide him? I'd rather he were here than out there, killing people,' Becca hissed.

'Speaking of which, he is going to get hungry, if he isn't already and I don't feel comfortable being in the same building as him. Any thoughts?'

'I can put a containment spell on the attic so…'

'I'm not talking about that,' Ellie said. 'I'm talking about what are we going to get him to feed on?'

'Ummm, not sure,' Becca said, looking towards Antony, who was patiently waiting by the front door. 'Let's get this done first and worry about that later.'

'Let's just hope he doesn't get the munchies in the meantime,' Ellie muttered.

CHAPTER 41

'Okay, we're here. So, where is it?' Becca said as she stared through the windscreen of her beaten-up Fiesta, glad they'd decided to come in her car and not Ellie's.

Burnt-out cars resided in driveways, upturned dustbins littered the streets, picked apart by the pack of dogs limping across the road, no doubt. A gang of teenage boys, hoodies hanging from their wiry frames, cigarettes glowing in the dark, watched them as Becca crawled through Scarsdale in second gear. Probably not a good idea.

'El?'

'I don't know. It's not like I had GPS co-ordinates to go off. This is the best I can do.'

'Dammit. How are we going to find it without something more specific?'

'Don't have a go at me,' Ellie growled.

'Ladies. Please,' Antony said and the retort died on Becca's lips. 'Did you say you had something that Ebenezer would want, Rebecca?'

'Ummm, yes,' Becca said, patting her pocket to make sure it was still there.

'What is it?'

'The amulet that Anna stole from him.'

'Amulet?'

'Yes, didn't you know? No, I don't suppose you would, would you? He used to use it to see people or spy on them to be more precise. Anna used it to summon him and I was hoping to do the same thing.'

'Why not do it here then?' said Ellie.

'Because you have to be in his home to summon him.'

'The lycan…Ellie may have a point,' Antony said, correcting himself, following a look from Becca.

'What do you mean?' Becca said.

'Enchanted objects, such as the one you have, will usually pick up the presence of their owner and respond in some way.'

'Respond how?'

'Now that, I'm afraid, I don't know. Each object is different.'

Becca took the amulet out of her pocket and snatched it away as Antony reached for it.

'I just wanted to take a look.'

'Look with your eyes,' Becca said. 'It doesn't look or feel any different than it did when I first found it,' she said.

'Maybe you should get out of the car and walk along the street, with nothing between it and the atmosphere, and see what happens?' Ellie said.

'Are you mad? Have you seen this place?'

'It'll be fine. Antony and I won't be far behind you.'

Becca looked up at Antony, who nodded his agreement, and with a sigh, she pulled the car over and got out.

CHAPTER 42

As she walked, Becca shivered and goose-bumps rippled across her skin. Although the evening was cool, she was wrapped up warmly. It was the feeling she was being watched that was causing her discomfort. She glanced over her shoulder and relaxed a little as she saw Ellie and Antony not too far behind.

Becca knew of Scarsdale. She couldn't help but not know, given it was always in the papers and on the news, but this was the first time she had ever set foot there. She shivered again and looked across the street to where the gang of youths had been. They were nowhere to be seen.

She looked over her shoulder again and smiled a half smile at the thumbs up Ellie gave her. She took the amulet out of her pocket and held it by the chain, with nothing but the air to surround it.

She held it out in front of her, swinging it from left to right; her gaze fixed on it – mainly because she didn't want to focus on where she was and what was around her.

She could feel that hollow feeling in the pit of her stomach start to form, as hope began to fade as she rounded a corner. Soon Scarsdale would end and she'd be back on the main road heading back into town.

She had just turned, to let the others know it was a waste of time, when she thought she felt a vibration through the chain. She turned back and stared intently at the amulet. Nothing happened. She continued walking around the bend and, sure enough, a vibration went through the chain.

A ripple of excitement suffused her body. She looked up, but all she could see was a clump of trees to the left. Undeterred, she turned to the others and beckoned for them to catch up as she quickened her pace.

As she approached what now emerged in the moonlight as a copse, the vibrations intensified and the blue stone in the centre of the amulet flickered with a very weak glow.

'What is it?' Ellie said, as she and Antony caught up to Becca.

'Look,' Becca said and held the amulet up so they could see.

'How long has it been doing that?' Antony said.

'It started vibrating as I neared the bend back there, but the light has only just started.'

'We must be near. What's beyond those trees?' Antony said.

'Not sure to be honest,' Ellie said

'Only one way to find out,' said Becca and started running towards the trees. The closer she got, the brighter the light became until it seemed to reach the peak of its intensity and started to pulsate. Becca stopped running and looked up.

Surrounded by the copse of trees stood a church.

CHAPTER 43

'This can't be it,' Becca said as the others joined her.

'Why not?' said Ellie.

'A church built on the site of an evil warlock's home? Really? Sounds like something out of a cheesy horror film,' Becca said.

'The perfect disguise,' said Antony.

'Why?' Becca said, wandering passed the church to see what would happen. The pulsating stopped and the light started to weaken. She turned and walked back to the church and, sure enough, the light started to pulsate. 'No question about it. According to the amulet, this is the right place. Sorry, Antony, why is this a perfect disguise?'

'Think about it. No one would expect to find a holy place in the same place as something evil, would they?'

'So, are you saying this isn't a real church, but merely a façade?' Ellie said. 'An illusion, if you will,' she clarified, at the look of confusion on Antony's face.

'Not necessarily. I'm just saying it is a good disguise.'

'Not that good if we've found it,' Becca said.

'But we've had help,' Antony said, indicating the amulet, which was still pulsating.

'Shall we?' Becca said.

'I'm afraid you'll have to do this without me,' Antony said. 'I cannot enter a holy place.'

'Go on. I'll keep an eye on him,' Ellie said.

'Here goes nothing,' Becca muttered and walked up to the entrance to the church, the pulsating quickening the closer she got to the building. She reached out for the door handle, not expecting it to be unlocked, not in this neighbourhood, but it was. She pulled the door open and stepped inside.

Candles burned from alcoves in the walls and from plinths flanking the alter. Aside from this, no other lights were on. The glow from the candlelight cast eerie shadows against the stone walls, causing her to jump more than once at her own shadow.

'Hello?' she called, more as an afterthought. There was no response. She walked the circumference of the church, checking each door. Those that were unlocked she opened and checked inside, to make sure no one was around.

Satisfied she was alone and a little alarmed at the unattended candles, she returned to the main aisle. The amulet looked like it was about to explode and Becca set it down on the floor in the middle of the aisle.

She sprinkled the herbs the spell book had indicated around the amulet and placing herself inside the circle, she began to chant the spell that Anna had used to summon Ebenezer all those years ago.

When she had finished, she stayed where she was, unsure whether she should break the circle, unsure how long it would take for him to come.

It was in this same position that Ellie found her an hour later.

'Becca, come on, we need to leave,' Ellie said, holding the door open. Becca turned and could see the first tendrils of dawn on the horizon. Her shoulders sagged.

'It didn't work,' she said. 'Maybe I should wait a little longer?'

'I'm not leaving you in this neighbourhood and we need to get Antony back before the sun comes up,' Ellie said.

'It has to work, El. After everything I said to Antony, it has to work. What am I going to tell him?'

Ellie walked towards Becca, sliding her hands into the pockets of her jeans.

'Didn't I hear you say that he didn't appear straight away when Anna did the spell?'

'I guess,' Becca said, struggling to mask her disappointment. 'I just thought…maybe…oh, I don't know…'

'Look, Becca, not to belittle your gift, but if a powerful witch like Anna couldn't make him appear on the spot, then what makes you think you'd be able to?'

'I just hoped,' Becca said and sighed. 'You're right, though. It's going to take some time.'

'Speaking of time. We don't have much, so grab your stuff and let's get back before Antony turns to dust…although, thinking about it, that would solve your problem.'

'Don't start, El,' Becca said and playfully pushed her friend as they exited the church.

CHAPTER 44

'Quick, get him inside,' Becca said as she skidded to a halt in her driveway. She looked through the windscreen to see the sun now rising over the horizon. It wasn't far to the front door, but she had no idea of the speed of the sun's effects. 'Hang on a sec,' she said before Ellie got out of the car.

Becca jumped out and opened the boot. It was in here somewhere, she was sure of it. Sure enough, under all the rubbish she kept in her boot, she found the blanket she kept there – just in case.

'Here, put this over your head and make sure your hands are covered,' Becca said as she threw the blanket at Antony, who was crouched down as low as possible in the car. Becca could see wisps of smoke rising from his clothing already.

'Is the window in the attic covered?' Ellie said as she fumbled in her pocket for her front door key.

'Not yet, but there are plenty of dark places up there. I'll cover it when we get him inside.'

'Okay, give me two secs to get the front door open.'

Becca nodded and tapped Antony on the shoulder. He glanced up and she could see the burn marks forming on his face.

'Come on, let's get you inside,' she said. 'We're coming.'

Becca virtually dragged Antony out of the car and towards the house. She gagged at the smell of burning flesh as they ran the short distance, a pang of guilt clutching her heart for leaving it so long.

Antony never made a sound, although Becca had no doubt he was in pain; he had to be.

Ellie barely had the door open before Becca and Antony barrelled through.

'There should be some heavy drapes in the spare room. Can you grab them and the toolkit out of the garage?' Becca called over her shoulder as she dragged Antony upstairs to the relative safety of the attic and away from the harsh dawn light flooding through the unshaded windows.

Finally in the attic, she pulled Antony into the darkest corner and unhooked his arm from around her shoulders. He collapsed to the floor without a sound.

'Antony? Are you okay? Antony?' Becca shook him, but got no response. She clasped his jaw in her hand and turned his face towards her. His eyes were closed.

'Antony?' she said more loudly and slapped his face, wincing as the charred skin flaked off at her touch.

'Shit,' she muttered as she smelt smoke and looked down to see Antony's clothes still smouldering. As gently as she could, Becca removed his heavy brocade coat to reveal a white smock style shirt, which was sticking in places to his skin. Not wanting the fabric to adhere to his wounds, Becca ripped the shirt down the front and carefully peeled it from his charred and bloodied torso.

How the hell had the breaking sun managed to wreak this much damage? As she uncovered his remaining arm, her breath caught in her throat.

'Oh my God,' she muttered. 'Ellie!' Becca shouted as panic placed its firm grip around her heart. 'Ellie!' she screamed, backing away from Antony's inert form and staring at what she could only describe as a black ink stain spreading from the wounds Ellie had inflicted, up his arm and starting to reach across his chest. It was more than just the sight though, it was also the smell. Becca fought against her gag reflex for, underneath the smell of burning skin was something far worse, something that caused dread to fill Becca's stomach and fear to clutch her chest. For underneath that smell, was the smell of rotting and decaying meat; the smell of death.

'Ellie!' Becca screamed again.

'Jeez, Becca, I'm going as fast as I can. Your toolkit wasn't where you said, but I found a hammer and some old nails. What's the…oh, Christ,' Ellie said and dropped the drapes on the floor.

'What's happening to him? Why isn't he healing? I thought vampires healed quickly?'

'When was the last time he fed?'

'How the hell should I know,' Becca sobbed, tears running freely down her face. 'What do we do? We can't let him die, El, not like this.'

'He needs to feed is my guess. He can't have fed since you released him, otherwise he would be healing – from his burns anyway.'

'What about that black stain? Is that the venom?'

'Yes,' Ellie said, lifting his arm and using one of the nails to pierce the skin. 'His body is dying. See, no blood.'

'But I thought it took longer than this. I thought…'

'It should,' Ellie said. 'But, in his weakened state and then with the exposure to the sun, his body isn't fighting the venom anymore.'

'We have to help him. We can't just let him die.'

'Why the hell not, Becca? Your life would be back to normal if he did. No obligation, no death threats, nothing.'

'No! I won't let him die.'

'There's nothing you can do. He is already unconscious. The venom is spreading rapidly. He needs blood to regain his strength so his body can repel the venom again.'

'Then let's give him some blood, El.'

'Absolutely not.'

'Well if you won't, I will.' And before Ellie could stop her, Becca bit into her wrist and thrust it into Antony's mouth.

'Becca, no!' Ellie said and grabbed Becca's shoulder and tried to pull her away, but Becca shrugged away from her, with a strength she didn't know she had.

'I have to help him, El. Please understand.'

As the blood dripped down Antony's throat, his body responded and within seconds he gripped her arm; she cried out as he drew on her.

'Becca!' Ellie said and grabbed her arm again, her grip much more secure.

'In…a…minute,' Becca said. 'Let…him…feed.' She tried to shrug away from Ellie, but she didn't have the strength. She could feel the darkness closing in on her with every draw of Antony's hunger. She couldn't stop him. She had gone passed that point. He was going to get his freedom after all. Just as she was about to surrender to the darkness, she felt as though her left arm was being yanked out of its socket and she heard herself cry out as her right wrist was torn open.

Becca felt weightless for a moment and then she landed on something relatively soft, but her head smashed against the corner of a trunk and she blacked out.

CHAPTER 45

Becca could hear raised voices breaking through her dulled mind. She fluttered her eyelids open, the movement causing pain to sear through her head. The room was in darkness, but she knew she wasn't alone. For underneath the voices she now recognised as Ellie and Frank, she could hear a tapping sound on the wooden floor.

'Antony?' she said and tried to push herself up into a sitting position, the pain in her wrist making her collapse to one side. As she moved, she disturbed Spook and he jumped out of the way.

'Why did you do it, Rebecca?' His deep gravelly voice sounded from across the room, drawing a guttural growl from Spook. Becca turned her head in the direction of the armchair and she could just about make out his shape against the paler wall.

'Why did I do what?' she said and reached for the bedside lamp and switched it on. The harsh yellow light seared through her head and it took a moment for her eyes to adjust. She saw Spook sitting on the edge of the bed, positioned between her and the armchair in which Antony was sitting. She felt her breath catch in her throat and her stomach flip as she looked at him.

Antony was sitting back in the chair, shirtless, his dark wavy hair loose and falling around his broad shoulders. Her gaze travelled across his toned torso, lingering in the wisps of dark hair descending from his belly button.

Becca forced herself to look away as her body responded in a way it hadn't for such a long time. She looked instead at his wounded arm and was relieved to see the venom hadn't spread any further. In fact, it appeared to have receded somewhat, as the black tendrils no longer leeched onto his chest.

Her gaze continued to travel upwards, over his full red lips, to his dark eyes and hooded brows; furrowed now; frown lines marring his alabaster skin.

'Why did you save me?' Antony said and leaned forward, steepling his hands under his chin, resting his elbows on his knees.

'Your arm, you can move it,' Becca said, as Antony looked down at it, before stretching it out and flexing his hand.

'Yes, I can move it, but the feeling has long gone.' He turned his gaze back to her, his eyes boring into hers. She saw that softness once again, which only fuelled the unexpected feelings she was developing towards him.

'Why, Rebecca?'

'Because I couldn't bear to see you die.'

'But why?'

'Because you don't deserve any of this, Antony. You deserve the chance to live a normal life and I made a promise to help you do that.'

'But I could have killed you.'

'But you didn't.'

'Only because the lycan…Ellie pulled you away.'

'You wouldn't have killed me.'

'How do you know that, Rebecca?'

'Aside from the fact the venom would have killed you, I think, deep down, you too believe there must be another way.'

'But your spell failed.'

'Maybe, maybe not,' Becca said, aware of the increased volume as Ellie seemed to be trying to stop Jakes coming up the stairs. 'It took a little while for him to come when Anna called, so don't give up yet.' She smiled at Antony and thought she saw a half smile in return, before her bedroom door banged open and Jakes limped in.

CHAPTER 46

'Is this true? Have you been stupid enough to tackle him again?' Jakes said as he grabbed her wrist, bound tightly with bandages. 'For Christ's sake, Becca, what is wrong with you? Do you have a death wish or something?'

Spook, not being one to like raised voices, shot out of the open door and out of harm's way.

Becca opened her mouth to speak, but Jakes didn't give her chance. 'When are you going to learn? When are you going to realise he is just a monster and his kind cannot be helped?'

'Frank, you know why…'

'Oh, don't give me that crap again. Maybe he didn't deserve it, but he certainly doesn't deserve the benefit of your kind heart and your help. Christ, he almost ripped you to shreds in the crypt and Ellie has had to pull him off you twice now, in as many days.'

Becca looked up at Ellie, who was standing in the doorway and had the good grace to look down at the floor.

'Frank, it's not as simple as…'

'It is perfectly simple. Put him back in that box and forget about him!'

'Mr Jakes is right, Rebecca. Why do you care so much?' Antony said from the armchair in the corner.

'You!' Jakes said, whirling round and going for Antony, punching him in the jaw.

'Frank, don't!' Becca said as she saw anger flash across Antony's eyes and his features ripple as the monster fought to take hold. Antony didn't retaliate; he just took the punch.

'And you,' he said, rounding on Ellie. 'You didn't tell me she'd let him in the house, that she was actually sheltering him.'

'You didn't give me chance,' Ellie said, clenching and unclenching her fists.

'Enough!' Becca said, as she jumped out of bed and threw a glass vase against the wall to emphasise her point. 'Enough,' she said again, reaching her hand out to steady herself against the wall. 'I don't want to hear any more arguing and shouting about this, okay?'

The three of them stared back at her, but didn't respond. Becca started to feel a little woozy and sat back down on the bed, putting her head in her hands.

'Becca, are you okay?' Jakes said coming to sit next to her.

'I'll be fine. I guess it takes a good while to recover from blood loss twice over,' she said without thinking. Jakes grabbed her bandaged wrist and tore the dressings off.

'You fed on her?' he said, jumping up and facing Antony again.

'I fed him,' Becca said. 'Sit down, Frank.'

Jakes didn't move. He looked from Antony to Becca and finally at Ellie, before shaking his head and turning to leave.

'Frank, let me explain,' Becca said.

'Explain what?' Jakes said as he stopped and turned to face her.

'Frank, look at his arm from the wound Ellie inflicted after I released him.'

'Shame she didn't rip him to shreds.'

'Frank! He's going to die unless I can find a cure for the curse; die a slow and painful death.'

'I thought Ellie knew how to cure him?'

'She won't, not until we have found a way to break the curse and he is no longer any threat to me.'

'First piece of good news I've heard. Let him rot.'

'No! I'm surprised at you Frank and disappointed. You, who has devoured every word of Carla's journals and who has told me how much she adored Antony and what a good man he was before this. It makes me sad to think you would turn your back.'

'I have no doubt about who he was,' Jakes said, almost spitting the words in Antony's direction. 'But you have no proof that there is an alternative cure to this curse and so I believe what I know and what I have seen. The only thing I give a damn about is your safety,' he said, gesturing to include Ellie in his statement. 'I don't, quite honestly, give a damn about him.'

Becca pushed herself up off the bed and walked over to Frank and took both his hands in hers.

'Look at me,' she said and slowly Jakes raised his gaze to meet hers. 'I do care and I am going to help him. I firmly believe there is another way to break this curse and I am going to find it and I'm going to give Antony his life back.'

'I thought that's what you would say,' Jakes said with a sigh and released Becca's hands. 'Good luck. You'll need it.' He kissed her on the forehead and then turned and left.

CHAPTER 47

Becca slumped back down on the bed after Jakes had left.

'He'll come around,' Ellie said and sat down beside Becca, putting her arm around her shoulders.

Spook came and positioned himself in the doorway, a clear exit should he need one, and looked at Becca reproachfully, through slitted eyes.

'I feel like I've let him down somehow, but I have to do this, I have to help you,' she said, looking at Antony as he came and stood before her.

'The infection is spreading again,' she said, standing up and tracing her fingers across the black tendrils starting to snake across Antony's chest. Antony placed his hand over hers and pressed it to him. Becca shivered.

Ellie cleared her throat and Becca pulled away from Antony, the moment broken.

'He needs to feed and I don't mean on you. I have rung around a few butchers and have found one who will provide us with a regular supply of pig's blood, no questions asked,' Ellie said. 'I was just going to pick it up when…' The sound of breaking glass and a thud against the wooden floor interrupted Ellie. Spook scattered.

'What the hell was that?' Becca said and grabbed Antony's arm as he made for the door. 'You can't go! The curtains are open downstairs. I don't think you could take another burst of sunlight.'

Becca released his arm and headed downstairs, Ellie in her wake.

The hallway was clear. It was as they entered the living room that Becca saw the rock with a piece of paper tied to it with string. It lay in the centre of the rug.

'Another bloody window to replace,' Ellie said as Becca went and picked up the rock. She untied the string and unfolded the piece of paper to reveal spidery scrawl across the page:

I'll be waiting when the sun has set.

E.L.

'What is it?' Ellie said.

'Looks like he got my call after all,' Becca said, handing Ellie the note.

CHAPTER 48

Unable to dissuade Ellie from leaving her alone with Antony, the three of them stood just before the bank of trees that hid the church from view.

'Are you sure this is where he'll be?' Ellie said as Antony walked forward, passing the line of tress. He laughed, causing the girls to look at him.

'What is it?'

'Oh, this is where he is. I have no doubt of that,' he said and gestured for them to come forward.

A little nervous, Becca hooked her arm through Ellie's and the two moved forward as one. As they passed the barrier of trees, Becca gasped.

The church was gone.

'How the hell..?' Ellie let the question hang.

Becca slipped her arm out of Ellie's and walked up the steps from the street. Instead of leading to the huge church entrance, the once immaculately kept path was now uneven and overgrown and wove its way through previously non-existent bushes to a tumbledown shack, whose chimney emitted a thin wisp of smoke.

As Becca approached, she could see a faint flickering light between the boarded up windows. She walked up to the front door and reached her hand out.

'Rebecca, wait!' Antony said, but it was too late, she had already knocked.

The door creaked open as she heard Antony and Ellie running along the path behind her.

'Why, Ms Martin, I presume? Do come in,' a cracked voice sounded from inside the shack and a frail old man, with long wispy white hair and papery skin came into view. 'My name is Ebenezer Lightwoller. Why, I do believe you requested my presence?' He stood aside and opened his arms, gesturing for Becca to go in.

She took a step over the threshold just as Antony grabbed her arm to try to pull her back.

'Why, Mr Cardover, I didn't expect to see you again. Do come in,' Ebenezer said and both Antony and Becca were almost sucked inside the shack. 'Why, I'm afraid there's no room for lycanthropes,' he said to Ellie and slammed the door, making Becca jump.

Ebenezer vanished into the shadows cast by the two candles burning on the windowsills. A weak fire was the only other source of light in the shack. Becca looked around her, searching for Antony; a friendly face in this situation. The irony was not lost on her. He was nowhere to be seen, hidden too in the shadows, no doubt.

'Why, I do believe you have something that belongs to me, Ms Martin,' Ebenezer said, emerging from the shadows and extending a boney hand towards her. Becca recoiled and fell backwards into a chair.

'Not…yet,' she said and squeezed the amulet tightly into her fist for fear the old warlock would summon it to him. 'I want something in return,' she continued, her voice stronger now.

'Why, do you now? And what might that be?'

'I would like to know how to break the curse you have placed on Antony.'

There was a pause and then Ebenezer started to laugh, the sound emerging as a cackle from his haggard features.

'Why, that's perfectly simple and Mr Cardover is well aware of how to break the curse are you not, Mr Cardover?'

A growl sounded from somewhere behind Becca, sending goose-bumps racing across her skin.

'No!' she said, causing Ebenezer to turn and look at her. 'The other way. There has to be another way.'

'Why, what makes you think there is another way?'

'Anna taught me.'

'Ah, yes, dear Anna.'

'In all the teachings and spells she left behind there is always another way. So, why should a curse be any different?'

'Why indeed?' said Ebenezer, looking up and smiling as he clapped his hands together. 'Why, I don't believe we'll be needing another way, dearie. It looks like Mr Cardover is ready to follow the original plan.'

'What?' Becca said and jumped out of the chair. She turned to find Antony bearing down on her, the monster in full control of him yet again.

'Antony, stop!' Becca said backing away from him. 'Remember the venom. It will kill you.'

'Why, dearie, the lycanthrope's venom has no hold over him in here,' Ebenezer said and a cackle erupted again.

Becca screamed and called out for Ellie.

'Why, she can't help you in here, dearie; no one can.'

Becca wasn't listening anymore. As Antony reached out to grab her, Becca closed her eyes and raised her palms towards him, focusing her mind on creating the ball of energy, muttering the repelling spell over and over. Nothing happened. The energy didn't come. The ball didn't form. She opened her eyes just as Antony gripped her by the throat and dragged her towards him.

'Why, didn't I mention, dearie, your magic has no place here either,' Ebenezer said.

Becca could feel the blood thundering in her head; the black dots forming already.

'You…don't…need…to…do…this…Antony,' she whispered, trying to gulp air into her screaming lungs.

'Why, of course he does, dearie, if he wants to be free again.'

'Antony…please,' Becca croaked and tears ran down her cheeks as she felt his teeth pierce the skin of her neck. 'Please…let…me…help…you,' she said as he drew on her. She knew it wouldn't take him long. Her body hadn't yet fully recovered.

'Noooooo!' she said, adrenalin finally kicking in as she punched him hard in the chest, catching him off guard and causing him to let go.

'Why, you are a feisty one, aren't you, dearie? Maybe I do have another option for you after all.'

'Tell me what it is,' Becca said, bracing herself against the table to catch her breath. 'I'll do anything.'

'Why, you should be more careful with your words, dearie, or you may regret it.'

'I will do anything if it means that Antony gets his life back,' Becca said, looking Ebenezer in the eyes; eyes that belied the shell in which he stood before her.

'Why, have it your way, dearie. I will give Mr Cardover his miserable human life back, if you take his place.'

CHAPTER 49

Aside from the crackling of the fire, silence reigned in the shack as Ebenezer's proposal hung in the air, waiting to be accepted or rejected.

Every ounce of Becca's being screamed for her to tell him to go to hell. She looked at Antony. The monster had receded back inside for now, leaving behind someone more gentle, someone more real.

She squeezed her eyes shut tight, imagining Jakes' reaction if he were here now, imagining Ellie's reaction. Becca's heart ached, for she knew there was only one decision to be made.

'Done,' she said.

'Why, that is excellent news,' Ebenezer said and turned to Antony. 'It would appear there is someone who thinks your soul is worth saving, Mr Cardover. You are a lucky man.'

Ebenezer turned back towards Becca and waved his hand in front of her. A goblet of thick red liquid appeared on the table before her.

'Why, I just need you to tell me that you would give your life to save Mr Cardover here and then I need you to drink that, dearie.'

'What is it?' Becca said.

'Why, an essential part of this deal, dearie. Now, do as I ask or the deal is off,' Ebenezer said, his frail fist thumping the table with more force than it ought, causing the goblet to teeter. Becca jumped and reached for the goblet.

'I would gladly give my life so that Antony Cardover can have his back,' Becca said and lifted the goblet and then hesitated.

'Why, come along, dearie, one more little step and the deal is done.'

Closing her eyes, Becca raised the goblet to her lips.

'No, Rebecca, don't!' Antony said and strode forward, snatching the goblet out of her hand. 'Why? Why would you do this for me?'

'Because I made a promise and you don't deserve this,' Becca said and reached out for the goblet, but Antony held it out of her reach.

'Neither do you,' he said reaching out and touching her face. Becca rested her cheek against his cool skin.

'Why, this is all very touching, but there is a small matter of a deal that Ms Martin has made.'

'The deal is only made if she drinks the blood from this goblet,' Antony said. 'That is never going to happen.' Antony hurled the goblet into the fire, the wood catching immediately.

'Why, that wasn't a very wise move was it, Mr Cardover? You had your chance to rid yourself of your curse twice this evening and yet here you are, still cursed.'

'I wouldn't wish this curse on anyone,' he said and turned to look into the fire.

'Why, the Antony Cardover I know wouldn't have let anything stand in his way,' Ebenezer said, but Antony didn't bite.

'There has to be another way,' Becca said, going up to the old warlock and facing him.

'Why, you keep saying that, dearie, but there isn't.'

'I don't believe you,' she said and looked Ebenezer in the eyes. 'Please, please help him.'

'Why, I did help him,' he said. 'And there is no going back on the deals I have made. If he wants to break the curse, then he knows how to do it. Now, return my amulet and stop wasting my time.'

'Never!' Becca said, gripping the amulet even tighter and staring into Ebenezer's eyes.

'Why, have it your way. I've lasted this long without it.' Ebenezer went to clap his hands, but Becca reached out to stop him.

'Wait,' she said, shuddering at the stone-like feel of his skin. Ebenezer recoiled from her touch, but she could swear she saw a flush of colour across his waxy complexion.

'Why, dearie, what else could you possibly want?'

'Please,' Becca said, reaching out to grasp his hands again as she looked into his eyes. 'If this was someone you cared about, wouldn't you keep trying?'

'Why, dearie, you mistake me for someone with the capacity to care,' Ebenezer said, without breaking her grip or her gaze.

'I believe you did, at one time, a very long time ago.' Ebenezer snatched his hands away and turned his back on her.

'If any of that is still inside you somewhere, please tell me how we can break this curse, without either of us having to die.'

Ebenezer whirled round and a light glinted in his eyes as he rubbed his hands together.

'Why, you both don't have to die, dearie.'

'Fantastic,' said Becca, jumping up and down and clapping her hands. 'What do we have to do?'

'Why, solve the puzzle that is me, then ye two will both be free.'

'What?' Becca said, her heart sinking, but Ebenezer just smiled at her and clapped his hands.

Becca and Antony found themselves standing, once more, in front of the church.

CHAPTER 50

Becca stood and stared up at the spire of the church and shivered.

'Oh my God, are you okay?' Ellie said as she came running along the path towards them.

'We're fine,' Becca said, raising her collar so Ellie wouldn't see the puncture marks. As she started towards Ellie, Antony grabbed her arm, his touch so gentle that Becca felt her heart lurch.

'Why do you care so much about helping me?' he said, his brows furrowed. Becca could swear she saw tears in his eyes, but it could just have been a trick of the moonlight.

'As I said in there, none of this is your fault. You…'

'As the inspector would say, cut the crap, Rebecca. This is more than that. What is the real reason?'

'That is the real…'

'Rebecca!'

Becca sighed and looked at the ground before looking him in the eyes again.

'You were there for me when I needed you, all those years ago.'

'What happened? One minute you were here and then you just vanished into thin air. The shack too. Gone,' Ellie said as she grabbed Becca, breaking Antony's grasp, and hugged her. 'What happened? What did he say?'

'Not a lot, to be honest,' Becca said and glanced at Antony who was rubbing his chest, a pained expression on his face.

'He must have said something, you were gone for over an hour.' She looked round at Antony. 'How bad?'

Antony growled in response and Ellie shrugged.

'Suit yourself,' she said and turned back to Becca.

Becca shrugged out of her grasp and walked over to Antony.

'He was trying to goad Antony into killing me and breaking the curse.'

'What?' Ellie rounded on Antony, but Becca stepped between them and held her hand out.

'It's fine. I'm still here. He said there is no alternative, basically, or if there is, he's not telling.'

'Great,' Ellie said. 'Back to square one then.'

'But,' Becca said, 'he said something strange before we ended up back here.'

'What?' Ellie said.

'Give me chance to tell you, El,' Becca said and watched as Ellie opened her mouth to retort and then closed it again, resorting instead to clenching and unclenching her fists.

'After I said there must be a way that doesn't involve us both losing our lives, he said something weird.' Becca held up her hand to stop Ellie from jumping in. 'He said, "solve the puzzle that is me then ye two will both be free".'

'What the hell is that supposed to mean?'

'I think it means we need to delve into his past and find out how he became what he is.'

'And that's going to help break the curse how?' Ellie said and Becca shrugged. 'What else did he say?'

'Nothing. Only that we both don't have to die. He said that before he said about solving the puzzle.'

'Ha!' Ellie said. 'Of course you both don't have to die. If he kills you,' she said, gesturing towards Antony, 'then only one of you dies. Honestly, Becca.'

'But he will die too, from your bite, remember.'

'Ah, yes. There is a silver lining.'

'El!'

Ellie shrugged.

'You could cure him,' Becca said and looked at Ellie, who turned and walked back towards the car.

CHAPTER 51

'Come on, El, please. He could have killed me in there, but he didn't. Even though your venom had no effect in there, he didn't kill me,' Becca said, holding Ellie by the arms as the coffee brewed.

'But he certainly had a go, didn't you?' Ellie said, turning to Antony and gesturing at the now exposed puncture marks on Becca's neck.

Antony didn't respond. He sat slumped in a kitchen chair, rubbing his chest, the pain evident by the rippling changes across his face. Becca felt her heart ache as she looked at him.

'How bad is it?' she said and came to kneel beside him, tilting his chin up to the harsh kitchen lights.

'Christ, El, look at him. His skin is turning grey,' Becca said and reached up to move his hand from his chest. She then proceeded to undo the buttons of his shirt, slowly and carefully, her fingertips grazing the firmness of his chest as she did so, making her shiver. She opened his shirt and gasped.

'Oh my God. Ellie, we have no choice. Look!' Becca stood up, allowing the light onto Antony's chest. Ellie gasped and her hand flew to her mouth.

'It…isn't…supposed…to…happen…this…quickly,' she said, recovering her composure and stepping forward. She reached out to touch Antony's chest. He growled and jerked away from her, his skin crumbling from her touch as he did so. 'He's fed. This shouldn't be spreading so quickly,' she said, almost to herself.

'But it is, El. You have to cure him,' Becca said, stamping her foot, but

Ellie didn't seem to hear her. Her gaze was somewhere in the middle distance, her lips moving, but no sound coming out.

'It has to be the blood,' she said, snapping back to reality and causing Becca to jump.

'What do you mean?' Becca said.

'It has to be the blood. The pig's blood I gave him earlier. It's the wrong sort. It seems to be accelerating the process, not slowing it down.'

'Let's get some cow's blood or sheep's blood or…'

'No,' Ellie said. 'It has to be human blood. That's the only thing that can slow it down.'

'Or you could just give him yours and make it go away altogether,' Becca said, looking down at Ellie, her hands planted on her hips.

Ellie stood up and walked to the cafetière, her back to Becca, and started to pour coffee into three mugs.

'Well,' Becca said.

'I can't, dammit. Why can't you just accept that?' Ellie said, a growl erupting from inside her as she turned towards Becca, her eyes flashing red. Becca stepped away from her, putting herself between Ellie and Antony.

'Up until now, it has always been "won't", so when did this change to "can't"?' Becca said.

Ellie turned her back again and picked up one of the mugs.

'It's the lore of my pack. The rules we all live by.'

'What are you talking about?'

Ellie turned round, almost tripping over Spook, who had come to referee the situation, judging by his positioning, and handed two mugs to Becca. Becca gave one to Antony, who cried out as he reached for it with his decaying hand. Becca took it from him and placed it on the table. She then touched his cheek as she pulled another chair out and sat down to face Ellie.

'I think it's time you enlightened me a bit more on your life,' Becca said.

'You really care for him, don't you?' Ellie said.

'Yes, I do. Now, spill.'

Ellie sighed and pulled herself up to sit on the kitchen counter.

'I don't know how much you know about werewolves…'

'Assume nothing. Just tell me the pertinent facts. It's not like we have a lot of time to exchange full life stories.'

'Okay. Well, as you may imagine, being a werewolf means I need to belong to a pack. Every pack is led by an Alpha and all werewolves are governed by a lore - a code of conduct, rule of ethics, whatever you choose to call it.' Ellie paused to drink some of her coffee.

Becca waited, sipping her own coffee, her foot tapping at an increasing rate. Antony just looked at Ellie, his chin resting on his chest, his eyes turned upwards.

'As long as I can remember, our pack master, who is the Alpha, has preached to us about vampires and werewolves being sworn enemies. Stems from some war, way back when. Our advantage over the vampire is the venom from a bite or a scratch. Werewolf blood, as I have said, will also cure a vampire poisoned by venom.'

Becca tried to interrupt, but Ellie raised her hand to stop her.

'However, the lore says that we are never to use it to cure our enemies. We all have to agree to this in a blood pact.'

'So, what is the point in having the power to cure and never being able to use it?' Becca said, slamming her mug down on the table.

Ellie shrugged. 'All I know is that it has been used as a torture technique. You know, poison them, leave them until they're almost dead to try to get information, cure them and do it all again. The increasing pain as the venom spreads has elicited results. Or, so I'm told. Christ, Becca, I never in a million years expected to see a vampire. I thought they were just ancient myths and folklore.'

'What, just like in the same way werewolves are?' Becca said.

'Touché.'

'So, this pact, is it a physical can't be broken or a verbal promise that can't be broken?'

'Promise.'

'Well then, you can cure him,' Becca said, jumping out of her chair and going over to Ellie. 'Please Ellie, if you don't, he probably won't survive long enough for us to find a cure. I can't keep feeding him and I don't want him killing anyone. Do you?'

Ellie shook her head and looked at Becca. The anguish Becca saw in her friend's eyes broke her heart, but she had to stand firm.

'Jesus, Becca. You don't know what you're asking. If my pack finds out, they'll kill me. Literally.'

'How are they going to find out, El?'

Ellie shrugged.

'Please, Ellie, this is important to me. He's important to me,' Becca said. Ellie looked at her and sighed.

'Just remember this when they're hunting me down.'

'I will,' Becca said and hugged her. 'Thank you,' she whispered.

CHAPTER 52

'Shouldn't it have started working by now?' Becca said, pacing, the black tendrils of venom still evident across Antony's torso. 'It's been hours.'

'It's supposed to work straight away. I don't know why it isn't, Becca,' Ellie said.

'I do,' a voice sounded from the attic doorway. 'You know, you really need to lock the front door Becca and why on God's green earth is your living room window boarded up again?'

'Frank,' Becca said. 'What're you doing here? I thought you wanted nothing to do with this.'

'I did. I do, but I care about the two of you more. So, as the saying goes, "if you can't beat them, join them." How much did you give him?' he said, taking hold of Ellie's heavily bandaged wrists.

'As much as I could,' Ellie said, sitting down suddenly on one of the trunks.

'Too much it would seem, but you could have let him drain you and it still wouldn't work.'

'Why? I don't understand. The lore. The pact,' Ellie said, resting her elbows on her knees to support herself.

'Why? Because of bleeding hearts like yourself, because vampires are very charismatic and charming creatures; creatures who no one – human or supernatural – has any power to resist, unless you are an Alpha.'

'What are you saying?' Becca said.

'The power to cure lies solely with the Alpha, a creature immune to the vampire charm.'

'How did you…'

'Research,' Jakes said.

'So, what do we do now?' Ellie said.

'Solve the puzzle that is me, then ye two will both be free,' muttered Becca.

'What was that?' Jakes said.

'That's what Ebenezer said,' Becca said.

'Ebenezer? How have you..? When..?'

'I summoned him using the amulet. I didn't think he'd respond, but he did, eventually, hence the broken window.'

'I don't understand. What has the broken window got to do with anything?'

'It doesn't matter really. The long and short of it is that we met with Ebenezer,' Becca gestured to Antony. 'And he said there was no alternative cure, other than the obvious…'

'So, I was right. There is nothing you can do, so you should have just left him where he was.'

Becca was shaking her head. 'I begged him, Frank. I asked if he'd ever cared about anyone and I think I hit a nerve. That's when he said that – solve the puzzle that is me, then ye two will both be free.'

'What the hell is that supposed to mean?'

'Maybe there is something in his past, in his story that will help,' Antony said, his voice weak.

'And you know this for sure?' Jakes said.

Antony shrugged and slumped back against the wall.

'Maybe in the journals or on the Internet,' Becca said.

'Well, there's nothing in Carla's journals, I can assure you,' Jakes said.

'Well, we need to find something soon because he isn't going to last much longer,' Becca said, going over to Antony and laying a hand on his shoulder, causing him to growl.

'Sorry,' Becca said.

'I have something that should help buy us some time,' Jakes said and headed back to the front door.

'What?' Becca called after him, but got no response.

The three of them remained in the attic, silence between them, until Jakes retuned carrying a cool box with him.

'Here, give him this,' Jakes said and threw a pouch of blood at Becca.

She only just caught it and turned it over and studied the label. 'This is donor blood,' she said. 'Where did you..?'

'Ask no questions, Becca. Just give it to him.'

Ellie and Becca stood and stared at him, mouths slightly agape.

'Rebecca?' Antony muttered.

'Sorry, sorry. Here, drink this,' she said, holding the bag to his mouth to make it easier for him.

'Now, when he's finished that and perhaps another,' Jakes said, handing Becca another pouch. 'I suggest we let him rest and get to work researching Ebenezer. Did you read all of Anna's journals?'

Becca didn't answer. She was watching Antony feed, watching to see if the tendrils started to recede, but nothing happened.

'Becca?'

'What? Sorry, Frank. What did you say?'

'Anna's journals. Did you read them all?'

'Er, no, just a few. How about you?'

'Nothing in the ones you gave me,' he said. 'Did you read them in chronological order?'

'Don't know really. I just grabbed a handful and started reading.'

'Okay, well, that's where you and I need to go back to. I know you mentioned about Anna and others daring each other to approach his cottage, so there is a story there somewhere, a story they were told as kids.

Maybe she wrote about it? Ellie, I need you to trawl the Internet. Let's see where we get to. Failing that, we'll hit the library.'

Nobody moved.

'Well, come on. Let's get moving. I thought we didn't have time to waste?'

CHAPTER 53

Becca dropped yet another journal on the floor and sighed.

'This is hopeless,' she said and slapped the arm of the chair, causing Spook to jump and grumble about being awoken from his nap. He promptly indicated his displeasure by sinking his claws into Becca's thigh.

'Ow Spook, stop it!' she said and pushed the grey cat off her lap. He hit the floor with a thud and then gathered himself up and stalked out of the room, tail held high.

'What's wrong?' Jakes said, his eyes never leaving the page in front of him.

'These last few journals just don't make sense. They don't flow.'

'Have you checked the dates? Are they..?'

'Yes, but these are early ones and the entries are sporadic. They appear to be in order, but something's missing. I'm going to have another look in the trunks. I refuse to believe she wouldn't have mentioned anything, even if only in passing. Here, you have a read and make sure I haven't missed anything,' Becca said to Jakes who grunted in acknowledgement.

'Right,' Becca said as she threw open the lid of one of the trunks. 'You've got to be in here somewhere.'

'Hey, Rebecca, what the hell are you doing?' Antony's voice sounded from the shadows and Becca winced. She had forgotten he was up there, trying to rest.

'Ah, sorry Antony, I'm looking for some more journals.'

'I thought you had them all?' he said and she heard movement as if he was trying to get up.

'Hey, don't move. You stay there and relax. You're supposed to be conserving your strength.'

'I'll give you a hand…'

'No, it's fine. I shouldn't be long. If I'm right, there should be another journal or two in this trunk. I just need to find them.'

'Let me…'

'No, honestly, I'm fine.'

'Suit yourself, but if you don't want my help, could you at least keep it down please?'

Becca didn't respond as she focused all of her attention on what may, or may not, be hiding in the recesses of the trunk.

'Gotcha,' she muttered after a few minutes, as her fingers detected the uneven nature of the back of the trunk. She pulled at the raised block-like shape and managed to wedge her fingertips behind it and then, very slowly, she pushed her fingers fully into the gap. She was rewarded with a tearing sound as the block she had hold off came away from the back of the trunk.

Careful not to disturb Antony again, Becca took her find out of the attic and into the light.

'Bingo,' she said and raced down the stairs and into the living room. 'I knew there were more,' she said, brandishing the water stained journals under Jakes' nose.

'Bloody hell, Becca, you nearly gave me a heart attack,' he said, placing his hand on his chest to emphasise the point.

'Sorry, but I knew there had to be more,' she said, flopping down into the armchair and prising the journals apart as carefully as she could. 'Let's just hope they bear fruit,' she muttered and within minutes was, once again, lost in the past.

CHAPTER 54

Ebenezer closed the door softly behind him and shuffled over to the battered wooden table. He dropped his medicine bag on the worn surface and allowed his weary body to sink into a chair, which creaked under his meagre weight.

He let his head drop into his boney hands, his lank greasy hair falling forward, and he started to cry.

Nothing. A day of tramping through the village, of knocking on every door, of speaking to every person and still nothing.

'Damn, witches,' he muttered. 'They'll be the death of me.'

He let his hands drop down to the table and lifted his head to stare around his home. The place was almost bare; everything sold to try to keep Henry and himself warm and fed.

The trouble was, there was nothing left to sell and he needed to fix the wheel on the cart to be able to travel further to sell his medicines to make money to put food on the…

He thumped his fist down on the table and winced. It was a vicious circle. He couldn't do one without the other and he couldn't ask for credit, as he still hadn't finished paying for the last repair.

'Damn witches,' he muttered again. If they hadn't come to Breccan his business would still be booming. He'd even suggested they share the trade and complement, not compete against, each other. But no, they came in under the guise of a "friend", just helping out a neighbour, and bam! Not only had they undercut his prices, but they'd stolen all of his customers.

For a while, he'd managed to make ends meet by travelling further afield, but the witches were taking over everywhere and, not only that, he'd also buckled both wheels on his cart trying to avoid the farmer's stray sheep. What thanks had he got for that? None. All he'd got was accused of reckless driving.

He sighed and leaned back in the chair, almost falling as the last spindle gave out and the back fell to the floor. Ebenezer's shoulders sank. What next?

As if to answer his question, there was a hammering on his front door. Ebenezer winced as he heard bits of the rotting wood hit the floor. He pushed himself up from the table and shuffled to the door.

'Who is it?' he said without opening the door.

'Open the door, Lightwoller,' a gruff voice sounded.

'Not until you…'

'Papa, help me,' a young voice sounded.

'Henry!' Ebenezer called and yanked the door open.

'Papa, get them off me,' his son shouted as he struggled to get away from his captor.

'What is the meaning of this?' Ebenezer said, as he looked up into the full swarthy face of the large man in front of him.

'You have been summoned to face the Gypsy Council, Lightwoller, to answer for the actions of your offspring,' the man said, as he continued to stand over Ebenezer.

'Why, what has he done? What have you done now, Henry?' Ebenezer said, stepping around the big man and moving towards his son.

'Nothing, Papa, I swear,' Henry said, still struggling against his captor.

'Liar!' the captor said and pulled down on the ropes binding Henry's wrists behind his back, causing the boy to cry out.

'I asked you what he'd done!' Ebenezer said, turning to face the large man who had banged on his door.

'You need to come with me and all will be revealed,' the man said.

'I haven't done anything,' Henry whined.

'Oh be quiet, Henry, and stop lying,' snapped Ebenezer. 'I have no doubt you've done something. My concern is how far you've gone this time. I am not going with you until you tell me what he's guilty of,' Ebenezer said, planting his feet and folding his arms across his chest.

There was silence for a moment and then the big man erupted with laughter.

'You are no threat to me, Lightwoller,' he said and grabbed Ebenezer by the scruff of the neck, pulled a sack over his head, and dragged him away.

CHAPTER 55

Ebenezer blinked, as the harsh light seared his eyes when his captor pulled the sack off his head.

His eyes adjusting to the brightness, he allowed his gaze to travel around the spacious room, taking in a long wooden bench with a row of five dark haired olive skinned men seated behind it, all staring back at him.

Uncomfortable under such scrutiny, Ebenezer shifted his position, the numbness in his tethered hands now unbearable, and tried to look behind him, but was slapped hard in the side of the head forcing him to look towards the bench.

'Mr Ebenezer Lightwoller, you have been called before the Gypsy Council to answer for the heinous crime committed today by your only son against the son and heir to the Gry family, the founding family of our troupe. How do you plead?' the man at the centre of the row said.

'I don't plead anything until someone tells me exactly what Henry has been accused of doing,' Ebenezer said, only to be rewarded with a kick in the back of the legs, which sent him to his knees before the Council.

'Do you doubt these accusations, Mr Lightwoller?' another member of the Council said. 'Do you doubt that a boy so irresponsibly raised and so renowned for his appalling behaviour, should have taken his bullying of smaller children too far this time?'

'I object to you accusing me of not raising my son better. Do you have any idea what it is like to try to raise a child after the tragic loss..?'

'We are well aware of your domestic circumstances, Mr Lightwoller. That does not excuse the fact that your son spends his time persecuting other children…'

'That's not my fault!' Ebenezer interrupted, holding his head high. 'I did everything I was supposed to do. Some children are…'

'Just born bad. Yes, we know this, Mr Lightwoller, but if you'd have been harsher with your discipline then…'

'Never!' Ebenezer said and stamped his foot. 'I was beaten to within an inch of my life by my father for the slightest thing and I swore that I would never do that to any child of mine.'

'That is unfortunate, Mr Lightwoller,' a man said and Ebenezer turned to see a tall, muscular man, tears streaming down his face, the body of a young boy draped across his open arms.

'Oh my God,' Ebenezer said and felt his skin turn cold and clammy, and a knot form in his stomach. 'Henry, what have you done this time?' he said under his breath.

'If you had,' the man, who Ebenezer now knew was the head of the Gry family. 'Then my only son, my heir, would still be alive.' The man fell to his knees in front of Ebenezer and Ebenezer felt the anger and hate emanating from him.

Ebenezer looked down at the boy and immediately wished he hadn't as he swallowed back the bile that had flooded his mouth.

The boy's clothes were soaked, the musty smell of lake water drifting up from the heavy fabric. His tiny hands were puckered from his time in the water and Ebenezer saw the open wounds on his cheeks where the fish had started to feast. His lips were a shade somewhere between blue and grey, but it was his eyes that turned Ebenezer's guts to liquid.

As he looked into the glazed milky stare of this small boy, Ebenezer could see the fear and horror of his ordeal etched there forever.

'How? What…happened?' he said and looked up into the cold hard eyes of Emile Gry and then over towards the five Council members. 'How do you know my son did this?'

'How dare you insult me!' Emile Gry said and spat in Ebenezer's face as he was surrounded by several women and ushered out of the room. 'You will pay for this, Lightwoller. You and that devil child you spawned,' he shouted before the doors were closed and silence descended on the room.

'How do you know it..?'

'Oh, we know. We have three witnesses who will testify against your son,' the head of the Council said and nodded towards the back of the room.

Ebenezer heard a door open and some shuffling. He tried to see what was going on, but was again forced to look forward.

After a few minutes, three boys Ebenezer recognised as Henry's friends, were ushered passed, heads bowed.

'And you believe the words of these three?' he said, unable to hide the sarcasm in his voice. 'They are just as bad as Henry. How do you know one, or all, of them isn't responsible and they're just trying to blame Henry?'

'Oh, believe me, Mr Lightwoller, we know,' the head Councilman said and nodded again. Ebenezer gasped as one of the boy's heads was raised revealing a severely swollen and bloodied face.

'We have our own way of getting to the truth, just as we have our own way of obtaining justice. An eye for an eye, as they say,' the Councilman said and nodded once again.

This time when he heard the door open, Ebenezer heard the protests of his only son, a boy he had tried and failed to raise to be a kind decent human being, a boy who had exhibited the signs of the devil at an early age in his treatment of small animals; signs Ebenezer had hoped he'd grow out of.

'Oh Henry, what have I done to you?' he said.

'Do my ears deceive me or have you just pled guilty to the actions of your son, Mr Lightwoller?'

'No, I…' but he couldn't finish the sentence for, deep down, he had no doubt that Henry had killed that little boy.

'Excellent! Now we can proceed with the punishment,' the Councilman said and banged his fist on the table.

CHAPTER 56

Ebenezer stared, mute, as Henry was hauled forward, his hands bound tightly behind his back and his legs clamped in shackles he didn't know existed outside of a prison. Once in position, so both the Council and Ebenezer had a clear view, Henry's head was dragged upright and Ebenezer could see exactly the punishment the gypsies had already started to eke out.

Like the other boys, Henry's face was battered and bloodied, his eyes swollen so all that was visible were slits, where tears now seeped from. His lips, also swollen, were split and bleeding, the blood dripping onto his ragged open shirt; a shirt revealing the blackening skin as bruises were forming around the welts, inflicted by a whip no doubt.

'Papa…help…me,' Henry said, the words muffled by the bubbles of spit that formed as he tried to speak.

'What have you done this time, Henry?' Ebenezer said, his teeth gritted as he attempted to control his conflicting emotions – the revulsion at what his son had done and the protectiveness only a parent can feel, regardless of what their child had done.

'Nothing…Papa, I…swear,'

'Don't lie to me, Henry!'

'It…wasn't…me…Papa.'

'I said don't lie! They already know it was you, so stop lying!'

'I'm…not,' Henry spluttered and Ebenezer watched, his heart aching, as tears flowed freely down his son's cheeks. He desperately wanted to believe him, but he had witnessed Henry's bullying before and had no doubt he had been the ring-leader. If only…

'Enough of these protests,' the head Councilman interrupted Ebenezer's thoughts. 'It's time to discuss punishment. Do you confirm that this boy is indeed your son, Mr Lightwoller?'

'I do.'

'And do you confirm that this is not the first time he has been involved in the bullying and persecution of others?'

'But, this isn't…'

'Yes or no, Mr Lightwoller.'

'Yes, but…'

'And do you believe that bad behaviour should be punished?'

'Of course and I will…'

'And do you take responsibility for your son, Mr Lightwoller, and for his behaviour?'

'I do and I will ensure he is appropriately punished.'

'I'm afraid, Mr Lightwoller, that based on the failure of your past efforts to control and punish your son, we, the Council, do not feel you have the stomach to eke out the punishment that fits this crime. As such, we will take this deed out of your hands.'

'You have no right, do you hear me. He is my son and…'

'Oh, we have every right, Mr Lightwoller. You see, young Henry here committed his crimes on land leased to us and as such, under the common laws of Breccan and Carlford, he is subject to our lore.'

Ebenezer felt the knot form in his stomach and the clamminess return as the words sank in and the seriousness of Henry's fate became apparent.

'No, no, he's just a boy. Punish me instead, please,' Ebenezer pleaded. 'He doesn't deserve your…' he let the sentence hang.

'Oh, but we will be punishing you, Mr Lightwoller, as is our lore. As for him not deserving his fate, I think we both know that's not true, don't we?' the head Councilman said and nodded towards Ebenezer.

'Let's go,' a gruff voice said in his ear and Ebenezer felt himself being pushed towards his son and the exit.

CHAPTER 57

'Why have you brought us here?' Ebenezer said as he stood on the shore of the lake and gazed out across its still grey surface. He knew why they were there, but he still felt he had to ask. Ebenezer shivered as he looked across at his son, forced to stand waist-deep in the murky water.

'An eye for an eye, a life for a life, Mr Lightwoller.'

'You can't mean that. I know what he did was…'

'Heinous, unforgivable, unnecessary, avoidable if only his father had disciplined him properly in the past? Yes, all of those things, which is why you are both here, to be taught a lesson; one which you will not forget,' the head Councilman said and nodded.

The man holding Henry placed his paw like hand on the back of Henry's head and thrust him forward, sending the young boy head first into the lake. Instead of letting him surface again, however, Ebenezer watched in horror as the man held Henry's head firmly below the surface; Henry's legs beating as much as they could, his tethered arms useless.

'Stop! Please stop!' Ebenezer said, throwing himself on his knees in front of the head Councilman, who had his eyes closed and was murmuring in a language Ebenezer could not understand. 'Please. Punish me instead, but give him another chance. He is only a boy. He can learn.' Ebenezer nudged the man with his shoulder and the murmuring stopped.

Ebenezer looked up to find the man staring down at him, his mouth set in a thin line.

'Do not interrupt me, Mr Lightwoller.'

'Please take me. Punish me. Do what you want to me, but let him go. Please. Give him a chance.'

'That boy is beyond redemption. You know it and I know it. As for punishing you, we will get to that. Now, will someone keep him quiet!'

Ebenezer felt himself being dragged away and a foul smelling piece of cloth being shoved into his mouth. He tried to resist, but the pressure of his captor's hand squeezing his jaw was too much. The same hand that had silenced him then held his head firmly, forcing Ebenezer to watch as Henry, his only child, was drowned.

'An eye for an eye,' he muttered as Henry finally stopped struggling and his inert body floated to the surface. He squeezed his eyes shut tight, waiting for his son's lifeless corpse to be dropped in front of him. Instead, however, he heard the sound of a boat being dragged across the shore and opened his eyes to find a huge boulder had been tied to his son's legs and his body was being manhandled into the boat.

Ebenezer tried to spit the gag out to protest, but he couldn't. He struggled against his captor, but to no avail. All he could do was watch; watch as the head Councilman placed a hand on Henry's corpse and uttered something in that unintelligible language; watch as the boat was pushed away from the shore and rowed out to the centre of the lake; watch as his son's body was pushed over the side of the boat, the boulder in its wake, to spend eternity in a watery grave.

His gaze shifted as the Councilman turned away from the shore and walked towards Ebenezer.

'And now for you,' he said and removed the gag from Ebenezer's mouth.

CHAPTER 58

'How could you?' Ebenezer said and spat at the tall olive skinned man standing before him. 'How could you? He was just a child?'

'As was his victim, Mr Lightwoller. Now, enough! It's time for your punishment.'

'Haven't I been punished enough? You've taken my child.'

'Silence!' the Councilman said and snapped his fingers, rendering Ebenezer speechless. 'Now, for the crime of murder, carried out against a Gry, by your son, Henry Lightwoller, you, Ebenezer Lightwoller, will carry the Curse of Souls. This curse requires you to collect the souls of twenty people, all guilty of the murder of an innocent. Once said souls have been collected, you will once more appear before this Council for us to decide whether your debt has been repaid. What say you?' The Councilman snapped his fingers and Ebenezer coughed, as if some invisible hand had been released from around his throat.

'Well?' the Councilman said.

'Why should I do as you say?'

'Well, Mr Lightwoller, you really don't have much of a choice. That's the trouble with curses, you see, they tend to carry consequences.'

'Such as?' Ebenezer said, coughing and massaging his throat.

'Such as the fact you will find yourself ageing very quickly and dying long before your time if you do not collect these souls.'

'That's not really an incentive since I no longer have anything to live for.'

'Oh, and your son will never be at peace, unless you do as we say.'

'Meaning what?'

'Meaning that his spirit will continue to roam this plane until you have fulfilled the terms of your curse. For every soul you take, he will deliver a note to their loved ones, telling them what has happened. Once this letter is delivered, their name will appear in this book,' the Councilman waved a leather-bound book in Ebenezer's face. 'Once twenty names have appeared in here then we will summon you again to decide whether you have repaid your debt and whether your curse can, therefore, be lifted and you can go back to live out your life, aged only by the years it has taken you to collect the souls.'

'Why twenty?' Ebenezer said, his shoulders sagging.

'One for every person your son ever harmed.'

'Why the letters?'

'It's only fair the family should know and, besides, the letters are linked to this log, so you can't lie to us. This log cannot be written in, so the only way you can hope to be released from this curse is to do as I say.'

'And how am I supposed to take peoples' souls, for goodness sake?'

'Oh come on, Mr Lightwoller, I thought you were a healer; able to cure people of their ills?'

'I am, with herbs and plants. I am not a witch. I cannot do this, nor do I want to.'

'Then you wish to allow your son's spirit to roam the earth for eternity? I thought you professed to love him, Mr Lightwoller, regardless of his sins?'

'I do, but…'

'Then there we have it and, besides, it wouldn't be right to curse you without giving you the means to fulfil your debt to us?'

'What do you mean? I don't understand.'

'We will give you the means to take the souls, Mr Lightwoller. You just need to work out how to use it. That is, if you wish your son to rest in peace. But, don't take too long to figure it out, for it is these souls that will enable you to maintain your youth, otherwise you will grow old and die very quickly.'

'But, I…'

'There is nothing else you can say, Mr Lightwoller. The curse has been cast.' The Councilman stepped to one side to reveal Emile Gry standing behind him, eyes downcast, murmuring in that strange language.

Ebenezer stared, his mouth agape, as Emile Gry raised his head and flicked a ball of light in Ebenezer's direction, hitting him in the chest and knocking him off his feet. He cracked his head on the ground and white lights pricked at his eyes before he blacked out.

CHAPTER 59

'Anything?' Ellie said as she walked into the living room carrying a tray of steaming mugs of coffee.

'Nope,' Jakes said and stretched. 'Christ, what time is it? I'm stiff as a board.'

'You don't want to know,' Ellie said. 'I've struck out too. I guess it's down to Becca or the library.' Both Jakes and Ellie looked over towards Becca, but she remained oblivious.

'Yoo hoo Becca. Anybody there?' Ellie said, wafting the strong coffee under Becca's nose.

'What? Oh, great. Thanks El,' Becca said and took the mug from Ellie's hand and went back to reading.

'Becca!' Jakes said, forcing her to look up.

'What?'

'Have you got something?'

'Er, yes, I think I have. I'm not sure how much yet.'

'Why don't you share it with us, so we can all decide,' Jakes said.

'Okay,' Becca said and went back to the first journal. She took a gulp of her coffee and cleared her throat.

'The info is a bit sketchy, as you may imagine, and scattered across these journals so it may not be…'

'Becca, just tell us what you've found,' Ellie said and sat down on the arm of Jakes' chair.

'Okay, well, it would seem Ebenezer used to be some sort of medicine man for the Breccan and Carlford villages.'

'You mean like in voodoo?' Ellie said.

'I think you're getting carried away…'

'No, I think she means a healer or a doctor for want of a better description,' Jakes said.

'That's the word – healer,' Becca said. 'My sleep deprived brain couldn't think of it. Anyway, he was a healer, but a really poor one. It would seem that the witches stole a lot of his business, as they would do the same work for less reward.'

'It's always money,' Ellie said.

'Sshhhh!' said Jakes. 'Go on, Becca.'

'Well, as you can imagine, this didn't exactly endear him towards witches. As if this wasn't bad enough, he also had a wayward son. Apparently, the son, Henry, and his friends used to bully other kids in the village, sometimes pretty aggressively. Henry, probably due to his father's situation, also taunted the witches. Nothing too bad from what I can tell, but that could be because he was also afraid of what they might do to him.'

'No mother?' Jakes said.

'Uh-uh. She seems to have died in childbirth.' Becca lapsed into silence.

'Anything else?' Jakes said.

'Yeah, Anna talks about a troupe of gypsies coming to Breccan. I'm just trying to find their name. Ah, here it is. Gry. G-R-Y. From what Anna says, they were pretty widely known at the time. It would appear that young Master Lightwoller and his friends wanted to test the theory that gypsies were actually witches and they lured one of the boys away from the camp, fashioned a dunking stool…'

'A dunking stool? Really?' Ellie said.

'Yep and guess what? The boy drowned.'

'There's a surprise,' Ellie said and snorted.

'Yeah, well, the kid happened to be the son and heir to the Gry gypsies and to say Papa Gry was upset was an understatement.' Becca fell silent again.

'Oh, for God's sake Becca, get to it,' Ellie said.

'The gypsies murdered Ebenezer's son,' Becca said.

'Jesus, what did they do?' Ellie said.

'Drowned him. An eye for an eye, Anna says, and Frank?' Becca said, looking towards Jakes. 'The boy whom Carla mentions in her journal. You know, the one who visited Anna when Antony disappeared?'

Jakes nodded.

'Well, that's him, Henry.'

'What about Ebenezer though? As horrible as it is, I can see why they retaliated against the boy, but was it the Grys who made Ebenezer into what he is?' Jakes said and Becca nodded.

'Now, on this Anna has added quite a bit of detail. Apparently, as punishment for not controlling his son, Emile Gry, the head of the family and the father of the drowned boy, placed a curse on Ebenezer.'

'What kind of curse?' Ellie interrupted.

'Well, if you'd let her finish, we'd all find out,' Jakes said and Becca watched Ellie bite back a retort and fold her arms across her chest.

'The curse caused Ebenezer to age prematurely at a rate that would have meant he would be dead within a few months.'

'So, how is it he is still here after all this time?' Jakes said.

'Souls,' said Antony from the doorway. 'He takes people's souls to regain his youth. I saw it when he cursed me. At first, he was an ancient old man, at least his body was, like he was last night, Rebecca, but then….when he'd tricked me into drinking from the goblet, tricked me into giving him my soul, he changed in an instant. He became younger, his body finally matching his voice and his eyes.'

'Antony's right. The curse that Emile Gry placed on him required him to take the souls of twenty evil people; twenty being the number of kids Henry persecuted. Once the twenty was reached, in theory, the debt would be repaid, Henry's spirit would be set free and…'

'What about Henry's spirit?' Jakes said.

'His spirit – that of the boy – was cursed to roam forever on this plane.'

'Unless Ebenezer took those souls,' he said.

'Correct.'

'But how would they know he'd done it?'

'The names magically appeared in a log, once Henry's spirit had delivered the letter to the family.'

'Okay, so why is he still alive now?' Ellie said. 'Surely, he should have still aged and passed away?'

Becca shrugged.

'No. When he took my soul he became young again, the age he was when Emile Gry cursed him,' Antony said.

'So, it's like a reset then? Every time he takes a soul, he goes back to the age he was when he was cursed?' Ellie said. 'How did he end up being so nasty? I mean, he didn't used to be, from what you've said,' she continued.

'No, but the loss of a child will do that to you. Wait until you've dealt with the aftermath of a child murder and you'll see what I mean,' Jakes said.

'Kind of,' said Becca. 'From what Anna says, based on the stories passed around, he initially just took the souls of criminals, as he was told to do, but the villagers believed that, over time, the evilness of these souls corrupted Ebenezer's basic good nature. In the end, he took the soul of anyone who had wronged him or those desperately wanting help or restitution.' Becca fell silent.

'Like me,' Antony finished.

'Like you,' Becca said. 'And, in return, cursed them in different ways, from what Anna says. From what she'd seen, no two curses were ever the same.'

'Again, I ask why is he still here? I get the ageing thing, but surely he's taken more than twenty souls over the years?' Ellie said.

'Yes, but probably not the twenty evil souls he was supposed to take, to repay his debt,' Antony said. 'It would seem he changed paths and took the souls of the good and hence, never repaid his debt to the Grys.'

They all lapsed into silence at this point, Spook sitting in the doorway as if overseeing proceedings.

'Anything else?' Jakes finally said.

'No, that's it,' Becca said, slapped the journal shut and sighed. 'Now what?'

'We find the Grys,' Antony said.

CHAPTER 60

'Are you sure that's the right move?' Jakes said.

'If anyone is going to know how to stop Ebenezer, it is the Grys. They made him what he is, just like he made me what I am.'

'Yes, but we're looking for an alternate way to break your curse, not on a mission to rid the world of that piece of scum.'

'No, he's right,' Becca said, jumping out of her chair, a bubble of excitement and hope rippling through her. 'If they know how to stop him, they may also know how to break his curses.'

'And if they don't?' Jakes said.

'They will,' Becca said, sure for the first time in all of this, and squeezed Antony's arm, causing him to wince.

'Sorry,' she said. 'How do you feel?'

'Stronger.'

'And the venom?' Becca said, reaching out to open his shirt to take a look.

'It's not spread any further,' Antony said, taking hold of her hand and pressing it against his chest as he looked down at her.

'Okay, well, I suggest you go and get yourself some more blood, while the three of us try to figure out what to do next,' Jakes said, coming over to propel Antony out of the living room away from Becca. Spook ambled into the room to let them pass.

'Right ladies,' he continued. 'Becca, if you do an Internet search, looking for…'

'No,' Ellie said, sitting up suddenly. 'I've got it. I knew that story seemed familiar.' Without saying anything else, she hurried out of the room, bumping into Antony as she did so.

'Where is the lycan…Ellie going?'

'I have no idea,' Becca said and was going to ask Jakes to continue, when Ellie swept back in, clutching a laptop and a few paperbacks.

'The name is spelt differently, but names do evolve over time, but it is the story. I had heard it before on a radio interview, a few weeks ago,' Ellie said.

'El, what on earth are you talking about and why do you look all flushed all of a sudden?' Becca said.

'I'm not flushed,' Ellie said, dropping her loot on the coffee table and raising her hands to her face.

'Well, are you going to explain what you are talking about or do we have to play twenty questions?' Jakes said, picking up one of the paperbacks. 'I didn't know you read all this fantasy rubbish.'

'It's not rubbish,' Ellie said, snatching the book back off him. 'It's actually quite good.' She looked down at the photo on the back cover and Becca watched the colour rise to the roots of Ellie's hair. Intrigued, she picked up the other paperback.

'Well, well, now I can see why you look all hot and bothered. Little bit young for you, though, isn't he, El?' Becca said and smiled, winking at Antony.

'He's not that much younger than me,' Ellie said, a little too quickly. 'Anyway, I'm not interested in him. He's not my type and…'

'Can we please get to the point,' Jakes said and turned to look at Ellie.

'Look at the name,' she said, tapping the front of the novel.

'Luca Gryse. Yes, and?'

'Take away the "SE" and you have Gry. He also pronounces it that way.'

'Really? And you would know this how?' Becca said, trying to bait Ellie again.

'Don't start again,' Jakes said.

'I know this because of the interview I mentioned, the interview in which he talks a little about his past.'

'And what has that…'

'Just listen, okay,' Ellie said and clicked play on the laptop screen.

CHAPTER 61

'Well, good afternoon, Mr Gryse,' the interviewer said.

'Luca, please,' a gravelly voice sounded from the laptop, sending shivers down Becca's spine.

'Luca it is then. Thank you so much for taking the time to come in and talk to us today.'

'It's my pleasure,' he said and gave a small throaty laugh.

'Oh no, I can assure you the pleasure is all ours, or should I say mine. Cold shower in here, please,' the female presenter called and then laughed, an annoying jackhammer kind of laugh.

Becca heard a chair shifting and could imagine Luca Gryse trying to get as far away from this woman as possible.

'Now, before we start, let me just create the fantasy for all of our female, and probably some male, listeners out there. Mr Luca Gryse, award winning author of more than ten dark fantasy novels is sitting before me in dark skinny jeans, that fit in all the right places, ladies...' The interviewer paused to allow that horrendous laugh to take over. 'And a rather, how shall I put it, leaves nothing to the imagination t-shirt over that toned muscular chest. That, together with the shaggy dark hair, olive skin and come to bed eyes, well, I don't know why I'm doing this interview and not ravishing you.' Her laughter filled the air and Becca groaned, hiding her face in her hands, feeling extremely sorry for the poor guy. Even Spook had his head bowed, his gaze fixated with something on the floor.

'Phew, allow me to calm down before I continue,' she said and Becca heard Luca's nervous laugh in the background.

'Right, I am calm, for now. You must have women falling all over themselves to get to you?'

'Erm, not really. I keep pretty much to myself.'

'And where might that be?'

Becca groaned again. 'I can't listen to any more of this. Can you forward to the important bits, El, before I throw up?'

'I'll try. I know it's pretty bad. I did feel for the guy when I listened to it.'

The room lapsed into silence as Ellie skipped through the interview.

'Okay, here we go,' she said.

'So, Luca, your next book is in complete contrast to your usual work, in that it is a biography, isn't it?'

'Not so much a biography, Jenny, more like a historical account, based around the lives of my ancestors, from as far back as the sixteen hundreds, all the way through to present day.'

'So it is biographical?'

'To some extent, yes,' he conceded with a sigh.

'Would you care to share with us a little of your ancestry?'

'Of course. My family, the Grys, spelt G-R-Y, have lived in this part of the world for centuries…'

'Why is your name spelt differently?' the interviewer interrupted.

'The family split and my side broke away, wanting to integrate more, wanting to go mainstream, I guess you could say. Part of that was to alter our surname slightly.'

'And yet you pronounce it the same. Interesting. So, why the breakaway?'

'Well, if you let me finish you would find out,' Luca said, making Becca snigger.

'I like him,' Becca said.

'Me too,' said Ellie and sighed. Becca looked up and saw Ellie gazing into space, a dreamy look in her eyes.

'It was the early sixteen hundreds and my family were making their annual trip to Breccan, for trading and entertaining, when it happened.'

'When what happened?' the interviewer said.

'God, she can't help herself can she,' Becca said and slapped her hands on her thighs.

There was a pause in the interview and Becca could well imagine that Luca was trying to compose himself, before he spoke again.

'The eldest son of the head of the family was killed by some local kids.'

'Oh my God,' the interviewer said. 'What happened?'

'I'm afraid you'll have to read the book to find out,' Luca said and laughed, the sound causing Becca to shiver again. 'Suffice it to say, it was the aftermath of this incident on my family and on Breccan itself that created the rift that finally drove the family apart.'

'And when can we get our hands on a copy of "The Curse of Gry"?'

'It's actually released today,' Luca said. 'And I'll be starting a national book tour later this week.'

'Excellent. So, all our listeners can come and feast their eyes on you soon then and pick up a copy of "The Curse of Gry" of course.'

'Of course,' Luca said.

'Well, Luca, thank you so much for coming in to talk to us, you scrummy specimen, and I hope the book does really well.'

'Thanks for having me.'

'You are more than welcome. So, that's it for today. Don't forget to check out the gorgeous Luca Gryse at a bookstore near you very soon.'

Ellie pressed stop and silence filled the living room.

'Who the hell was that awful woman?' Becca said.

'Jenny Nightingale. She's one of the daytime presenters on B&C Radio.

Quite popular apparently,' Ellie said.

'Goodness knows why,' Becca said.

'Anyway,' said Jakes. 'It would appear that Mr Gryse's story bears a strong resemblance to that told by Anna, not to mention his name.'

'So, how do we get in touch with him? His agent?' Becca said.

'Well, coincidentally, or not, depending on your viewpoint, he lives in Scotsford. The cabin on the lake.'

'Ooohh, I always wondered who lived there. That place is stunning. I'm guessing we're not just going to be able to turn up on his doorstep, though?' Becca said.

'No, not unless we have to. But, what I thought was we could approach him at his book signing. His last one is in Scotsford tomorrow. What do you think?' Ellie said.

'I think this is the perfect excuse for you to meet him,' Becca said, observing the colour creeping up Ellie's neck.

'I was going anyway.'

'Yes, but this will give you an excuse to have a real conversation, though, won't it?'

'Becca!' Jakes said. 'It was you who wanted us all to take this seriously?'

'I do, but no harm in a little fun and maybe matchmaking on the side.'

'Becca!' Ellie said, her face now crimson.

'Okay, okay. Let's just focus, shall we?' Jakes said. 'How are you proposing to open up a line of conversation with him? It's not as if you can just come out and tell him what you need.'

'Why not?' Antony said, stepping into the conversation for the first time since Ellie started the interview replay. 'In my time, it was always best to state your business from the start. In that way, there was less confusion.'

'I guess you've got more chance of him listening to you if you use the direct approach,' Jakes said. 'Otherwise, you're just another couple of pretty girls trying to get his attention.'

'Thanks for the vote of confidence,' Becca said. 'You could always go instead.'

'No, I think this is something you need to do,' Jakes said.

CHAPTER 62

Becca and Ellie decided to leave it until towards the end of the day, hoping they would get more of a chance to speak to Luca Gryse, but as they walked through the doors of the Watersones in Scotsford, Becca felt her heart sink.

'Christ, this guy has quite a female following,' she said to Ellie, as they observed the length of the line still waiting to see the illustrious author.

'Yeah, but I wonder how many of them actually read what he's written,' Ellie grumbled.

'Yes, I wonder.'

'Hey, I read them,' Ellie said, grabbing a copy of "The Curse of Gry" off the stack as they walked passed.

'Sure you do. The guy writes about werewolves, something you are well acquainted with and yet you still like his writing? Please.'

'You'd be surprised how accurate his information is. It's almost like he has inside knowledge.'

'Maybe he does,' Becca said, picking up a copy for herself too.

'Mmmm. I'd really like the chance to ask him,' Ellie said, fidgeting from one foot to the other as they neared the front of the line.

'Well, can we solve the predicament we're in first, please?' said Becca, looking up and catching her first real look at Luca Gryse.

'Wow, he is way more good looking than this picture gives him credit for,' she said, tapping the book jacket, but she might as well have been talking to herself. Ellie stared at him, her mouth slightly agape.

'Well, that's one way to get his attention, but not for the right reasons,' Becca said and nudged her friend. 'Could you at least pretend to be less star-struck! You might get us thrown out,' Becca whispered as she caught the two security guards watching them.

'Hello, ladies. How are you today?' Luca Gryse said as they reached the front of the queue. He fixed them with an easy smile, his dark eyes warm and friendly.

'Oh my,' Ellie muttered.

Oh God, Becca thought. *So much for Ellie doing all the talking.*

'Hi, I'm Becca and this is my friend, Ellie. We're both big fans of your work.' Becca cringed at the sheer corniness of her comment. 'I'm sorry. I bet you've been hearing that all day and are getting pretty fed up of it.'

'I have been hearing it all day, but very few have been genuine unfortunately. Jenny Nightingale's interview seems to have unleashed a new form of fan,' he said and ran his hand through his tousled hair.

'Think positive. It's all sales,' Becca said and handed her book over to him and then wrestled Ellie's out of her hands.

'True, but the writer in me wants them to be interested in my work, rather than in me.' He smiled a crooked smile and then signed their books with a flourish.

'Ummm, confession time then,' Becca said, causing Luca to stop signing. 'Ellie here is the fan, not that you would know it from the way she is behaving.' Luca glanced at Ellie and then back at Becca.

'And you?' he said, a small smile on his lips.

'I, well, although I have to confess, I had never heard of you up until yesterday, I…' A gasp went up from behind them and Becca turned to see a line of women still waiting to see Luca.

'Go on,' Luca urged, his hands now steepled under his chin.

'Well, I am interested in this book,' she said, pointing at the volume lying open in front of Luca.

'Why this one?'

'Well, that's what I was hoping to talk to you about. In private.'

At this point, the smile vanished off Luca's face and the security guards stepped forward.

'I think it's time you left, Miss,' one of them said and placed a hand on Becca's shoulder.

'What's going on? What did I say?'

'You wouldn't believe how many times I've heard similar offers today,' Luca said and handed the books to her. 'Thank you for coming out and buying my novel. I hope you enjoy it.'

'Luca. Mr Gryse. You've got it all wrong,' Becca called back to him as she and Ellie were man-handled towards the exit and a star-struck bimbo stepped forward.

Seeing their chance disappearing, Becca took a deep breath, flexed her palms and muttered under her breath, causing the guard to release his grip. She ran back towards Luca and pushed in front of the now giggling bimbo.

'This is no joke,' she said, leaning on the table, her nose inches from his. 'Lives are at stake and I need your help.' She pulled an envelope out of her pocket and pushed it across the table to him.

'Read this, please. Your ancestors are linked to mine and to a four hundred year old curse. Please,' she said, just as the security guard caught up with her and dragged her away from the table.

'Please,' she said again. Luca didn't reply, but she did see him take the envelope and slip it into his jacket pocket, just as she and Ellie were ejected from the store.

CHAPTER 63

'You got barred from a bookstore? Seriously?' Jakes said, hands on hips, as Becca and Ellie stood before him.

'In my defence, it was all Becca,' Ellie said, wandering into the living room and slumping onto the sofa.

'Only because you were standing there with your mouth hanging open, like some blithering idiot,' Becca said and slumped down next to her and then burst out laughing. 'You should have seen your face, it was hilarious. You certainly didn't wow him with your charms, did you?'

'Oh, shut up, Becca,' Ellie said, folding her arms across her chest.

'Never mind all that. Did you manage to ask him before you were ejected?' Jakes said.

'No. I think if I hadn't mentioned wanting to speak to him in private, I might have got a bit further. We seemed to have clicked, unlike some people,' she said, nudging Ellie.

'So, you didn't get anywhere?'

'I didn't say that,' Becca said, feeling her blood pressure spike at Jakes' tone. 'Before they threw us out, I managed to get the copies of Anna's journal to him and he put the envelope in his pocket.'

'So?' Jakes said.

'So, now we wait,' Antony said, coming into the living room, massaging his dying arm, Spook at his heels.

'So, now we wait,' Becca concurred.

CHAPTER 64

The sound of Becca's mobile phone ringing from the kitchen, where she had left it on charge over twenty four hours ago, reverberated around the house.

Becca raced from her room, her feet thundering down the stairs two at a time, praying she wouldn't fall in her haste.

'Hello?' she said, breathlessly, as she caught the call just before the answer-phone kicked in.

'Hello, is this Becca Martin?' the gravelly male voice on the other end of the line said. Becca felt her heart flip. It was him.

'Yes,' she said, still trying to catch her breath.

'This is Luca Gryse.'

'Yes, yes, I recognise your voice. Thank you for calling.'

'I nearly didn't. I have to admit.'

'Okay,' Becca said. 'May I ask why?'

'You may, but I'd rather not talk about this over the phone. Would you be willing to come to my place this evening? We can talk then. It's th…'

'House on the lake,' Becca finished.

'Yes, in Scotsford,' he said, sounding distracted.

'Is it okay if I bring a friend?'

'Yes, yes, fine. Shall we say eight o'clock?'

'That will be fine. Thanks again, Mr Gryse.'

'Luca, please.' And with that, he cut the connection.

Becca stared at the phone for a while after Luca hung up.

'Was that him?' Ellie said, hurrying into the kitchen.

'Yep,' Becca said, still staring at the phone.

'And?' Ellie prompted.

'And he wants me to go round to his place tonight to discuss it.'

'That's brilliant,' Ellie said, clapping her hands together.

'He sounded pretty nervous, though, El. He certainly didn't want to discuss it over the phone.'

'That's understandable. Plus, gorgeous house.'

'Really, El, this is serious. I wonder why he is so nervous.'

'Why do you think? For the same reason you are, probably. It can't be nice for him, delving into his family's murky past.'

'But he's just written a book about it.'

'Yes, but I bet the dirtier laundry has been missed out. Anyway, you can ask him when you go over later.'

'Will you come and act normal?'

'Oh, ha ha. I'd love to come, but I have to work. Take Frank.'

'No, he's at some family function of Jan's.'

'I'm sure he'd drop out if you asked.'

'But I don't want him to. I'll just go up there with Antony.'

'Whoa, hang on a minute. You're going to go to a remote location, to meet a man you don't know with a man who wants to kill you? Are you insane?'

'Oh, for God's sake Ellie, will you step out of the police uniform for a minute,' Becca said. 'Antony is just as invested in this as I am. There is no benefit in him killing me, thanks to you, and I will text you when we get there and when we leave, if it makes you feel any better.'

'Not really.'

'El, Luca is our only chance and so I'm going, with Antony. This is all for him, after all,' Becca said and turned and walked away.

CHAPTER 65

'Wow, this place is enormous,' Becca said as she and Antony climbed out of her battered Fiesta.

'It is rather large,' Antony said. 'How many people live here?'

'Just one, as far as I know,' Becca said and headed up to the double oak doors of the oak and glass structure. Before she could lift the iron knocker, the door was opened.

'Good evening, Ms Martin,' Luca said.

'Becca, please. This is my friend, Antony Cardover; the one I mentioned,' Becca said and gestured towards Antony, who was still standing at the bottom of the wooden steps.

'Yes, yes, please come on in, both of you,' Luca said as he stepped aside to allow Becca and Antony inside. 'Oh, and I apologise for the symbols, Mr Cardover. I just need to make sure you are no threat whilst inside my home.'

Becca felt herself bristle at this and was about to reply when she felt Antony's hand on her shoulder. She turned to look at him and he shook his head.

'I understand your caution, Mr Gryse. Please call me Antony,' Antony said and reached his right hand out towards Luca.

'Luca,' Luca said as he shook hands. 'Please take a seat while I get us some refreshments,' he continued, gesturing towards an open plan seating area with huge picture windows overlooking the lake.

'Wow, I bet this view is stunning,' Becca said.

'It is,' said Luca. 'Maybe you and your friend could come back and see it sometime. Where is, er, Ellie, tonight?'

'Oh, she's at work. Terrible hours working for the police,' Becca said, smiling to herself at the look on Ellie's face when she told her Luca had asked after her.

'I can imagine. Tea, coffee, water?'

'Coffee please,' Becca said.

'Nothing for me,' Antony said and went to stand close to Becca, in front of the window. She closed her eyes and allowed herself to rock back so that her back rested against him.

'Apologies for dragging you over here,' Luca called from the kitchen, breaking the moment. 'But what you want to know isn't really something to be discussed over the phone. At least here, I can protect against eves-droppers.'

'You said you almost didn't call. Why?' said Becca, moving away from Antony and walking towards the kitchen area, part of the open plan ground floor of the house.

Luca handed her a large mug of coffee and gestured for them both to sit down on the expanse of sofa. Becca obliged and Luca sat across from her. Antony remained standing in the window, but did turn to face them. Becca noticed his gaze was now fixed intently on Luca.

'When I read the excerpts from your ancestor's journal and read about your predicament,' Luca directed this point at Antony, before turning back to face Becca, 'it evoked memories of stories I'd heard as a child; unpleasant stories; stories that were the cause of the rift in my family. I couldn't remember the details and knew I would have to contact members of the family that we hadn't had anything to do with for centuries. To do this, I would need to speak to the elders and I wasn't sure I wanted to. I wasn't sure I wanted to dredge up this part of our past.'

'But your book?'

'There are certain skeletons that should remain locked within the privacy of family and this is one of those. Some things are just best left in the past.'

'So, what changed your mind?' Becca said.

'You, Becca. You seemed so desperate when you asked and when I read about Ebenezer and what he had been up to and probably still is, from what you told me, I couldn't just leave it. At the end of the day, the Grys created him.'

'Do they even know what they created? Do they even care?'

'Of course they do,' Luca said, his voice hard, his teeth clenched. Antony stepped forward and stared down at him.

'Then why didn't they stop him?' he said.

'Because at first he was doing everyone a favour, taking the souls of convicts, but something changed. The magic from the curse and the evilness of the souls corrupted and changed him, imbuing him with power he was never supposed to have had, power he used to inflict pain and suffering on others.'

Antony snorted and walked back towards the windows. 'Why didn't they stop him then? Why didn't they stop him when they realised what had happened?'

'Because they couldn't find him. His power was such that he could vanish at will and no one knew when or where he would reappear. There was a rumour that he could be summoned with some kind of stone, but my family never found it.'

'The amulet,' Becca said.

'What?' Luca said.

'There is an amulet that can summon him. Anna had it. I have it. We summoned him.'

'You did what? Are you out of your mind? Why would you..?'

'To ask him for a way to break the curse he'd placed on Antony, other than by killing me. The terms of his curse are for him to kill all of his adulterous wife's descendants and I am the last.'

'And yet, here you both are. Rather friendly for mortal enemies aren't you?'

'It's a long story and I will be happy to tell it to you another time, but right now is not that time. We need to find an alternative cure, otherwise Antony will die very soon.'

'Why?'

'Werewolf venom. Another long...'

'Ah yes, werewolf venom. Not good for a vampire and I presume you don't know an understanding Alpha either?'

'Er, no, how do you…never mind. Again, a conversation for another time.'

'So, I take it Ebenezer didn't give you an alternative?'

'Correct. He said there wasn't one. That's why we're here. He said that if we solved the puzzle that was him, then we would both be free,' Becca said and looked across at Luca. He had his head down and was shaking it. 'I thought you had something, that's why you asked me to come over?' Becca said, clenching her fists and glaring at Luca.

'Rebecca, relax. I'm sure he hasn't called us here for nothing,' Antony said, walking over and resting a hand on Becca's shoulder.

'I haven't called you here for nothing, but it probably isn't what you're looking for.'

'We're looking for a way to break the curse,' Becca said.

'I realise that, but Ebenezer is right, there is no way to break Antony's curse per se. I thought you were looking for a way to stop Ebenezer.'

'So, there's a way of breaking the curse your ancestors placed on Ebenezer, but not for the one placed on Antony? How the hell does that work?' Becca said, feeling the anger building within her and the power pulsating in her palms.

'Let him speak, Rebecca,' Antony said, taking hold of her hand and squeezing it. The feel of his skin against hers made her shiver, but also seemed to calm her.

'The reason I didn't contact you straight away was that I did get in contact with the elders and showed them what you gave me. After some deliberation, they agreed to share their knowledge and to allow me to share it with you, but the details cannot be shared outside of this house, hence the symbols you see around the place. They are spells to stop the wrong people overhearing.'

'You mean Ebenezer?'

'Yes.'

'What did they tell you?'

'As I said, there is no way to break Ebenezer's curse or any curse, for that matter, other than the way originally intended…'

'But there are for spells…'

'Spells and curses are different. They arise from different motivations and curses have something attached, some punishment, which may or may not be permanent. In Ebenezer's case, there was more to it. As well as the curse, which wasn't supposed to play out the way it did, there was also a debt to be paid; an eye for an eye if you will.'

'Taking his son,' Becca murmured.

'Exactly. Ebenezer's son had been responsible for the heinous death of my ancestor's son and so needed to suffer an equally heinous death. His spirit was then linked to Ebenezer's curse; the ghost of the boy being a constant reminder of what he'd lost, mirroring the loss of the Gry's too.'

'How should the curse have played out,' Antony said.

'Ebenezer's curse was double edged. The curse element is the part that forced his body to age at an alarming rate, thus rendering him dead within a few months. The second side to it was more of a penance. The Grys recognised Ebenezer hadn't been the one to kill the boy, but they did hold him responsible for the actions of his son. His penance was to take the souls of twenty people. The souls were to be of those who had taken someone else's life, murderers. The log was completed once the letter was delivered to the families of his victims. The souls would ward off the ageing.'

'And when the penance was done?' Becca said.

'He was to present the log to us and he would get his life back, aged only by the years it had taken him to complete his penance.'

'So, what happened? I mean, he has taken more than twenty souls over the years, surely,' Becca said.

'Yes, that he has. As I said, the souls he took corrupted the magic used for the curse and created something the Grys didn't foresee.'

'So, if the curses cannot be broken, why did you call me here? There must be something, something you don't want Ebenezer to know about?'

'There is,' Luca said and started to fidget.

'Just tell us…please,' Becca said, her heart thudding as her pulse increased, wondering what on earth he was going to say.

'Ebenezer can be stopped, but neither way will be easy, as both of them mean getting close to him, close enough to kill him.'

Becca didn't know what to say. Killing Ebenezer hadn't really been on her agenda. Only saving Antony had.

'Killing him? But…what good will that do? I'm trying to help Antony here. I don't understand. I…' her voice trailed off and she clutched Antony's hand even tighter.

'Bear with me,' Luca said. 'As I said, there are two ways to kill him, but both involve getting up close and personal and it can only be done by those he has cursed. The first way is to stab him, through the heart, with a silver object, as he is a supernatural creature. This method will release all those he has cursed…wait,' he said, holding a hand up to stop Becca from interrupting him. 'It will release those he has cursed, but they will die.'

Becca felt her heart sink and tears sprang to her eyes.

'The second method also involves stabbing him through the heart, but this time with a dagger made from the water of the lake in which the Gry boy died. Killing him in this way will release all those he has cursed to live out their lives.'

'So, there is a way to break the curse?' Becca said, jumping up off the sofa. 'Oh my God, I knew there would be. There had to be. Antony, there is a way,' she said, sitting down again and throwing her arms around Antony.

'I detect a problem with this?' Antony said.

'The Gry boy was drowned in Soul Lake. Soul Lake isn't here anymore,' Luca said.

CHAPTER 66

'What? How can a lake not exist anymore? I thought it was this lake, Drydale, but they'd just changed the name of it?'

'No, it couldn't be. Soul Lake wasn't far from the village,' Antony said. 'It wasn't very large either. Nowhere near the size of this one,' he said, gesturing into the darkness beyond the picture windows.

'Antony is correct,' Luca said and got up and stretched. 'As the populations of Breccan, Carlford and Scotsford grew, a larger water supply was needed.'

'But there's the reservoir..,' Becca said.

'Yes, but it wasn't enough. At the turn of the last century, they decided to redirect the Swan River and to drain and dam Soul Lake, flooding a huge expanse of low lying ground that you now know as Drydale Lake.'

Becca slumped back into the sofa, her head spinning, her heart thumping, but most of all, her hopes fading.

'So, again, why are we here if you can't help us?' she said, staring up at Luca.

'Just because the lake is gone, doesn't necessarily mean there is no water,' Luca said.

'Of course it does,' Becca snapped and jumped up off the sofa and started for the door.

'We just need to dig down to find it,' Antony said. 'As if sinking a well.'

'But hopefully not that deep,' said Luca.

'And if we still don't find any water, what then?' Becca said, rounding on them both, struggling to contain her anger and frustration.

'Then there is always option one,' Luca said.

'Oh, yes, great idea, then Antony will die. How..,'

'Not necessarily,' Luca said.

'You said that if we kill Ebenezer with a silver object then all those cursed by him will die.'

'I did, but…'

'But what, for God's sake, Luca. Nothing you have said is filling me with much hope so far, so why should this be any different?'

'Let him finish, Rebecca. We are here now and might as well hear all our options.'

'Fine!' Becca said and marched back into the seating area and dropped back down onto the sofa.

'There is a potion that Antony could take which may protect him from death.'

'May?'

'Yes, well, it has never been tried before. The elders mixed it yesterday.'

'And what does this potion do?' Antony said, once again placing a hand over Becca's.

'It will hold you at the brink of death, as a human, until Becca can revive you.'

'And how would she do that?'

Luca coughed and looked down at the floor, rubbing his hands together.

'This is the part you're not going to like.'

'And you think I like any of this?' Becca said. 'There are too many uncertainties, what ifs and obstacles.'

'How would she revive me?'

'By feeding you her blood,' Luca said and looked up at Antony.

'But that would mean she would have to be…absolutely not. I won't allow it,' Antony said and Becca watched as his features started to morph.

'What? What would I have to be?'

'It is irrelevant. It is not going to happen.'

'Tell me,' Becca said. 'I have a feeling this will be my decision to make.'

'You would need to become a vampire,' Luca said before Antony could stop him.

The news hit Becca like a punch in the stomach and all the fight, all the hope finally left her. She allowed her body to mould into the sofa and her chin to drop down onto her chest as she brought her knees up and hugged them tight into her chest.

'That's not going to happen,' Antony said.

'But if that's the only way,' Becca said, her voice barely more than a whisper.

'Then I'll stay as I am.'

'And you'll die,' Becca said. 'The venom will kill you and I..,' she paused for a moment, wrestling with the emotions inside her. 'I won't let that happen. I don't want you to die. I want you to live, with me,' she said and looked up, catching Luca's raised eyebrow. 'Not like that,' she said. 'I just meant I want you to have a real life and I'd like to get to know…oh, never mind.'

To Becca's relief, Luca stepped in before she made even more of a fool of herself.

'Even without the venom coursing through your veins, you couldn't stay as you are. The curse Ebenezer placed on you would win through in the end. The monster inside you is too strong to be kept at bay forever. Becca would never be safe.'

Becca wasn't listening to Luca, as her mind was in overdrive over what he had said.

'Sorry to interrupt,' she said. 'But what if Antony turns me into a vampire. Effectively, I'd be dead so the curse would be broken and he would be free.'

'It doesn't work like that, Becca. The wording of any curse, spell or cure is critical. Antony's curse tasked him with "destroying" all of his wife's descendants. That means removing them from the face of the earth,' Luca said.

'Then the only valid option is to try to find some remaining water from Soul Lake,' Becca said.

CHAPTER 67

The front door slammed as Becca and Antony were laying out the maps of the town, once again.

'What you doing?' Ellie said, yawning loudly as she leaned on the doorframe of the living room.

Becca didn't turn from her kneeling position as she weighed down the corner of the old map.

'Trying to find the location of Soul Lake,' she said, holding down the edge of the new map, while Antony grabbed something to hold it down.

'Soul what?'

'Soul Lake. Spook, buddy, shift your butt off the map will you,' Becca said as she tried to push the grey cat off the map without damaging it.

'I think he misses you,' Antony said and ruffled Spook behind his ears.

'Blimey, when did you two become best pals?' Becca directed the question at Spook who simply blinked his large orange eyes and appeared to shrug, before slouching off the map and adopting a position not too far from the action.

'Hello? Soul Lake? I've never heard of it,' Ellie said.

'That's because it isn't here anymore. Pass me that tracing paper would you,' Becca said to Antony.

'So, why on earth are you looking for…you know what, I don't want to know right now. I need sleep. It's been a hell of a night.'

'Yeah, yeah, no worries. I've texted Jakes to ask him to be here at ten.

Can you be around too? We're going to need your help,' Becca said, turning and looking at Ellie.

'Yeah, sure. Give me a knock. You need sleep too, Becca. Remember you're still human.' With that Ellie disappeared and a few minutes later heavy footsteps could be heard on the stairs.

'Hold that in place, would you?' Becca said and, once Antony had the tracing paper firm, Becca drew around the outline of the lake. She then lifted off the paper and laid it over the modern map of Breccan. As she smoothed the paper out so that the details of the map became visible in the outline of the lake, Becca's heart sank.

CHAPTER 68

'So, let me get this straight,' Jakes said. 'You want us to help you salvage water from a long dried up lake so you can fashion some form of dagger to kill Ebenezer and thus free Antony from his curse?'

'Yeeeeees,' Becca said.

'Oh, but it wouldn't just be Antony, it would be every criminal he has ever placed a curse on? And non-criminal?'

'Yeeeeees,' Becca said again and when Jakes didn't continue with his rant, she continued. 'Will you help us?'

'Are you out of your mind?' Jakes said. 'C'mon Ellie, back me up here,' he said, turning to Ellie, who remained a silent observer, Spook sitting next to her, also reserving judgment.

'And you're okay with this I suppose?' Jakes said, rounding on Antony. 'Bringing all those felons back just to save your worthless life?'

'Frank!' Becca said, feeling her anger starting to boil. 'You are out of order saying that.'

'What, and allowing goodness knows how many criminals free reign again isn't out of order?'

'We could track them down, round them up and…'

'And how do you propose to do that?'

'The log of the people he cursed. Remember the letter that Anna mentioned in her journal, the one the boy brought to advise of Antony's fate?'

'What's that got..?'

'Well, don't forget it's those letters that form the log. If we get hold of the log, we will have the names and crimes et cetera.'

'How do you propose to track down these people?'

'Anna's spell books have locator spells detailed in them. I'll learn. I'll finally be able to put my gift to good use.'

'And what will you do with them if and when you find them? Stalk them until they do something wrong?'

Becca looked down at her feet. She couldn't answer him because she hadn't thought that far ahead. All she cared about, at the moment, was freeing Antony. Everything else was secondary to that.

'You haven't even thought it all through properly, have you? You haven't considered the long term ramifications…'

'Frank, I think you're being a little unfair. I'm sure between us all we can work something out,' Ellie said.

'So, you're okay with all this, are you?' Jakes said, rounding on Ellie.

'It's not about being okay with it, it's about doing the right thing and…'

'And unleashing goodness knows how many criminals is the right thing?'

'No, but we'll deal with it. It may not even come to that.'

'Good point. How do you even know any of this is true? How do you know the log exists, that the ice dagger will work? Need I go on?' Jakes said, turning back to Becca.

'I don't, to be honest,' said Becca. 'Luca said he'd consulted the elders and…'

'Yes, and gypsies are known for their honesty. How do you know you can trust anything this guy has told you?'

'I don't Frank, but Antony is running out of time so I'm willing to give it a go and, anyway, it's better than the alternative..,' Becca let the sentence drop, knowing she'd said too much, knowing Jakes wouldn't let the comment go.

'Oh, it's all coming out now, isn't it? So, what is this alternative that you clearly weren't going to share with us exactly?'

'It doesn't matter what the other option is, it isn't viable, hence why I haven't mentioned it.'

'Becca!' Jakes said and Becca watched as the colour rose in Jakes' cheeks. This was the last thing she needed. All she wanted was his and Ellie's help. Her shoulders slumped as she resigned herself to his anger. It wouldn't stop her, but it would be easier with him on their side.

'The other option is to stab Ebenezer through the heart with something silver – my poker, for example. It wouldn't be the first time it's been used after all, would it?' Becca folded her arms and stared at Jakes.

'So far, this option is sounding more favourable to the one you've chosen. I detect the side effects are the reason you've voted against this option?'

'Everyone Ebenezer ever cursed would be freed from their curse…' Becca held her hand up to stop Jakes interrupting. 'But they would all die.'

'Ah,' said Jakes.

'And the only way to save Antony, but there is no guarantee this would work, would be for him to take a potion that Luca gave us.'

'And the potion does what?'

'It holds Antony at the brink of death, giving me chance to revive him. But, even Luca said he didn't know if it would work, as it has never been tried before.'

'Hang on. The only way you could revive him were if you were…'

'A vampire,' Becca finished.

'Over my dead body,' Jakes said.

'Hence option two,' said Becca.

Jakes fell silent and turned his back on them. He walked over to the window and stared outside.

Becca listened to the clock counting down the seconds to Antony's demise. Her heart thudded in her chest as she waited. She hated falling out with Jakes, but with or without him, she was going to do this. His help, however, would be invaluable further down the line.

'I'm in,' said Ellie and came over and squeezed Becca's hand.

'Thanks, El,' Becca said and turned her attention back to Jakes, who was looking down at his hands and shaking his head.

'Frank?' Becca said.

Jakes sighed and turned to face Becca. 'What do you need us to do?'

'Really?' Becca said. 'You'll help?'

Jakes nodded and Becca ran over to him and threw her arms around him.

'Thank you so much. I don't know what I'd have done without your support.'

'Given time is of the essence, what do you need us to do?' Jakes said, hugging her back briefly and then pushing her away from him.

'In a nutshell…help find some water,' Becca said. 'The problem is, most of the lake area has now been built on so we only have a really small area to work with.'

Her mind now in "to do" mode, Becca went to grab the map she and Antony had looked at earlier and spread it out on the floor. Everyone knelt down to take a better look, Jakes groaning as he lowered himself down.

'Sorry, Frank. We can do this in the kitchen…'

'I'm here now,' he said waving her away.

'Okay, well, the south end of what was Soul Lake now forms part of the woods. I don't know what is growing in that part as I've never really ventured that far. The rest is given over to Breccan Park. Now, a lot of the park is a no go area due to landscaping, buildings et cetera, but there is an area here,' Becca said, pointing to an area almost half the size of the park. 'This has been left to go wild, some eco project or something. So, I think we would be okay looking here as there's never anyone around.'

'That's a hell of a lot of area to cover, Becca,' Ellie said.

'I know. So, the sooner we get started the better. Can you and Frank do the day shift and Antony and I will come out as soon as the sun goes down?'

'And how much water are we after?' Ellie said.

'As much as you can find, but we need at least enough to make one dagger. Ideally, I'd also like a backup, but…'

'Well, we better get moving then. Half the day has gone already,' Jakes said, holding onto Ellie's arm as he hauled himself to his feet.

'Thanks again, Frank,' Becca said.

Jakes nodded and kissed her on the forehead as he hobbled passed.

CHAPTER 69

'Okay, we're good to go,' Becca said as she watched the sun sink below the horizon. 'Are you sure you're up to this?' she continued as she turned to look at Antony.

Whilst the venom didn't seem to be visibly spreading across his body anymore, his strength was failing him. Becca hoped they had enough time and that they could do this.

'Yes Rebecca, I will be fine. Please stop asking me,' Antony said, as he dropped the spades on the floor and slumped into an armchair, leaning his head against the back and closing his eyes.

'Of course you will,' she said, picking up the spades. Antony shot forward and snatched them out of her hands. *Speed is still there*, she thought, as she stepped away from him.

'Look, I can go on my own. You stay here and wait…' Becca was interrupted by her mobile phone ringing. 'Hi, Frank, how are you getting on? We're just about to head out,' she said, a smile lighting her face.

'Not good, if I'm honest,' Jakes said, between breaths.

'Are you okay?'

'Yes, yes, it's just hard work digging holes, especially when you need eyes in the back of your head and have to keep climbing out when someone appears.'

'Jeez, Frank, how deep have you been digging?' Becca said, her smile fading and her optimism waning.

'Pretty deep! Had no choice. Look, I'm beat. I've not found anything.

I'm sorry, Becca, but Ellie may have had more luck.'

'Where are you?'

'We started in the woods, but about an hour or so ago, I sent Ellie over to the park. It's probably best you head over there. I'll meet you there.'

'Okay, thanks, Frank. I'll see you shortly.' Becca hung up the phone and looked at Antony, who was watching her intently.

'It makes sense they didn't find anything in the woods. The trees have probably drained whatever was left of the lake,' he said.

'True,' said Becca, her heart heavy. 'Are you sure you can manage those?'

'Of course I can, Rebecca, have a little faith,' Antony said and, hauling his cargo over his shoulder, he stalked passed her to the front door.

The grimace on his face was not lost on Becca.

CHAPTER 70

Ellie and Jakes were waiting for them in the car park. Becca felt a pang of guilt as she looked at him, leaning against Ellie's car looking as if he were suffering from a high fever. Ellie, on the other hand, looked like she hadn't done a thing.

'Any luck, El?' Becca said as she gave Jakes a hug.

'Not entirely,' Ellie said and Becca felt a glimmer of hope flutter in her belly.

'But you found something?' she said.

'I found the possibility of something…let me finish,' she said as Becca opened her mouth to interrupt. 'As I dug down, and I have to say it was a couple of feet, water was oozing from the ground, but it wasn't sufficient to capture. I think there is a chance we could find some, but it may take a while.'

'Where were you digging?' Becca said, her adrenalin beginning to kick start once again.

'Just over the ridge there, out of sight,' Ellie said.

'Okay, can you stay any longer? I hate to ask as I know you are on nights…'

'Not a problem, Becca, I'll let them know I'm going to be late tonight. They will give me hell, but if we find something, it will be worth it.'

'Right, well, let's split up. Ellie, if you carry on where you are, I'll go midway across the field and Antony, can you go close to the far boundary?'

Ellie and Antony nodded.

'What about me?' Jakes said, trying to push himself up out of the seat of the car and failing.

'I think you've done enough manual labour for one day, Frank. Can you move the cars out onto the street somewhere, though, as I think they close the gates shortly? Then, can you keep a look out?'

'I suppose,' Jakes said, but Becca could see the relief on his face, despite his grumbling.

'Right, let's get moving,' Becca said and the three of them headed out in search of water.

Becca's back muscles screamed and the blisters on the palms of her hands had burst. She didn't know how much longer she could carry on.

She thought she'd hit the jackpot about six holes ago, but the water soon disappeared. She'd only managed to capture a few centimetres. Still, she tried to comfort herself, if they all managed a few then maybe, just maybe, they would have enough to make a dagger.

Becca had hoped to find enough to make more than one. She wasn't a gambling person, but having all their hopes resting on one dagger didn't sit well with her, especially after the bad luck they'd been having.

She wondered how Antony was doing. She really hadn't liked the look of him earlier. The blood Jakes kept bringing just wasn't enough to renew his strength. Little by little, as Ellie said, the venom was eating away at him.

'Dammit!' she said and thrust her spade into the ground. 'He doesn't deserve this.' She felt the power pulsate in her palms, which only frustrated her even more.

Why didn't she know more? Why couldn't she do more? She had naively believed she would be able to locate any underground water, without any ritual, without any spell. Why? Because she'd had a gut feeling that she would be just drawn to it.

'How stupid am I?' she muttered. What made her different from her grandmother or from Anna? 'Nothing, that's what,' she said, looking down into her seventh hole of the night.

Becca's heart seemed to stop as the moonlight glinted off something smooth and shiny. She closed her eyes and took a deep breath.

'Please, please,' she murmured as she dropped down onto her haunches and tentatively reached down into the hole.

Her fingertips brushed the surface of the water, causing it to shimmer in the moonlight. She didn't think she'd ever seen anything so beautiful.

Becca could barely contain the shout of joy that bubbled through her, but she caught herself just in time. She didn't know, after all, who might hear her.

She rummaged in her pocket for her Maglite and shone it into the hole for a better look. There wasn't a lot, but there might just be enough. Becca lowered an empty tub into the hole and pressed it down beneath the surface of the water into the hard packed earth below.

Although mud and other sediment also collected in the tub, Becca had a good feeling about it. She glanced at her watch and saw that it was passed midnight, passed the rendezvous time. She secured the lid on the tub and put it with the others in her ruck sack. She grabbed the spade, almost crying out as her raw blisters chaffed against the handle, and quickly filled the hole in, replacing the carefully dug out layer of grass when she'd finished.

Becca hoped Antony had remembered to check his watch. She smiled as she recalled the look on his face when she'd strapped it around his wrist and told him exactly what to look for. She turned and headed back to the car park and the exit.

CHAPTER 71

'Right, let's get this stuff sifted so we can see exactly how much water we've managed to collect,' Becca said as she unzipped her ruck sack and took out the containers. The others followed suit and soon there were tubs on the kitchen table, all containing various levels of water.

'How do we know this is lake water,' Ellie said, yawning and stretching her shoulders.

'We don't! We've just got to hope,' Becca said, refusing to let this doubt take root. 'Can you grab me a sieve out of the cupboard and a measuring jug?'

Becca took the sieve and jug from Ellie and removed the lid from the first tub. 'Here goes nothing,' she said and started to empty the contents of the tubs, one by one. When she'd finished, she held up the jug to read the measurements on the side.

'Just over half a litre,' she said.

'Will it be enough?' Ellie said.

'It will have to be,' said Becca.

'Okay, well, I've got to get to work, so I'll leave you guys to it,' Ellie said.

'Thanks for all your help El,' Becca said and hugged her. Ellie hugged her back and left.

'So, I guess we need to make some sort of mould?' Becca said and looked up at Jakes.

'Leave that one with me,' he said.

'We need to make it thick enough so it doesn't break on impact,' Becca said.

'I know. As I said, leave it with me,' Jakes said and pushed himself up out of the chair.

'How long will it take?' she said, looking Jakes in the eye and then shifting her gaze to Antony.

'Not long. Now, let's get some rest and we'll get together again in the morning.'

CHAPTER 72

'Why didn't you wait Becca, until someone could go with you?' Jakes said, thumping the kitchen counter.

'Because we are running out of time, fast,' Becca said and turned away from Jakes so he couldn't see her wiping the tears from her eyes.

'Do you need more blood?'

'It isn't working,' Becca said, her voice barely a whisper.

'She should be able to get hold of some more,' Jakes said.

'It isn't working, dammit!' she shouted and spun around to face Jakes.

'Hey, hey, calm down. Tell me what's happened,' Jakes said, pulling Becca into his arms and holding her. Becca couldn't stop herself. All the pent-up worry, frustration and fear came spilling out and she sobbed into his shoulder, large wracking sobs that shook her whole body.

When they'd subsided, Jakes pulled away from her and tilted her chin up, so she looked him in the eye.

'How bad is it?'

Becca felt tears threatening again and swallowed them back down.

'It's bad. His torso is completely covered and he is struggling to move. His affected arm is virtually useless. I'm afraid he may not be strong enough to do this; that's why I summoned Ebenezer last night.'

'But what if he'd appeared?'

'He didn't. He may take days. He may not. I just couldn't…' Becca's voice cracked as a sob escaped.

Jakes hugged her to him again, but said nothing.

'Okay, okay, I'm up. Three hours sleep, but I'm up,' Ellie said, yawning, as she made a beeline for the coffee machine. 'Nectar,' she said, inhaling the rich aroma. She flicked the switch and turned to face the others. 'What's going on here? Are you okay, Becca?'

Becca nodded as she pulled away from Jakes and wiped her eyes. 'I'll be okay.'

'Where's the man we're all losing sleep over? Shouldn't he be..?' Jakes held his hand up to silence Ellie.

'I told him to rest,' Becca said, fighting the urge to cry again. Christ, when did she get so soft?

'Great, we're all busting a gut to help him and he gets to take it easy,' Ellie said and grabbed her coffee from the machine, sloshing it on the floor.

'Ellie!'

'It's okay, Frank. He's too weak, El. The blood is no longer holding back your venom. I need him to conserve his energy as I can't tackle Ebenezer alone.'

Ellie opened her mouth to reply, but seemed to decide against it.

'How did you get on in mould making class?' she said, turning her attention to Jakes.

'Good,' he said, bringing out of a bag two wooden blocks, one slightly smaller than the other.

'Ah, ah,' he said. 'Let me explain how they work before you start ripping them apart.' He plucked the mould out of Becca's hand.

Becca and Ellie looked at each other and smiled before turning their attention back to Jakes.

'I carved out and sanded, as smoothly as I could, an icicle like shape within each of the blocks of wood. Obviously, half an icicle in each piece.' He held up the separate halves of the blocks to show them before continuing. 'I then screwed these plates onto the side. Before any water is poured in, these plates need to be as tight as possible to minimise leakage. I then drilled a hole through the top of each mould, wide enough to take the tip of a funnel, so we don't lose any water on pouring and also, large enough to take these.' Jakes held up two metal rods.

'What are they for?' Becca said, reaching out to take one off him.

'To give Antony something to hold onto and to try to slow down how quickly these things will melt.'

'But there is no heat in his body anyway. In fact, it is probably as cold, if not colder, than the ice,' Becca said, shuddering as she remembered the cold permeating her skin as she'd hugged him.

'Fair point,' said Jakes, 'but metal is easier to hold than ice, anyway.'

'Silver, by any chance?' said Ellie, pausing before she took the rod from Becca.

'Hardly,' said Jakes. 'But I do have this, Becca.' He handed Becca a silver dagger. 'I want you to use it, should the icicles fail.'

'Absolutely not,' said Becca, pushing the dagger away.

'But Ebenezer will kill you, you know that, don't you?'

'So be it,' said Becca and went to get the lake water. 'Let's get these made and in the freezer. His response could come at any time.'

CHAPTER 73

Antony leaned his head back against the brick wall of the attic, his eyes closed. He bit down hard on his lower lip, drawing blood, the wound taking longer to close than it should.

Damn lycanthrope! He dropped his chin down onto his chest, gritting his teeth as the venom continued to march through his veins. He rubbed his hand vigorously across his torso, but it did little to alleviate the burning sensation.

He felt the familiar ripple through his body and his features started to shift, his nails elongated; the vampire in him rising to defend him against this invasion. But, as soon as it had arisen, his demon vanished, overpowered by the lycanthrope taking over his body. He wrenched his nails across his stomach, determined to tear this imposter out, but all he did was create wheals on his skin; his sharpened nails having receded with his demon.

He looked up at the blacked out windows. A sliver of sunlight broke the barrier and slanted across the room towards him, spearing the wall just above his rotting shoulder. He raised his hand, like he had been doing every day, shortening the beam of sunlight so it focused on his palm. He thought he could feel its warmth, but could he, or was this simply a delusion; a symptom of the venom?

To test this, Antony shifted on the bed that Rebecca had set up for him, enabling him to raise his good hand to transect the sunbeam. He braced himself for the acute pain and instantaneous combustion that was the result of a vampire meeting sunlight, but nothing happened.

Emboldened, Antony pushed himself up off the bed and went over to the window, pulling the drapes back halfway.

He stood, shirtless, his eyes closed and allowed the warmth of the late afternoon sun to penetrate the coldness of his flesh. How long had it been since he'd felt this?

Antony remembered chasing Carla around Anna's backyard, the sun beating down on them both. Simple times. Happy times. He felt a smile tug at the corners of his mouth, but refused to acknowledge it. He couldn't. This wasn't real. It was an illusion. The venom was humanising him somehow, allowing him to feel, allowing him to remember.

'But for what purpose?' he said to himself and kicked one of the trunks, sending it crashing into the wall of the attic. He regretted his action and limped back to the bed, settling into the shadows.

Yes, the lycanthrope venom was definitely weakening him, in more ways than one.

'Are you okay up there?' Rebecca's voice sounded and Antony heard her determined footfalls on the stairs. She reminded him so much of Anna in her drive and refusal to give up, that he felt a pull at his dead heart. This confused him, as he didn't know who the pull was for.

'Antony? Are you okay? I heard a bang and…oh God, how long has the window been uncovered? You didn't get burned did you?' Antony watched her as she dashed across the room to fix the drape back in place. So much energy and vitality in that small body. If he had just a fraction of that then maybe, just maybe, he'd get through this. He felt his features shift as these thoughts flooded his mind and he turned away from her, focusing his attention on something else, willing the vampire away. He would not feed on her, no matter how good her blood made him feel.

'Antony?' Rebecca said and dropped to her knees in front of him. She took his chin in her hand and turned his head so he faced her.

He looked into her face, so young and still so innocent, despite everything. Her hair was longer now and not as black as it had been. It looked better, but it just made her look even more like Isabella. He closed his eyes against the pain of the memory of her betrayal, against the emerald eyes that were now staring at him, concern and something more in there. He couldn't allow himself to go there. Not now.

'Say something,' Rebecca said and shook him, the subsequent pain causing him to wince.

'I'm sorry, I'm sorry. I've brought you some blood. Jakes is trying to get hold of some more…' Antony wasn't listening to what she was saying, his attention was fixed on the carotid artery of her neck, which was throbbing due to her anxious state.

He felt his vision sharpen and his fangs elongate as the vampire in him rose. He shifted position, ready to strike, but the weight on his decaying arm sent shockwaves coursing through his body and he cried out.

'Are you okay? Here, drink this,' Rebecca said as she helped him to sit upright and held the bag of blood, straw inserted, to his lips.

'I'm okay,' he said and snatched the pouch from her, drawing on it long and hard, hoping it would somehow suppress his craving.

'Well, you don't look okay,' she said, standing up and folding her arms across her chest. 'Do you think you'll be strong enough to do this?'

'Of course,' he said and pushed himself to the edge of the bed.

'It's okay, it's not time yet. Still a couple of hours until sundown. Rest and I'll come and get you.'

Rebecca rested her hand on his shoulder, sending a shudder through his body.

'Make sure you drink all of that before we go,' she said and disappeared down the stairs.

What was that? Why did her touch, her closeness do that to him? It reminded him of the day Isabella first entered his father's workshop. The thought of Isabella caused the monster to flex again, but it subsided, replaced by the attraction and desire he'd first felt for Isabella, feelings he was starting to have towards Rebecca.

What was happening to him?

CHAPTER 74

Antony awoke to the sound of raised voices downstairs. He listened and groaned as he heard Rebecca and Jakes arguing yet again. He understood Jakes' animosity towards him. He had, after all, almost killed him not so long ago and Antony respected the fatherly protection he exerted over Rebecca. What Antony didn't understand was why the man still insisted on arguing with her. Even he, Antony, had learned it was a fruitless pursuit. Rebecca would do what she wanted to anyway, it was in her blood.

He hauled himself up off the bed and stretched, almost crying out at the pain shooting through his venom-riddled body. He flexed his dying hand and picked up a broken brick from the floor. He squeezed the brick in his hand, gritting his teeth against the pain. After a minute or so, the brick crumbled to dust and Antony wiped his palm on his trousers to clean off the dust. It might take longer, but his strength hadn't left him yet. Satisfied, he pulled on his shirt, grabbed his coat and headed downstairs.

'Why the raised voices?' Antony said as he walked into the living room, pulling up the collar of his coat, just as he liked it.

'Madam here is refusing to do something I have asked of her. What else?' Jakes said, raising his hands and letting them fall back against his thighs, creating a slapping sound.

'He wants me to take that dagger, that "silver" dagger, with us tonight, just in case,' Rebecca said, gesturing towards the small silver object lying on the carpet between her and Jakes.

'It's for your own protection,' Jakes said.

'We have the ice daggers, Frank, for God's sake!'

'Yes, but if they don't work or…'

'Or what?'

'Or they melt before…'

'They won't.'

'They might.'

'Oh my God, we're going around in circles again. I am not taking the dagger. To use it would mean Antony will die.'

'I'm dying anyway,' Antony said. 'Listen to Jakes. He is only trying to protect you.'

'Thank you,' said Jakes, turning to Antony.

'Well, I'm not…'

'No, but I will,' said Antony, leaning down and picking up the dagger with his handkerchief, before Rebecca had chance to stop him.

'Thank you, Antony,' Jakes said. 'I'm glad to see at least one of you is looking at this situation with some sense, if any of this can be deemed sensible.'

'Antony, don't…' Rebecca started to say, but Antony put a finger to her lips.

'I will only use it if there is no other option,' he said and smiled at her. He saw the tears well up in her eyes and turned away. He couldn't deal with that. He had to focus.

'I presume it is time?' he said, turning back to Rebecca, glad to see the tears hadn't fallen.

'It's time,' she said, looking down as Spook let out a pitiful meow. 'Don't worry, buddy, we'll be back soon.' She crouched down to cuddle him, but he shrank away from her. 'Let's go,' she said to Antony, as she stood up and headed for the door.

CHAPTER 75

'Okay,' Rebecca said as they stood on the pavement, just out of sight of the church. 'I don't know how long these will last, but I think we stand a better chance if you keep them pressed up against your skin.'

'That sounds sensible,' Antony said as he crouched down to help Rebecca remove the moulds from the packed ice.

'Don't,' he said. 'The warmth of your skin will start them melting. Let me.' He took the mould from Rebecca and removed the largest dagger, placing it in the waistband of his trousers, against his side.

'Put the other one somewhere else,' Rebecca said. Antony looked at her and was about to ask why when she continued. 'Just in case we need it. We don't want to risk him seeing both daggers.'

Antony nodded and slipped the second one at his back.

'Right. Let's do this,' Rebecca said, putting the cool-box back in the boot of the car and starting towards the church.

'Rebecca?' Antony said, catching her by the arm and turning her to face him. 'I just wanted to say thank you.'

'You don't have to thank me,' she said, pulling away.

'Yes, yes, I do,' he said, holding her firm, giving her no alternative but to face him. 'Whatever transpires with Ebenezer, I just want to extend my gratitude for all you have done. In spite of my past actions towards you, you have remained resolute in trying to break this curse. For that, I am eternally grateful.' He cleared his throat as he finished and looked at Rebecca, to see tears glistening in her eyes once again.

'You're very welcome,' she managed to say and dropped her gaze to the ground.

'You remind me so much of her. Your stubbornness, your determination, your loyalty.'

'Who? Isabella?'

Antony felt the familiar rage surge through him at the mention of his adulterous wife, but he managed to suppress it before his body responded.

'Loyalty is not a word I would use to describe Isabella. Though you do resemble her, your temperament is wholly unlike her. I was meaning Anna. You remind me of Anna.' He watched as colour invaded her cheeks and it made him smile.

'Is it difficult for you?'

'Is what difficult?'

'Me looking like Isabella?'

'Sometimes. Now, shall we get on with this task?' he said, not wanting to discuss his wife any further.

'I would have used the word "battle", but yes, I suppose we should. The sooner we face him, the sooner we break the curse.'

Or not, Antony thought.

CHAPTER 76

'Don't forget, we need to get him to show us the log,' Rebecca hissed in his ear as they walked along the winding path to the shack.

'It isn't just a case of seeing it, Rebecca. We need to get hold of it,' Antony said, stopping and looking down at her.

'Why? As long as we know where it is, we can find it after we've got rid of Ebenezer,' Rebecca said, not managing to stop quick enough and bumping into him.

Antony decided to wait a few minutes to see if she would realise the error in her statement, but she didn't, she just fidgeted from one foot to the other, impatient as ever.

'What makes you think the log will still be here once we have killed him?'

'Why wouldn't it be?' she said, looking towards the shack.

'What happened to the shack once Ebenezer had finished with us last time?'

'It disappeared…God, I'm so stupid sometimes,' she said as Antony saw realisation dawn in her eyes. 'The magic he uses to create this.' She gestured to the winding path and the shack. 'Will dissolve when we kill him?'

'That is what I'd expect. Any magic only stays alive as long as the person casting it remains.'

'How are we going to get it off him?'

Antony reached up to run his finger over the furrows now decorating her brow.

'Do not worry, Rebecca. Have faith that an opportunity will present itself.' He let his hand drop and proceeded up the path.

CHAPTER 77

'Well, well, well, the explorers return,' Ebenezer said as the door opened before Antony had chance to knock. 'Why, do come in.' Ebenezer stepped aside and Antony felt himself being sucked inside the shack.

The door slammed behind them and for the third time in his existence, Antony was standing in the damp and dark hovel, the fire barely alive in the grate, facing this ancient little man; a man with more power than Antony could imagine.

'Why, my dear Mr Cardover, you don't look very well at all. Never mind, a few minutes here and you will feel like your old self again.' He waved his hand in Antony's direction and Antony jolted.

'Why, Ms Martin. You look fit to burst. Does this mean you have done what so many have failed to do in the past and solved the puzzle that is me?'

'Yes, we found out all about you and your son and what he did. We…'

Antony tuned out from what Rebecca was saying. Something was happening to him, happening to his body. It was the venom, it felt like it was being sucked out of him. He could feel the movement in his veins. As the venom left he could feel something taking its place, something that had been receding, something he had been managing to control, something he didn't miss, something he didn't want.

'…there is no way of removing your curse, the…'

'No!' shouted Antony, cutting Rebecca off. 'What have you done to me?' he said, advancing towards Ebenezer.

He could feel his features morphing, could feel the anger and hate suffuse his body, but worst of all, he could feel that deep dark desire for vengeance trying to break free. He grabbed Ebenezer by the throat and slammed him against the wall, the silver dagger against his skin, causing it to start to burn.

'Antony, don't!' Rebecca said, running over and trying to pull his arm away. 'You can't use that. Remember what Luca said. If you kill him…'

'Why, Mr Cardover, Ms Martin is correct. If you kill me with that dagger, then you too will die and I know that's not what you came here for. Or, Ms Martin didn't, anyway.'

'How did you know about the dagger?' Rebecca said.

'Why dearie, do you honestly think you are the only naïve fools that I've sent on that wild goose chase?'

'I don't understand. If you know, then why did you send us?'

'Why, I like to check up every so often, to see if the stubborn old fools have softened any, to see if they will accept my log of souls as penance.'

'So you lied to us?' Rebecca said, stepping away from the two of them.

'Why no, dearie, I never tell lies. The two of you can be free.'

'How?' Rebecca said.

'Why, I do believe Mr Cardover knows.' Ebenezer looked Antony in the eyes. 'Feel it, Mr Cardover. Give in to it. Let the monster rise once more and take what it is owed. Then, you will be released from the curse, free to live your life. Ms Martin will be free too, free of her obligation to you. Isn't that what you both want?'

Antony squeezed his eyes shut, willing the thoughts and desires away. He could hear Rebecca's heart beating. He could smell her; so like the bitch who wronged him.

'No! I will not kill her!' he said and pressed the dagger further into Ebenezer's neck.

'Antony, don't!'

'Get away from me, Rebecca. It's better this way,' he said and shoved her hard in the chest, sending her flying across the room.

'Why, that's more like it. Feels good to release that anger, to allow that hatred to flow, doesn't it? A wild animal will always be wild, Mr Cardover. No matter how you try to tame it, its true colours will win through in the end,' Ebenezer said, his voice dropping to a gentle lull. 'Go on, Mr Cardover, there's no use fighting it. Give in to it. Free yourself from this torture, from this torment.'

Antony tried to shut out the hypnotic voice, but it was as if it was seeping into his ears, drawing the monster's desire forward.

'Never!' shouted Antony and released Ebenezer, allowing the old man to crumple to the floor.

Antony strode over to Rebecca, who was on her feet again. 'I can't hold on much longer. We need to do this. We need him to show us the log.' Antony continued to the back of the room, not trusting himself to be close to her.

'So, what makes you think they won't accept your log?' Rebecca said, stepping between Antony and Ebenezer. Ebenezer was standing serenely by the fire as if nothing had happened.

'Why, dearie, do you not think I'd have had word by now?' Ebenezer said and stepped to one side, so he could see Antony. 'Why, Mr Cardover, you do know you are fighting a losing battle, don't you? Just give in to the desire. Smell her, smell her blood. Listen to that heart pounding in her chest. Why, I do believe even she is starting to have her doubts.'

'Don't listen to him, Antony,' Rebecca said.

'Why, come along, Mr Cardover. Your pain and suffering could be all over if you'd let it. Why, you'd even be helping me out by letting me cross you off my list, getting me one step closer to redemption.'

'And why would I want to help you?' Antony said through gritted teeth. Rebecca's heartbeat was thundering in his ears and he was struggling to keep his focus off her carotid artery.

'Why, I would have thought that you would want me to be redeemed. Think of how dull the world could be again.'

'What makes you think that breaking curses will lead to the Grys forgiving you?' Rebecca said.

'Why, I didn't say anything about forgiveness, dearie.'

'So, what the hell's the difference between forgiveness and redemption then? And, why on earth would you think they would ever redeem you?' Rebecca said and spat in Ebenezer's direction.

'Rebecca!' Antony hissed, his gaze fixed on her neck as her flare of anger made her pulse quicken.

Rebecca raised a hand behind her in a gesture he wasn't familiar with, and continued to taunt Ebenezer.

'I bet you're just lying, preying on Antony's humanity, trying to get him to kill me for your own perverse pleasure. Prove it,' she said and, for a moment, the monster in him stilled as he waited to see what Ebenezer would do.

'Why, I don't have to prove anything to you, dearie, and as for Mr Cardover, his humanity left him a long time ago. Why, if you just take a look, you will see what I mean.'

Don't turn around, Rebecca, please don't turn around, Antony prayed, but it was no good. Curiosity always got the better of people. Antony watched in dismay as Rebecca turned around and screamed. She staggered backwards, away from him.

'Rebecca, it's okay. I'm okay,' he said as Ebenezer emitted a cackle.

'Why, you're far from okay, Mr Cardover. You're minutes away from doing what you are destined to do. Why, just look at you,' Ebenezer said and shuffled over to Antony, tracing his fingers across Antony's ridged brows and down his cheeks to lift his upper lip, revealing the fangs Antony could no longer control. 'All you have to do is give in,' Ebenezer whispered in his ear, before making his way back towards the fireplace, beside which stood a sparse bookcase.

Antony clenched his fists, feeling his nails cut deeply into his palms. He had a chance now, while the old man's back was turned. In seconds it could be over, but they needed the log.

'Rebecca,' Antony growled and his heart jolted at the fearful look in her eyes. 'Don't listen to him,' he said and shifted his gaze to the bookcase and then back to her, several times, hoping she'd pick up the hint. Eventually, she shifted her gaze to the bookcase and then back to Antony and nodded. He closed his eyes for a moment and, for the first time, felt the dampness of fabric against his frigid skin. The daggers were starting to melt.

'Prove it,' Rebecca said again, stepping forward and facing Ebenezer. 'Prove to me that you meant what you said, that you really want redemption.'

'Why, oh why, dearie, would I need to prove anything to you?' Ebenezer said.

'Because I might be able to help you,' she said.

'Why, how on earth could you possibly help me and why would you want to?' His tone remained uninterested, but Antony detected a slight change in Ebenezer as his pulse quickened. Was it hope?

'I know someone, a Gry, he would help you, I know he would. I just need to see the log, so I can tell him you did keep it, that at one time redemption was something you wanted and that it is something you are now looking for again.'

'Why, dearie, you really are a "little Miss Fixit", aren't you? Why, I'm starting to think that the two of you lied to me and you really did find something out about me, something useful?' Ebenezer stepped towards Rebecca and tilted his head to one side. Antony watched her break his gaze and knew Ebenezer was trying to read her mind.

'We'll tell you what we found out, if you show us the log of souls,' Antony said, distracting Ebenezer.

'Why, the log, the log. I don't know what your fascination with it is, it is just a book of names.'

'It used to be more than that and it could be, again,' Rebecca said. 'Wouldn't being redeemed also free your son from the purgatory he is in?'

At the mention of his son, Ebenezer's demeanour completely changed and Antony saw a glimpse of the man he used to be, before he turned away to face the bookcase.

'Henry,' Ebenezer said, his voice cracking as his shoulders slumped. For a moment, the evil warlock was gone, leaving behind a parent who had lost a child in a horrific manner. Antony felt a pang of sympathy for him.

He glanced at Rebecca, whose gaze was fixed on Ebenezer, and he carefully removed the largest dagger from its hiding place and held it by his side.

'Oh, Henry, why?' Ebenezer said and raised his hand to run it down the spine of a thin volume, sandwiched between two tomes.

Antony glanced at Rebecca, who had turned to look at him, and nodded.

Within seconds, he was upon Ebenezer. He grabbed him by the throat and dragged him away from the bookcase, to allow Rebecca chance to grab the log.

'As if someone like you should ever be given the chance of redemption,' Antony said, his face inches from the old warlock's.

'Got it,' he heard Rebecca say.

'You have caused far too much pain and suffering, destroyed too many lives…'

'Antony! Just do it!' Rebecca shouted, cutting him off.

'I hope you rot in hell,' he said and thrust the dagger upwards and into Ebenezer's heart. He stepped back and watched as the warlock staggered backwards, his hands coming up to surround the protruding metal handle of the dagger and then, to Antony's horror, Ebenezer started to laugh, a deep wracking laugh.

'Why, Mr Cardover, it would appear you did find something out from the Grys, after all. Why, I think you just needed to find a little more water,' he said and straightened himself up.

'Hopefully, this will be enough,' Rebecca said and Antony watched as Ebenezer's back arched. Antony reached his hand around to his waistband and found only damp fabric. Clever girl.

He turned his attention back to Ebenezer and felt Rebecca pressing her small hand into his. He squeezed it, but didn't take his gaze off what was happening in front of him.

Ebenezer was frantically trying to grasp the handle of the dagger Rebecca had plunged into him. The fight was slowly leaving him though, and Antony watched as his body started to fracture, like glass breaking, from the stab wounds outwards.

The old warlock stopped fighting and looked at them both, his watery eyes sharp as ever.

'Why, I do believe you both have your wish. You have broken your curse, Mr Cardover, but will it be what you hoped for?' With that, he folded his arms across his chest and bowed his head. A few seconds later, his body exploded into thousands of pieces, each turning to water as it hit the floor of the shack, the liquid seeping into the wooden boards as if sucked from down below.

Rebecca opened her mouth to speak, but before she could utter a word, the ground seemed to ripple underneath them, knocking them both over.

'What just happened?' Rebecca said.

'I don't know, but I don't think it's over,' Antony replied as the shack started to crumble. He reached out and grabbed Rebecca's arm, yanking her to her feet, and headed for the door, dodging the falling debris as he went. He pulled open the door, but before he could step through it, he felt the air being completely sucked into the shack. Instinctively, he braced himself, pulling Rebecca in close, just as the full force of the explosion hit them and catapulted them through the door and into the night.

EPILOGUE

Antony heard the sound far away in the distance, but couldn't make out what it was. He tried to turn his head, to lean in towards it, but pain shot through him and he groaned. The last time he remembered feeling like this was when his horse had refused a jump and had sent him careering head first into a tree.

The sound seemed to be getting closer to him and he gritted his teeth against the pain and turned towards it; blinking rapidly to try to clear the hazy image that was all he could see. He tried to push himself up onto one elbow, but that was too much and he slumped back down again and closed his eyes.

Moments later, he felt himself being shaken and the sound was clear now, an alarm of some kind based on its tone; but as he focused in, he realised it was his name being called, in a rather high-pitched panicked voice.

'Antony! Antony! Wake up!' The owner of the voice was also the one responsible for the assault on his body and he dragged his arm up and tried to push her away. Her - his foggy mind had managed to work that out at least.

'Ger' off me,' he mumbled and wafted his hand in the general direction of his assailant.

'Antony, are you okay? Are you hurt? My God, I landed on you. I might have broken something. I…' He tuned out of the incessant high-pitched chatter and focused on clearing his mind.

Drawing on all his resolve, Antony forced himself to sit up and shook his head, sending pain radiating through his skull. He brought a hand up and massaged his temples and then his eye sockets before slowly opening his eyes.

Dark, thank God, he thought and opened his eyes fully, focusing on his feet before starting to flex muscles and gently move limbs. *Good*, he thought, *no breaks*. Lots of bruises, but thankfully no breaks; they never did heal properly.

'What the hell happened?' he said as he finally turned his attention to his assailant.

'I don't know. Some sort of explosion. After we killed him, the place just self-destructed and…'

'Whoa, slow down. What are you talking about?' He still couldn't see her, due to the moonlight that shone from behind her, casting her purely in silhouette. As she started to babble again, Antony eased himself up to standing, only hearing bits of what she was saying as he focused on trying not to make his pain any worse.

'Okay, stop,' he said as his back made a disturbing crunching sound as he straightened up. 'First of all, who the hell are you?'

'It's me, Becca.'

'Who? Come closer so I can see you,' he said.

Antony felt a pain in his chest, as though his heart had stopped beating. The girl who became visible to him was the image of Isabella, except for her strange garments and hairstyle. He felt his anger flair at the thought of his whore of a wife and everything came flooding back to him, fuelling his body once more.

'Who the hell are you?' he said and stepped towards her, a small smile tugging at his mouth at the sight of her recoiling from him.

'It's me, Becca. For God's sake, Antony, what's wrong with you? Did you hit your head or something? You're not making sense.' She stepped forward, raising her arm towards his head, but Antony caught her and dragged her towards him until she was eye to eye with him and her feet hovered off the ground.

'Ow, you're hurting me. Let go!' she said and kicked him hard in the shin. He let her go and she cried out as she hit the ground. He dropped down on his haunches and grabbed hold of her jaw, forcing her to look at him.

'I don't know you! Who are you? Why are you here, with me, at this hour? It isn't proper.' He stared into her emerald eyes and felt a tug at his heartstrings, a familiarity he couldn't place. Maybe it was just the resemblance to Isabella. The thought of his selfish wife brought a flash of anger once more.

'Are you family – to Anna, to Isabella?' he said and released her and stood up, turning away to try to bring his anger under control, at least until he got to the bottom of what was going on.

'In a manner of speaking, yes. You know I am, Antony. What's wrong with you?' the girl said, massaging her jaw.

'Where is she? Where are you hiding her?' Antony said, rounding on her and standing over her. The girl looked up at him and the look on her face almost convinced him she was telling the truth.

'Who?'

'Who do you think? That bitch of a wife, who else? Anna isn't hiding her and she has to be somewhere. Why not with another family member – something else I knew nothing about! Now, where is she?' Antony said and grabbed the girl by her short hair and dragged her to her feet.

'You're hurting me,' she sobbed as she grappled with his arm until he let go. 'What the hell is wrong with you? This isn't funny, Antony. Why are you asking about Isabella? Why are you talking about Anna as if you've just seen her? Did Ebenezer do something to you before he died? I don't understand. I…just…don't…' Antony watched as the girl collapsed to the ground in front of him and buried her face in her hands and started to cry.

Even Carla didn't weep as easily as this, he thought and took deep breaths to quell his anger as he waited for her sobs to subside.

'Finished?' he said after she had been silent for a few minutes. The girl nodded. 'Let's try this again then, shall we? I'll speak slowly so you can keep up. You, judging by your resemblance to her, are clearly related to my wife and have no doubt been engaged in this whole plot to hide her from me, so that I can't dole out the punishment she deserves for turning me into the laughing stock of Breccan. So, for the last time, where is my wife?' He saw her close her eyes as he shouted these words, inches from her face, his spittle decorating her delicate features.

She didn't recoil from him though, which surprised him. Instead, she turned away from him as she stood up, drawing herself up to her full diminutive height before turning back and looking him straight in the eyes.

Antony saw the muscles in her jaw flex as she clenched and unclenched her teeth and his gaze shifted downwards, drawn by the pulsating light he saw emanating from her clenched fists.

'I don't know what the hell you're playing at, but here's a few home truths for you. Isabella is dead. Anna is dead. This all happened four hundred years ago. You were turned into a vampire by Ebenezer Lightwoller – cursed by him. You stupidly believed that he would help you find your precious wife. Where did that get you, hey?' she jabbed him in the chest as she spoke, forcing him to step backwards, his mind reeling with what she was saying. 'Banished by Anna for killing Isabella, for killing half of Breccan. Unfortunately for me, Anna's spells were broken and then you came after me because, yes, I am related to Anna and to Isabella and, to break your curse, you had to kill your wife and all her descendants. So, you came after me. You nearly succeeded too.'

'You lie!' Antony said, refusing to believe what she was saying, unable to believe it. It was impossible. How can they be dead? He only saw Anna yesterday. 'You lie!' he said again and pushed her away from him. She stumbled, but didn't fall.

'No, I'm not. You're only here now because I stupidly believed I could help you; I wanted to help you and we did it. We destroyed Ebenezer. We broke the curse, but look at you!' she said and gestured towards him.

'You lie! I see it now. They've sent you to mess with my head, haven't they? It's not enough that the bitch humiliated me. Now you all want to make out I'm losing my mind, that I'm mad. No! I'll not let you! Now, tell me the truth!' Antony grabbed the girl by the throat and dragged her towards him.

His mind was reeling. What was she saying? It didn't make sense. How can they be dead? How can four hundred years have passed?

Antony closed his eyes and gritted his teeth, forcing his mind to still, quelling his anger, rationalising his thoughts.

'Prove it,' he said and released his hold on her. 'Prove what you say is true.' He folded his arms across his chest and looked at her, confident she would fold.

The girl started to rummage in the pocket of her strange garments and pulled out a small object.

'Look at this,' she said and held it up. 'This is called a telephone. It enables me to talk to someone, wherever they are,' she said and Antony laughed. The girl clenched her jaw again and started pressing her finger against the object. She then put it to her ear and, after a few moments, held it out to him.

Antony didn't move. This could be a trick, a spell of Anna's maybe.

'Okay, fine,' the girl said and pressed the object again.

'Hello, hello. Becca, I can't hear you. Are you there?' A male voice emanated from the object.

Antony stared at the little box and felt an empty feeling start in his stomach as cold clammy sweat broke out across his skin.

'No!' he said as he staggered backwards. 'This is Anna isn't it? Trying to confuse me, trying to turn me into a lunatic?'

'No, Antony, it isn't,' the girl said with a sigh. 'I almost wish it was, but it isn't. For better or worse, you are now in the twenty-first century. Everything and everyone you know are long gone. All you have is me…and Frank…and Ellie.'

'No! I don't believe you. Just stop it! Whatever you're doing, stop it! Haven't I been humiliated enough?'

'Look around you, Antony. Look at the church behind you. The proof is everywhere if you look.'

Antony looked around, trying to take in his surroundings in the glow from the moon. She was right. Nothing was familiar. Not the neatly kept sod under his feet and certainly not the monstrosity of a building that stood behind him. He had never seen anything like that before, except in the grounds of the Duke's estate and he knew he wasn't there. Yet, this place felt so familiar.

He started to feel dizzy as the ramifications of what this girl said took hold. This girl, who was the image of the woman who had wronged him; a woman who had died at his hand four hundred years ago.

'I can't do this,' he said as he backed away from her.

'Antony, wait, let me help you,' she said, reaching out to him, but he recoiled, shaking his head.

'I can't. I have to go. I have to find Anna. I don't believe…I have to…' Antony turned away from the girl and started to run. Where to, he didn't know.

THE END

ABOUT THE AUTHOR

Broken Bonds is the second of four novels, centred around the unusual relationship between Becca Martin and Antony Cardover. It follows the huge success of Marie's debut novel, Bonds, which was published in February 2013.

In October 2013, Tales From A Scarygirl, a collection of Marie's short stories, was published, which included the individually published Three Silver Bullets and Sheer Hell.

Marie's novels continue to be read and enjoyed by thousands of people around the world.

In addition to being a writer, Marie is also a Chartered Accountant and a yoga teacher. She lives in an old stone cottage in North Wales with her three cats.

Why not follow Marie at the addresses below:

www.facebook.com/pages/Marie-Anne-Cope-Author

http://twitter.com/MarieAnneCope

www.scarygirl.co.uk

A MESSAGE FROM MARIE

I really hope you enjoyed BROKEN BONDS and that Antony and Becca are as much a part of your life as they are mine.

For those of you who are new to my writing, why not go and find out how it all began by picking up a copy of BONDS and settling down in front of the fire with a large glass of red wine. Or, you could lock the doors, barricade the windows and hide behind a cushion as you decide which story your nerves can take from TALES FROM A SCARYGIRL.

Whichever takes your fancy, I would love to hear from you, either through my website – www.scarygirl.co.uk – or subscribe to my blog at scaryramblings.blogspot.co.uk.

One final thing, just to whet your appetite, BONDS: RE-BOUND is currently being created. Check out the cover over the page.

May fear protect you when the darkness comes.

'Til next time.

The story will be continued..........

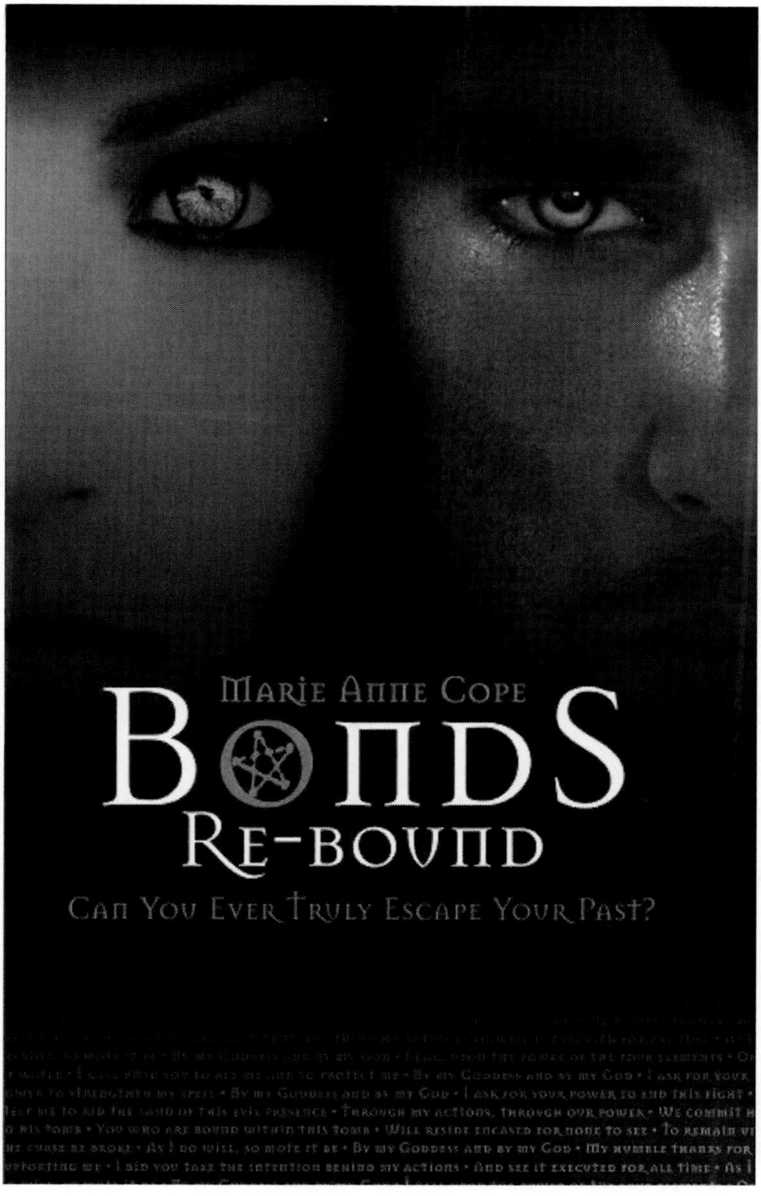

Tales to make you afraid, very afraid, of what lurks between the veil of this world and the next.

Tales From A Scarygirl

One: Dark and Scary

Marie Anne Cope

"Revel in the darkness, but keep your finger on the light switch!"